ASHES
ASHES

MURPHY MORRISON

Emily—
Thank you
for reading!
I hope you
enjoy!

HADLEIGH HOUSE
PUBLISHING

Hadleigh House Publishing
Minneapolis, MN
www.hadleighhouse.com

Cover design by Alisha Perkins

ISBN-978-1-7326347-5-6

ISBN-978-1-7326347-6-3 (ebook)

LCCN: 2020913017

HADLEIGH HOUSE
PUBLISHING

For Andrew

Ring-a-round the rosie,
A pocket full of posies,
Ashes! Ashes!
We all fall down.

CHAPTER 1

Lieutenant Charlie McMahon hoped his ten years at the fire-house would be enough to prepare him for his shift tonight. Riots had riddled the anti-violence protests all day and showed no sign of stopping once the sun went down. He knew his rescue squad would be summoned from Humboldt Park to downtown in only a matter of time. They'd spend the night responding to fires and medical emergencies.

They would save lives and pray they didn't lose others.

And after that, they'd go back home and try to sleep through the day—ghosts of victims more often than not paying visits to their dreams. They would wake up in time for their next shift and start all over again, the schedule that dominated Charlie's life, that first drew him to the job.

He ran a hand over his two-day scruff and merged into the far lane of traffic, not bothering to stifle a yawn. His cell phone buzzed and he answered the call.

"Hello?"

"Charlie?" His sister's voice came through the line, barely audible over the background noise. A group of people, from what he could tell. Her usual easygoing tone was formal and strained. She sounded upset.

"What's wrong?" he asked.

"I need you to come get me." There was an echo behind her words.

"I don't have time. You'll have to get a cab. Or call someone else." His shift started in twenty minutes. He couldn't be late, especially not tonight.

"I can't." She lowered her voice to a harsh whisper. "You have to come."

"Why?"

She didn't have a car and needed an occasional ride; he understood that. He was willing to help, but she couldn't expect him to drop everything the second she called. She had to remember he had a life of his own. He had a job, a schedule.

"Because I'm in the Cook County Jail."

"You're what?" He jerked his truck back toward the right, and horns blared in response. He swerved, suddenly feeling much more awake, and pulled onto the shoulder. "What the hell are you doing in jail?"

"I was arrested in today's protest."

"Jesus, Jen. Are you okay?" He hadn't considered that she'd been there. But of course she went. She was always fighting for something or other. She'd never been in any trouble, at least not that he knew of. But today, she could've been hurt or worse.

"I'm fine. Just come get me, please," she begged.

"I'll be there." He wasn't far from the jail. Fifteen minutes, tops. Getting her out would add more time, but leaving her in the cell wasn't an option. Calling their parents wasn't, either. Their mom would be too drunk to help, and their dad would lose his temper at the news. Jenny's friends might be available, but there was no guarantee they'd be able to get her out. And that left Charlie, shift or not.

"See you soon."

He hung up. He would have to be quick and get to the firehouse as soon as he could, hope any rescues held off until then. Pulling back onto the road, he weaved in and out of traffic, cutting the fifteen-minute drive down to ten.

After parking by the curb in front of the jail, the building's dark-gray façade blending in with the dusk-colored sky, he grabbed his phone and dialed a number.

Three rings and the line connected.

"Chief Freeman." Freeman's voice boomed as always, loud and clear, strong.

"Chief, it's Charlie." He jumped out of his truck and shut the door, hunching his shoulders against the brisk October air. "I'll be a little late for tonight's shift."

He made his way across the street. "Ten minutes," he guessed.

"A lot can happen in ten minutes," Freeman warned.

"I know." Charlie had seen people die in less. "But this can't be avoided. Can someone stay on until I get there?" The previous shift would want nothing more than to get home to their families. But they were all Charlie had.

Freeman didn't respond.

"Chief? You there?"

"You have a ten-minute grace period, that's it. Then I want you in my office."

Charlie had worked with Freeman long enough to know that he wasn't off the hook. Freeman didn't tolerate tardiness, and he wasn't about to start now. But that was fine, expected. Charlie had an extra ten minutes to get to work—thirty total.

That would be enough. That had to be. "Thank you. Bye, Chief."

Stepping over the curb, he ended the call and walked into the jail.

He sidestepped a correctional officer escorting a woman in handcuffs to a back door. The woman was crying. And she wasn't the only one. A handful of others had congregated in the waiting room. Some were upset while others sat silently, staring at nothing, waiting for something. Charlie approached the front desk.

A correctional officer sat behind the computer, scrolling on his cell phone.

Charlie cleared his throat, not about to waste his thirty minutes waiting. "I'm here to pick up my sister, Jenny McMahon. She was brought in from the protest."

"She and a hundred other people," the officer responded, still scrolling. "You can sit over there until she's out."

"I don't have time for that." Even if he did, he wouldn't be dismissed that easily, not with Jenny just on the other side of the waiting room wall.

"Listen . . ." Charlie read the nameplate on the desk. "Officer Anderson?"

The officer flicked his eyes in Charlie's direction, confirmation enough.

Charlie leaned forward. "I appreciate the process, but I'm due for a shift at the firehouse in thirty minutes."

They both worked for the city. Maybe they'd be able to see eye to eye, to come to an agreement and help each other out.

"That doesn't seem like my problem." Anderson put his phone down and leaned back in his chair. He laced his thick-knuckled fingers over his stomach and tapped his thumbs together. "I could make it my problem, for a price . . ."

"Really?" Charlie waited for him to cut the act.

Anderson didn't budge.

Charlie sighed. He glanced over his shoulder. No one in the waiting room was paying them any mind. If this was really happening—and he had a feeling this was really happening—then now was his chance to pay up.

He turned back to Anderson. "What do you want? Twenty bucks?"

"Try fifty," Anderson countered. No surprise. Charlie knew his type. His own dad was the same way, feigning authority and control, all to hide that he had none. If Charlie had to guess, any attempt at negotiation would only up the price.

He grabbed his wallet and handed Anderson two twenties and a ten, his preference for cash over credit solidified yet again.

"Happy?" he asked.

"Ecstatic." Anderson stuffed the money into his pocket, then ran his finger down a list of names. "Follow me," he said as he grabbed a set of keys and led Charlie through a door and down a hall lined with holding cells, fifteen to twenty people packed in each. The space reeked of alcohol, sweat, and weed.

They reached the last cell. "She's in there."

Jenny stood in the cell's far corner, away from the others sitting on the bench and the drunks passed out against the walls. She was twisting the ends of her long raven-black hair between her fingers, a telltale sign that her mind was somewhere else. Her pale skin, usually a stark contrast to her dark features, was flushed. She looked out of place. And she was—the Jenny he knew, at least, the sister who spent her time studying for law school and hanging out with a small group of friends.

And yet there she was all the same.

"Jenny," he called through the bars.

She looked up and spotted him. A flicker of relief passed through her gray eyes—eyes that were swollen as if she'd been crying. She started across the cell.

"How do I get her out of here?" Charlie asked.

"You don't, not until we hear back from the prosecutor. And based on the size of the riot on Michigan and Randolph, she'll likely be charged with disturbing the peace." Anderson smirked, apparently enjoying himself.

"I didn't do anything wrong." She joined them, still separated by the bars.

"They all say that." Anderson wasn't fazed.

"What if I guarantee she'll stay out of trouble?" Charlie didn't care about the details, not yet. He cared about getting her out of that cell without a record to taint the work she'd put into law school. "Could she leave with a clean slate then?"

Anderson chuckled. "No way in hell. Unless . . ." He cocked a brow at Charlie.

Charlie rolled his eyes and emptied his wallet. He handed Anderson another thirty bucks. "That's all I have. I hope you get a nice dinner out of this."

Anderson looked up and down the hall before taking the money. "Pleasure doing business with you."

Charlie made his way back to the lobby and waited for Jenny there. She emerged from one of the doors with her belongings in hand. They walked outside, Jenny on Charlie's heels. "I have to tell you something," she said.

"Why don't you start by telling me how exactly you ended up in a jail cell?"

If she thought he would look past the riot just like that, she was in for a rude awakening. He'd seen too much in his line of work to let this go.

"You could've been hurt or killed," he said.

"But I wasn't." She hurried to keep up. "Besides, that's not the point."

"And what about all of your good grades?" He crossed the street. "One mark on your record could've made those irrelevant. Did you even think about that?"

"This coming from the college dropout?"

"You sound like Dad." He reached his truck and turned to face her. Their gazes were almost level, her five foot nine to his six foot one. She looked different—swollen eyes aside, there was something he couldn't put his finger on. "If you keep this up, you'll end up just like him, ruined reputation and all."

"Will you please just listen to me?"

"When are you going to move out?"

She still lived with their parents, and not only for the free rent like she claimed. She stayed out of fear of what would happen to them if she left. Charlie would know. He'd felt the same way growing up. But he was twenty-eight years old now. He'd moved into his Humboldt Park apartment years ago and forged a path of his own. He'd moved on.

She could, too.

"That's not important."

"They're holding you back."

Jenny couldn't see that. She didn't understand. She hadn't been the ten-year-old tucking their passed-out mom into bed and begging their dad to come out of his study and help. She hadn't hoarded food at school so they'd have a meal at night.

Charlie had.

"I can help you find an apartment," he offered.

"I need your help with something else," she snapped.

His phone buzzed. It was a text from Chief Freeman, a reminder that he was down to nine minutes. And that didn't give him enough time to drop Jenny off anywhere else. He used his cell to order her a car, one just down the road.

"I'm late. I have to go."

"So that's it?" She stepped back. "You're really not going to help me?"

"What do you call this?" He gestured toward the jail. He'd already helped her in more ways than one. He called in late to work. But she didn't seem to register that, to care. "You do realize that your arrest impacted me, too, right? The firehouse?"

"How could I forget? Everything revolves around the firehouse."

"No, Jen. Everything revolves around you."

A Honda parked across the street.

"There's your car," he said, pointing.

He climbed into his truck, done with the conversation. "Do me a favor. The next time you need help with something, call someone else."

He shut the door.

She flinched but stayed rooted to the spot. There was something unsettling about the piercing look in her eye. He had just enough room to back up and pull away from the curb. So he did. He drove down the street and stopped at the intersection, glancing in his rearview mirror.

She was still standing there, watching him leave.

Her black hair blew in the wind, whipping around her face.

He turned the corner.

She disappeared from his view.

CHAPTER 2

Charlie sat at the firehouse's kitchen table. It was 3:00 a.m. and yet he knew better than to try for sleep, his mind always on the next fire. He pushed the newspaper aside, stories on Wednesday's protest only serving to agitate him further, to remind him that he hadn't spoken to Jenny since their argument two nights before.

"Can't sleep, Lieutenant?" Reggie Howell stumbled into the room. His black, buzzed hair was a contrast to Charlie's tousled light brown, and his deep black skin to Charlie's fair white. He reached up and grabbed a cup in the cabinet; he was shorter than anyone else on the squad, but stronger than everyone, too. He'd been with Charlie for six years now, his promotion to lieutenant right around the corner.

"Let me guess, woman troubles?" he asked.

"Not quite." Charlie laughed. He wasn't dating anyone and he wasn't interested in a relationship either, not since the last woman he saw demanded he drop his night shift three dates in. Someday, maybe. But not today.

"What's your excuse?" Charlie asked him.

"The usual." Howell filled the cup with water. "Adams is snoring."

The fire alarm blared, a high-pitched beep followed by a steady buzz. "Engine 78. Truck 59. Ambo 71. Fire at 2450 Galder Avenue, Berwyn." The dispatcher's voice rang through the overhead speakers and echoed down the halls.

Charlie sprung to his feet and Howell left his cup on the counter. They jogged to the garage and went for their protective gear.

Charlie threw on his uniform over his sweatpants and T-shirt and grabbed his hat and facemask. He climbed into the truck's passenger seat as his crew jumped into the back. Slinging his arm out the window, he hit the door with his open palm. "Let's go."

Davis jammed the key into the ignition and turned the metal. He pulled out of the garage and flipped a switch. The siren's wail and the truck's red, flashing emergency light sliced through the night. Engine 78 and the chief's car followed as they sped down empty streets.

Charlie's squad was quiet for the ride, their minds likely on sleep or on family back home. He tried not to think about either and watched buildings shoot past instead, a warehouse on one street, a McDonald's on the other.

"There it is." Davis eased on the brakes.

Bright orange flames marked the property down the street, standing out against the dark early-morning sky. Slate-gray smoke billowed from the roof.

Davis parked by the curb across from the house and Charlie jumped out of the truck, leaves crunching under his feet. He faced a group of bystanders that'd gathered.

"How many people live here?"

"No idea." A woman shook her head. "We never see them."

"Stay over there." He pointed at a lawn two houses down.

He turned back around and joined his squad. The wooden house was all but consumed with fire. Flames on the left side of the house were shooting out of the windows and reaching well beyond the roof. The right side was better off and the windows still intact, but flames danced behind the glass.

The gray smoke was turning black.

Engine 78 and the chief's car parked behind Truck 59. The engine crew jumped into action and unraveled the hose. Chief Freeman stepped onto the street, burly with a balding head and a strong jaw. He jogged over to Charlie.

"What's your read?" Freeman asked.

"Hold the water. Let us try and get inside." They'd have minutes to find a point of entry, nothing more. Once the water deployed, it would weigh down the smoke and choke off the remaining air. Any victims still alive wouldn't stand a chance.

"Okay," Freeman agreed.

Charlie turned to his men. "Howell, we'll take the left side of the house and the back. Jones, Adams, Chow, take the front right and the right side. No one goes in unless you can get back out in thirty seconds. Got it?"

They nodded.

"Let's move," he ordered.

Charlie and Howell cut to the left side of the house only to find the flames just as advanced as at the front, waves of yellow and orange rolling toward the sky.

They rounded the house's back corner and came into an alley separating the fire from the neighboring apartment buildings. Again, there was no point of entry, fire already growing behind the house's windows—on second glance, all but one.

Charlie ran to the farthest window in the row. He knelt to look through the metal grille covering the glass. Flames were in the room, low and by the door. Smoke covered the ceiling. Aside from a mass in the far corner, the room was empty.

Howell joined his side. "See anything?"

"Maybe." Charlie pointed to the shape across the room, a shape that could be something, someone, or nothing at all. He stood, grabbed his Halligan bar, and shoved the steel tool between the window's wooden frame and the metal grille. He added his body weight for leverage and pushed down on the bar.

The grille's top corner popped away from the house. He yanked the rest free, tossed the metal to the ground, and grabbed his radio. "I'm going in, Chief."

"It's too late," the chief's voice crackled in response. "Abort. Do you copy?"

Charlie copied, and he normally wasn't one to disobey commands. But a potential victim was right in front of him. He couldn't just walk away. He'd be out in thirty seconds, less.

He moved behind the window and struck the glass with his Halligan bar. The window shattered. He dropped the bar and elbowed the stray shards of glass away from the frame.

"Chief said to abort," Howell warned.

"Stay here." With the added ventilation, the fire would spread fast. Charlie had to move, now. He secured his mask over his face and lowered himself into the house. The air was dense with smoke, the heat heavy.

"Firefighter!" he yelled as he pushed across the room.

Plaster fell from the ceiling.

He ducked, debris bouncing off of his helmet.

A woman screamed.

The mass by the door wasn't stationary anymore. It was writhing—on fire. He lunged forward and threw himself on top of the woman, suffocating the flames. He pulled away. The right side of her body was burned, badly. Her eyes rolled back into her head.

Howell was there in seconds. He grabbed her legs while Charlie took her shoulders. No time to waste telling Howell to get back outside.

They lifted her and walked toward the window, jolting to a stop.

Something resisted their stride.

"Hang on." Charlie glanced over his shoulder.

The woman's arm extended into the air, angled backward. She had a handcuff around her wrist. A chain extended from the handcuff to the wall. Charlie's eyes met Howell's. She was chained to the wall. She was a prisoner of the room, of the house.

Not anymore.

He set her down, ran back to the window, and reached outside to grab his Halligan bar. Then he went to the wall and struck the chain's base.

Nothing gave.

"Come on!" He struck again. The metal square jerked.

He yanked the chain as hard as he could.

The base fell to the ground.

"Hurry," he shouted as he and Howell grabbed the woman again and started across the room. They made it to the window and Howell climbed back outside. He reached through the frame and pulled the woman out of the room, into the alley.

Something slammed into Charlie's head.

He fell to the ground and tried to stand, but he couldn't move. An increasing pressure pinned down his shoulders and pinched off his airway, making his vision blur. He heard Freeman yell something over the radio, but he couldn't respond.

He tried jerking to the side, grunting with the effort and moving less than an inch. There was no give. He sucked in air but couldn't get enough.

He couldn't breathe.

He'd die in that room. He'd burn alive.

The weight disappeared. "Move!"

Howell grabbed Charlie and pulled him to his knees. Charlie forced himself to stand. He reached for the windowsill, still coughing, and hauled himself into the alley while Howell climbed out beside him. They collapsed to the ground.

Charlie took off his mask. "We have a victim," he croaked into the radio.

The house would fall any second. They needed distance.

He grabbed the woman's arms and Howell took her legs. They lifted her from the ground and jogged to the front of the house, the chain dangling from her wrist. Charlie's lungs burned with each step; his head pounded. They turned the corner.

"Over here!" he yelled.

The front yard was chaos.

Police were clustered in the street and Engine 78 was pumping water into the house. Two medics raced toward Charlie and Howell, a gurney between them.

They lifted the woman onto the pad and started carrying her back toward the ambulances, all without reacting to the handcuff or the chain—as if they'd seen as much before.

Charlie and Howell followed them to the road.

Freeman was waiting, face red. "What the hell was that?" His voice boomed.

"She was too close to leave." Charlie braced for a verbal lashing.

"I don't give a damn! You two disobeyed a direct order."

"I made the call." Charlie disobeyed the command, not Howell. "He saved my life." He clapped Howell on the back. "Thank you. I would've been dead."

"You set a poor example," Freeman continued.

But Charlie wasn't about to back down. If given the chance, he'd jump into that room a hundred times over. "She was handcuffed, Chief. You would've done the same thing."

Just then an explosion erupted from behind. They ducked, Charlie's temple throbbing at the sound. He looked back to see that the house's roof had caved in. The motion made his head spin and the ground tilt beneath his feet.

He blinked, swayed.

Howell put a steadying hand on his shoulder. "He was hit with debris."

Freeman exhaled. "Go get yourself checked out."

"I'm fine." Charlie didn't feel fine, but he stood up taller all the same. His vision started to steady, his balance to return. "Were there any other survivors?"

"No," Freeman answered. "We know of one casualty so far, another woman. She was also in handcuffs, chained to the wall."

"Another woman?" Charlie had seen plenty on the job before, but nothing like this. They hadn't even searched the entire house. What else would they find?

He turned toward the officers. He had to tell them what he saw. He had to help.

Freeman stepped in front of him. "You already disobeyed one order tonight," he warned. "Don't make it two. Go to the hospital and get your head checked."

Charlie debated a retort, but he knew arguing wouldn't do him any good.

"Keep me posted," he said.

The ambulance had room for him to catch a ride to the hospital, sitting next to the victim's gurney. She was still unconscious and had light hair and a slight frame.

Charlie held on to her unburned hand as the medic worked. After what she'd been through, he wanted her to know she wasn't alone, that he was there. Her fist was closed, clenched, as if she had something in her grip. He pried her fingers open.

She was holding a pocketknife.

He took the knife. The red handle and the carbon blade were familiar. His dad owned the same model, his monogrammed with silver initials along the side. But how had the woman gotten her knife? And how had she planned to use it?

He turned the blade over in his hands. His blood stopped cold.

Silver letters snaked along the knife's handle.

ELM.

Edward Lawrence McMahon.

Charlie's dad.

CHAPTER 3

Detective Jeff Foley had seen three dead bodies at the house so far: two women and one man. The corpses were burned, badly; the women had been chained to walls. Three dead and one woman in the hospital—that's all he knew, nothing else about what happened inside of that house. He could venture a guess, sure, a sex trafficking ring, maybe. But his fifteen years with the CPD had taught him that facts were bible and speculation was taboo. Personal biases were to be left at home.

His past considered, that was easier said than done.

He stood outside of the house's charred remains. Aside from yellow leaves clinging to the one tree out front, there were no signs of life left after the fire.

His team was searching the area, the property otherwise empty. Firefighters were packing up their trucks across the street and the medical examiner had yet to arrive. Even the neighbors had scattered after news of the bodies spread. A quiet had settled in their wake, one he recognized well.

The calm before the storm.

"Detective Foley," Chief Freeman called as he crossed the street, walking away from the fire trucks. He ducked under the tape surrounding the site and stood at Jeff's side. "We're heading out. We took a preliminary look around."

"Anything interesting?"

"If you call accelerant along the back of the house interesting, then yes."

Jeff raised his eyebrows. "Arson?"

"Looks that way," Freeman confirmed.

"I'll get the investigator here and see what he has to say." If Freeman was right, then they had a triple homicide on their hands—considering the woman in the hospital, an attempted murder on top of that. If he was right, they had a murderer potentially still on the loose.

"Good luck." They shook hands. "I have a feeling you'll need it," Freeman said before heading back across the street and getting into his car. His men climbed into their trucks.

Jeff watched them leave.

If only I believed in luck.

Turning back around, he made his way to a white tent serving as a command post on the property's edge. He walked under the tent's front flap. Lieutenant Reid was in the corner, giving an update over the phone. Detective Strum was inventorying evidence, carefully handling charred objects with his white-gloved hands.

Jeff joined him. "What do we have?"

"These were found at the back of the house." Strum slid two matches into an evidence bag, both scorched. He grabbed a camera, took a picture, and set the bag into a bin for the lab. "Maybe they sparked the fire."

"Maybe." Or not. They didn't know how long the matches had been there. The lab's analysis might be able to tell them more.

"Did you get an update on the woman from the fire? Is she awake yet?" Jeff asked. He'd sent two officers to check on the survivor at the hospital.

"They called five minutes ago. The woman is still unconscious and on restricted status. They weren't allowed into her room." Strum grew quiet as he picked up the next object from his evidence pile and reached for another plastic bag.

"Keep me posted on that, will you?"

Jeff wanted to talk to the woman when she woke up. At the very least, he wanted to let her know that they were fighting on her side. At the most, to hear any information she had to offer. From what he'd seen, she wouldn't be able to talk for some time. She'd have an uphill battle ahead. But if she'd survived that house and the fire, then she could pull through anything.

"She had a belonging, too," Strum added.

"Which was?"

"A pocketknife. Apparently, a firefighter found it."

"Make sure that goes to the lab with all of this." Jeff gestured to the bins. Until they were allowed into the woman's hospital room, the knife was a place to start with prints. If the blade had been used as a weapon, they might even get DNA.

"Have you had a chance to look into the house's owner?" he asked next, unbuttoning the top button of his shirt and stretching his neck from side to side. Despite the chill in the air outside, the tent was a heat trap, uncomfortably warm.

"Tuco Alvarez. He's fifty-one, born and raised in the city, parents deceased and no other family. He was arrested once for shoplifting. His prints are in the database."

"Good." For all they knew, Tuco Alvarez was the dead man in the house. Only time would tell. In any case, Jeff would find Tuco, dead or alive. He'd find him and anyone else who'd been involved with that house.

He'd make sure they paid.

"Jeff!" Detective Keith Griffin called from outside of the tent. He was the only one at the CPD who addressed Jeff by his first name. Keith was one of the best detectives at the department and Jeff's friend on top of that, a father figure more than anything else.

"We'll talk later, Strum." Jeff gave Strum's shoulder a pat and left the tent. He made his way toward the back of the house, feeling his team's eyes on him as he moved. He picked up his gait and rounded what was left of the house's back corner.

Keith walked toward him with a slight slouch in his stocky shoulders. "We found something."

He held a plastic bag into the air.

"What is it?" Jeff could barely make out a red square. Leather, maybe.

They met in the middle of the alley.

Keith gave Jeff the bag.

"A wallet."

CHAPTER 4

Charlie waited in a makeshift doctor's office, a five-by-five space enclosed by a curtain hanging from a U-shaped rod. He ignored the nurse's direction to sit still. The woman from the fire and the knife she held in her hand were on his mind—a knife that couldn't possibly belong to his dad. The initials were a coincidence. They had to be.

Once the woman woke up, she'd tell him the same.

"Coming in." A man in a white lab coat stepped through the curtain, scanning a clipboard and adjusting his glasses. "Mr. McMahon?" He looked up.

"Call me Charlie."

"Dr. Corbin." They shook hands.

"Please tell me you have good news." Charlie's vision had stabilized since leaving the fire, and his nausea was gone. He was better, more than better; he was back to normal. There was nothing to discuss.

"You have a minor concussion," Dr. Corbin said plainly as he sat in the chair next to the cot. "The worst of the symptoms may have passed."

"That's great." Charlie went to grab his jacket and his turnout gear. As soon as he was cleared to leave, he'd go check on the woman from the fire.

"I recommend you take a week off of work."

"A week?" Charlie pulled back. He couldn't be out of work for a week. He didn't remember the last time he missed even a day. "You said the symptoms had passed."

"I said they *may have* passed," the doctor corrected. "I prefer to be sure."

Charlie's phone vibrated. He ignored the call. "I feel fine."

"We'll reevaluate you next Friday." Dr. Corbin stood.

"And until then?"

"You relax." He peered at him over his glasses, as if he already gathered that relaxing wasn't part of Charlie's DNA. "I'll pass the same onto your chief."

Great.

Once Freeman heard the diagnosis, Charlie wouldn't stand a chance at downplaying the results. His week of relaxation started now, whether he wanted the days off or not. Next Friday couldn't come soon enough.

"See you in a week, then."

"Good luck." Dr. Corbin stepped out of the space.

Charlie followed and went straight to the lobby. The receptionist behind the front desk was on the phone, scribbling on a notepad with her back to him. He walked over to a nurse standing at the desk's far corner, sorting supplies.

"Excuse me," he said.

"Yes?" She was petite, the top of her head just barely reaching Charlie's shoulder. Long, thick eyelashes and full eyebrows framed her dark-brown eyes and stood out against her mint-green scrubs. She looped a stethoscope around her neck.

"How can I help you?" she asked.

"I'm looking for a woman who came in this morning, a burn victim."

She eyed his uniform. "Are you family?"

"No. But I'm one of the firefighters who helped pull her out of the fire."

"Sorry, she's restricted to family visitation." She turned her attention back to the supplies.

"Please, it's important."

She had no idea how important.

"The police said the same thing." She arranged three items into a tray. "But she's not fit to see anyone today, and we don't make exceptions—uniform or not."

She picked up the tray. "Come back in a few days," she said as she walked away.

"Thanks for your help," he quipped, not deterred just yet. The receptionist behind the desk was still on the phone. He approached a nurse hanging bulletins instead. "I'm looking for a patient's room number. Could you help?"

"I sure can." She spun around. "What's the patient's name?"

"I'm not sure. But she was a burn victim from this morning."

"Hang tight. I'll grab someone from the burn unit." She moseyed away and disappeared around a corner. He went to follow and stopped when she came back into the hall with another nurse at her side—the nurse who dismissed him seconds before.

He couldn't turn away fast enough. Her eyes locked with his. She said something to the second nurse before striding his way. "You're kidding, right?"

"Listen, will you at least let me talk to the woman's nurse?" Any information he could get would be valuable at that point, medical status included.

"Sure." She smiled, only a twitch of her lips, but enough that hinted dimples on her cheeks. "Her nurse is Talia Griffin."

"Great." He relaxed. Finally, some progress. "And where can I find her?"

"You're looking at her." She put her hand on her hip. "And like I said before, you can come back in a few days." She turned on her heels and walked away again.

He followed. "She might not have a few days. Don't you understand that?"

"I understand that better than anyone." She turned around with a guarded look in her eye. "And I certainly don't need a reminder from you."

He held his hands in the air. Obviously, he hit a nerve, but at least he had her attention. "Okay. I'm sorry. But I'm not leaving until someone gives me an update."

"Why do you care so much?"

He wouldn't mention the knife or the initials, not to Talia, not to anyone. But he had to give her something. He could predict exactly how she'd react if she thought he was wasting her time, lying. She'd walk away. And he couldn't risk that. She was now the closest connection to the woman he had.

"I want to ask her about the fire," he said.

"And until she's able to talk?"

"I'll remind her to fight." He'd seen firsthand what the woman's life had become in that house, what she survived. "I want to help. But you have to let me."

A line creased her forehead. She considered him, taking her time.

"I'll show you her room, but that's it." She went to the front desk and told the receptionist that she'd bring Charlie in and that he would be right back. Then she took off without waiting for him to join.

He jogged to catch up, sensing that something had shifted. "Thank you."

"Forget it." She led him through a heavy set of doors and into the burn unit, casting not so much as a glance in his direction as they moved. They stopped in front of a room. An observation window spanned the wall. "She's here until she stabilizes."

The woman lay in a hospital bed with the right side of her body bandaged, her face included. A ventilator regulated her breathing and her eyes were closed, her left wrist purple and inflamed, scarred where the handcuff had been. She looked smaller than she seemed in the ambulance, more vulnerable somehow.

"Will she make it?" Charlie asked.

"She's a fighter." That's all Talia said, no guarantees, but hope in her voice.

"If I give you my number, will you update me if anything changes?"

She narrowed her eyes at him. "Are you ever going to go away?"

"Not unless she tells me to."

Her gaze drifted back to the woman and stayed there. Sighing, she took out her phone and entered a code. "Add your information."

She handed him the cell.

"Thank you." He typed in his name and number. "I'm Charlie, by the way. Charlie McMahon."

He gave her back the phone. Their fingers grazed.

She jerked her hand away. Her smooth brown cheeks grew flushed as she stuffed her cell back into her pocket and pushed a strand of dark, wavy hair behind her shoulder. "I have to get back to work."

"I'll show myself out." He suppressed a smile. After witnessing her stubborn front a moment before, he couldn't help but enjoy her fluster now. "Thanks again."

"Right. Bye." She walked away at a brisk pace and didn't look back.

His phone vibrated. He pulled it from his pocket.

His mom's name flashed on the screen. She never called, not unless she was so drunk that her words were slurred and remorseful. He could answer in case she was sober enough to check his dad's desk drawer and confirm that the knife was still there. But that would require an explanation, one he wasn't yet ready to share.

He ignored the call.

Seconds later, another buzz, this time his dad. *What the hell is going on?* Charlie asked himself. Something, otherwise they wouldn't have tried again.

He answered. "Hello?"

"Where the hell are you?" his dad barked in the same condescending tone as always, one he reserved for Charlie over the years. "Your mom has tried you twice."

"I'm at work," he lied, already regretting taking the call. "It's busy. I should go."

"Charlie."

"What?" He braced for the lecture to come, his dad's points always the same. The firehouse wouldn't lead to an actual career. College dropouts were always financially behind their graduate peers. The list went on, the same argument each and every time. But this time, the other end of the line was silent. "Dad?"

"Come home, Charlie." His dad's voice cracked. "It's Jenny."

CHAPTER 5

Charlie stopped at a red light. He grabbed his phone and called Jenny a second time. Her line went straight to voicemail, again. "Dammit!" He hung up. He had to relax. A dead phone didn't mean anything. She was probably just studying and she turned off her cell to focus. Or maybe her battery had run out and she didn't have a charger. There'd be a reasonable explanation. Jenny always had a reasonable explanation.

His sister was fine; she was just fine.

The light turned green and he stepped on the gas before swerving onto his parents' street. Their rambler with peeling brown paint and a flat roof was just up ahead—a childhood house that felt nothing like a home.

After veering into the driveway, he parked with his tail end still protruding into the road and jumped out of his truck. He ran up the short, crumbling brick walkway.

The front door was unlocked.

He went inside and hastened through the kitchen, past the used-to-be white walls and cabinets that had tinted yellow over the years.

"Dad?" he called, hearing nothing but the house's familiar creaks in response. "Mom?" No answer. He continued down the shaggy-carpeted hallway and stepped into the living room. "Hello?"

His parents sat in identical chairs, the fake white leather crinkled around their forms. Both of their heads were in their hands, the bald crown of his dad's on full display.

Charlie rushed over to his mom and knelt on the floor, placing a hand on her shaking shoulder. "What's wrong?"

She didn't so much as lift her head. The smell of vodka hung over her body and clung to her threadbare clothes, invading Charlie's nose. He leaned back and glanced at his dad. He'd never seen him shed a tear before. His mom, yes, but never his dad.

"Where's Jenny?" he asked.

"Are you Charlie?" A man walked into the room.

Charlie's eyes were immediately drawn to his thick copper-red hair. The man took a pen out from behind his ear and pulled a notepad from his jeans' pocket.

His movements were precise and fluid.

"I'm Detective Foley. I work with the Chicago Police Department."

"Detective?" Charlie stood. What was a detective doing in his parents' living room? He looked familiar, his red hair especially, but Charlie couldn't place him.

"Where's Jenny?" Charlie asked again and scanned the room, half expecting her to jump out from behind the couch. No one answered. His parents had yet to even look at him. "Where the hell is she?" He raised his voice.

"There was a fire in Berwyn this morning," Foley answered.

"A fire?" Surely, he wasn't talking about the same fire Charlie had been at hours before, the house that held the women captive and stood no chance against the flames. The house also located in Berwyn. "On Galder Avenue?"

"Yes." Foley squinted. "You were one of the firefighters."

"You were there, too." He remembered now. Foley had been with the officers.

"Wait a minute." His dad looked up at Charlie, his voice raw. The web of red, broken capillaries on the side of his nose looked angry against his porous skin. "You were at the fire?" His neck trembled under the weight of his head. "You were there and you didn't get Jenny out?"

"Get her out?"

Foley mentioned the fire, but not that Jenny had been inside of the house. That couldn't be the case. She wouldn't have survived.

"Where is she now?" Charlie asked. Again, no one answered. "Someone tell me what's going on!"

"She's dead!" his dad yelled. "She's dead, okay?"

"No." Charlie backed against the wall. Blood pounded in his ears. "She wasn't there." His voice sounded miles away, not his own. "I would've known."

He would've done something.

"I'm sorry," Foley said, apologies in his eyes. "There were three casualties. So far, we've identified two of the bodies. One as the house's owner, and the other as Jenny." He hesitated. "Her prints matched one of the bodies chained to the wall."

"You're lying."

Jenny, chained to a wall? The sister who still lived with their parents, who studied in her free time? The sister who never got into any trouble?

But she *had* gotten into trouble.

She was arrested on Wednesday. She tried to talk to him outside of the jail and ask for his help. And how did he respond? He lectured her about her grades, her record, their dad. He refused to listen and told her to call someone else.

He shut the door in her face.

"We're still investigating what happened."

"Stop." Charlie couldn't take another word.

He turned Jenny away on Wednesday night. But he still had time to make amends. She didn't die. Foley was wrong. Charlie didn't save another woman while Jenny burned alive.

But what if I did? What if she heard the sirens coming and was waiting for him to find her, and he never showed? What if he left his sister to die?

"You were supposed to protect her," his mom slurred, so quietly that Charlie almost didn't hear. But he did hear. She stared at the space of wall just above his shoulder, a twitch in her left eyelid pulsing at a steady beat. "She trusted you."

Drunk or not, she was right. He should've been there.

He had been there.

And had he gone to the right side of the house, he might've found another way inside. He might've found Jenny and gotten her out.

But he hadn't gone right. He'd gone left.

"Who did this?"

"We'll know more once we talk to the survivor," Foley answered.

"We can't wait that long." Charlie couldn't wait that long. The woman from the fire wouldn't be able to speak for some time. "We don't even know if she crossed paths with Jenny."

Then again, maybe they did know.

He ran to his dad's study, the one room in the house that'd been off limits growing up, a rule that failed to prevent Charlie and Jenny from snooping around as kids. Now, Charlie went straight for his dad's desk. He opened the top drawer.

"What do you think you're doing?" His dad followed.

Charlie pushed the pens, pencils, and notepad aside. "Where is it?"

"Where's what?" His dad stormed over.

"The knife." Charlie opened the next drawer, stuffed with folders. He pulled them out one by one and threw them onto the desk, the floor. "Where the hell is it?"

"Don't touch those." His dad shoved him away and grabbed for the folders.

"What's going on in here?" Detective Foley joined them.

"She took my dad's knife." Charlie stepped away from his dad, from the desk. His breath was heavy. His ears rang and his head pounded, and not because of the concussion—but because his sister had been at the house that burned down.

She must've been. How else could he explain the knife missing from his dad's drawer? A knife that was identical to the one the woman from the fire had been holding.

But why the hell would Jenny have been there in the first place?

Charlie needed answers, now. He needed proof that she was gone, something more than just a stranger's word, something he could see with his own eyes. Otherwise, for all he knew, Jenny could still be out there, alive. She could still be waiting for him to find her, to help.

He could still have time.

He looked at Foley. "Show me the body."

CHAPTER 6

Charlie felt numb. He stood with his parents and Detective Foley on the morgue's bottom floor. Any minute now and they'd be let inside of the room, be shown a body that could belong to his sister. A body he prayed belonged to someone else.

"How much longer?" he asked.

"Not much." Foley didn't sound sure.

Charlie's mom wrapped her arms around her torso. Cold air blasting through the vents blew wisps of her brittle hair around her face. "I can't do this."

"You don't have to come into the room." Charlie thought she shouldn't have come at all, not in her intoxicated state. But she didn't want to be alone, and his dad refused to stay behind. So there they were. Standing in the morgue.

All of them, together.

All of them but Jenny.

"How did this happen?" his mom wept, her bottom lip quivering.

"We don't know what happened," Charlie said.

His parents were ready to believe that Jenny was dead. And he couldn't blame them for that. They were running away from the flames. But he'd been trained to run the other way. "It could be someone else."

"The fingerprints matched. What more do you need?" his dad pleaded.

"I need to see the body." The CPD could've made a mistake.

Foley could've made a mistake. That's why Charlie was there, to make sure that hadn't happened. If his dad didn't understand that, he could leave. "No one is forcing you to be here."

The door opened.

"McMahon family?" A round woman with silver hair and a white lab coat stepped into the hall. "My name is Sheila." She didn't move to shake their hands, and she didn't seem to expect a greeting from them, either. "If you're ready, you can come in."

"We're ready." Charlie walked into the room and turned back around. No one followed. He met his mom's eye but was speaking to both parents when he said, "You don't have to do this."

His mom huffed a breath of stale vodka into the air. She pushed her narrow shoulders back and joined him. His dad followed and Foley brought up the rear.

They stopped just inside the doorway.

A blue sheet covered a body on top of an operating table in the middle of the room. Everything else was white and appeared sterile, bleached.

"We've compiled the deceased's belongings." Sheila grabbed a plastic bag from a linoleum countertop and walked to the table.

Charlie joined her and took the bag. There wasn't much inside. But there was enough. Jenny's red wallet, her driver's license, and her key ring were all scorched and distorted. A watch with a silver band and a white-and-gold-striped face lay at the bottom.

"Let me see." His dad grabbed the bag. Recognition crossed his face and his posture crumbled. He looked at Charlie, shaking the bag in the air. "Isn't this enough? She's dead! Why're you making us go through this?"

"I'm not making you do anything!" Charlie shouted. "You're more than welcome to leave." He pointed at the door, his muscles clenched. He didn't want to do this anymore, either. But he had to see for himself. He refused to turn back now.

"The body is badly burned." Sheila's words pierced through the air. "The lab was lucky to get a fingerprint, so I want you to be prepared."

"I can't be here," Charlie's mom said as she placed her hand over her mouth. "I'm sorry." She grabbed the doorknob and pushed. The door didn't budge.

She tried again and again, more urgency in each attempt.

Foley stepped forward and pulled instead of pushed.

The door opened.

She ran out of the room, her footsteps echoing as she stumbled down the hall.

The door slammed shut. Silence was heavy in her wake.

"Anyone else?" Sheila waited.

Charlie's dad dropped the bag of belongings onto the table. "We shouldn't have come here." He glared at Charlie, then turned and followed his wife outside of the room.

"And you?" Charlie demanded of Foley, needing someone to confront.

Foley didn't budge. "Whenever you're ready."

"Just show me." Charlie balled his fists. "Please."

Sheila grabbed the edge of the blue sheet and pulled.

Charlie stepped back.

The face before them was charred, one eye melted into the rest of the face, the other eye closed. Wisps of black hair clung to the hairline.

He hunched over, struggling to breathe. The body was too burned to look like his sister. It was too burned to look like anyone. Jenny had a beautiful face and a wide smile. She had long flowing, black hair, and dark-gray eyes. But she also had a watch with a silver band and a white-and-gold-striped face—his birthday present to her last year.

The watch now in the plastic bag.

The floor tilted. Charlie dropped to his knees, suddenly underwater.

A buzz started in his ears and grew louder until he couldn't hear anything else.

Until he wanted to die himself.

"It's her."

CHAPTER 7

Detective Jeff Foley pushed through the CPD's front doors and made his way to the conference rooms, head down. He didn't feel like talking to anyone, like answering questions. And that wasn't just because he spent the day swallowing yet another senseless loss of life, but also because the crime scene took him back in time.

Back in time to a day he'd do anything to forget.

He walked into room 4B. Detective Strum was sitting at a table in the center of the space, leaning over the inventory log. They hadn't spoken since Jeff left Strum in charge while he'd been with the McMahons.

"What do you have for me, Strum?" Jeff asked.

Strum startled and jumped to his feet. "I didn't hear you come in."

"Any update on the third body?" Jeff dove right in.

They were ahead of the game with Jenny McMahon. Her wallet had given them a place to start, and the medical examiner was able to pull prints from the body and find a match in the system. They matched prints for Tuco Alvarez, too. But the third body hadn't been as easy—the second woman.

"Her remains were too burned to pull anything," Strum answered.

"Look through the missing persons reports and see if anyone stands out."

If they found even so much as a potential ID, they could try and track family, dental records.

"Will do."

"And the woman in the hospital?" Jeff asked.

"Still unconscious."

Still unable to tell them anything about that house or how the women ended up there, what happened to them after they were chained to the wall.

"But we did find something," Strum added. "This was under a rock in the back alley." He handed Jeff a plastic evidence bag. A napkin was inside with writing scrawled across the middle.

They deserved to burn.

—Tuco

If Tuco Alvarez started his own house on fire, then he sacrificed himself to the flames. That, or he was unintentionally caught in the fire before he could make his escape.

"Looks like a murder confession. Did we identify his writing?"

"No. We didn't find any other writing samples to use as a base."

"Keep looking." There had to be something. Jeff handed the bag back to Strum. "Did the neighbors see anything? Know anything about him?"

"Nothing." Strum shrugged. "And our sources didn't, either. They'd never heard of him, not as a player in the sex trafficking market, not anywhere."

"Maybe he was a one-man show." He could've lured the women to the house himself and held them hostage from there. Either way, they'd find out. "Check for CCTV or security footage in the area. And put that log on my desk when you're finished."

He turned to leave.

A picture on the log's open page caught his eye; black, red, and blue foil stalled his step. "What's that?" He pointed at the binder.

"This?" Strum lifted the page so Jeff could see. "A cigar."

Jeff tensed. He recognized the cigar, the black snake in the middle of the label. "That was at the house?" He did his best to keep a level voice.

"Yes, on the front lawn. We sent it in for testing."

"Good." He tried to swallow, his throat suddenly too dry. He stared at the image, the same brand of cigar his brother had developed a habit of smoking in high school, all in an attempt to emulate the older men, to be years older than his age.

"You okay?" Strum asked.

"I'm fine."

Jeff's brother left home with a scholarship to college twenty-five years ago and Jeff hadn't seen him since. While he'd been busy at the CPD, his brother had been working his way up the legal sector—ironic, considering what he'd done. But still, the cigar didn't mean anything. Jeff's brother couldn't have been at that house. He'd been involved in something similar before, yes. But that was years ago. He'd grown up since then. Surely, he'd changed by now, his cigar preference, too.

"You look like you just saw a ghost."

Jeff attempted a laugh and stepped back. He needed a minute alone, a minute to clear his head.

"I'll see you later, Strum," he said as he strode out of the room and down the hall.

"Foley!"

Jeff recognized the voice; it belonged to the last person he wanted to see and the one person he couldn't ignore. He stopped and turned around. "Chief Nelson."

"What's the status on the case?" Nelson and Lieutenant Reid walked his way. Nelson's gut hung over his belt, and a caterpillar mustache crawled across his lip.

"It's going." Jeff wouldn't risk saying anything else, not with his brother on his mind. Their past was one he'd fought hard to keep in the dark.

"Should be an easy close, though, right?" Lieutenant Reid asked as he took off his wireframe glasses and cleaned them on his tie.

"I wouldn't say that." After seeing the cigar's picture in the log, Jeff wanted nothing more than to close the case and lock it away. But Reid's preference for a good quota over time spent on cases he considered low-profile rubbed Jeff the wrong way, always had. "It's a little too early to tell, don't you think?"

"If you say so." Reid prickled at the question. He didn't say anything more, likely holding his tongue with Chief Nelson at his side. With a tight smile, he clapped Jeff on the back. "We're late for a meeting. I'll check in with you later."

He and Nelson continued down the hall.

Jeff cursed. Reid's attention was now sure to be focused on the case. He'd start forcing the investigation and pushing for a resolution, just like he always did when he sensed an approaching close, another tally for his team. And before that happened, before Reid took over, Jeff had to look into the cigar, for his own sanity at least.

He went to his office and pulled up the case's files on his computer. Strum was right. The cigar had been sent for testing. A description of the label was documented in the notes.

The cigar's brand wasn't included.

Jeff opened a browser window. He typed the brand of cigar that his brother used to smoke into the search bar: Adolfo Elon. He deleted and retyped the words, stalling and praying the search result images would differ from the picture in the inventory log, that his memory was wrong after all of these years.

He held his breath and hit Search.

Images appeared on the screen, one after another, depicting the same cigar—black, red, and blue foil with a snake in the middle of the label.

Jeff's memory wasn't wrong.

The cigar at the crime scene had been his brother's favorite brand.

CHAPTER 8

Charlie sat in his parents' living room, Detective Foley's voice nothing but a distant hum. He couldn't focus. He hadn't been able to since seeing Jenny's face at the morgue. And now, he saw her burned skin, blistered lips, and wisps of black hair everywhere he looked, nowhere at the same time. He could still hear her voice.

He could still see the way she'd looked at him as he'd driven away.

"Charlie?"

He startled, blinked. Foley and his parents were staring at him, waiting for something. He shook his head. "Sorry. What were you saying?"

"When was the last time you saw Jenny?"

"Wednesday night."

He was tempted to hide the rest, the fact that he turned her away. But hiding anything wouldn't help the investigation; plus, it would give him an out he didn't deserve. "She tried to tell me something. She said she needed help."

Foley raised his eyebrows. "Help with what?"

"I don't know." She could've wanted to talk to him about family, friends, or school. She could've wanted to talk to him about the women chained to the wall. He would never know. But had he listened, things could've been different. She could still be alive. "I had to leave before she told me."

Foley leaned back in his seat.

His dad leaned forward. "You had to leave?"

"I was late for work. I didn't have time to listen."

"You're her older brother. You should've made the time!"

"You're one to talk." Charlie threw the accusation right back. "I made a mistake. One I'll regret every day for the rest of my life, every second. But if you'd taken the time to actually parent, maybe she would still be here."

"She was twenty-four years old. We gave her space."

"You've been giving her space since she was a little kid."

They sat there, staring at each other, eyes ablaze.

Detective Foley studied Charlie. "Did you and Jenny get along?"

"Yes," Charlie said, annoyed by Foley's tone. "Look, if you think for one second that I was involved in Jenny's death, you're wasting your time. We fought occasionally, but then we made up and moved on."

They would've moved on from Wednesday's argument had he just picked up the phone and called her to talk.

"The same as any other siblings," Charlie added.

Foley glanced down at that. After a moment, he cleared his throat and looked up again, his attention now on Charlie's parents.

"Did either of you talk to Jenny last night?"

"She said goodbye before she left." His mom's tongue was heavy but her words weren't yet slurred. She held a purple mug in her hands, chipped along the edge and filled with vodka and a splash of whatever else she had in the fridge, likely flat Dr Pepper. She'd carried the same mug from room to room when they were kids. When Jenny was still alive. "She was going to meet up with her friend, Shevy.'"

"What time was that?"

"Around 8:00 p.m.?" She looked at Charlie's dad.

"Yes," he confirmed. "Jenny seemed normal."

"Would you have noticed if she didn't?" Charlie couldn't help himself. He refused to sit there and listen to his parents pretend to be anything other than uninvolved. "When was the last time you had a real conversation with Jenny?"

"That's none of your business."

"Let me guess . . ." Charlie should've stopped. He knew he should've stopped. But he couldn't, the words all but rolling off of his tongue. He was hurting, and he needed to see someone else in pain. He hated himself for that. "Before the *Smith v. Kenton* case?"

"You shut the hell up," his dad seethed.

Smith v. Kenton was a case he lost eighteen years back, a case that turned him into the resentful man he was today, his wife into an alcoholic, and Charlie and Jenny's childhoods into chaos. He went from a respected prosecuting attorney to a man too embarrassed to step foot in front of a jury ever again. So he'd become a probate lawyer instead, specializing in wills. And still, he carried around a grudge over the lost case and the bruise to his ego.

"Please," Foley intervened, "let's keep our focus on Jenny."

"What else do you need to know?" Charlie spoke through clenched teeth. He wanted to be anywhere else but in that room. Anywhere at all.

Foley fidgeted with his pen. "We're exploring whether the house had been used to host a sex ring. Had Jenny ever been involved in something like that?"

"In a sex ring?" If he even had to ask, he had the wrong idea about Jenny. "No. She lived with our parents, studied all day and night. She rarely ever broke a rule."

"She was just in jail, was she not?"

Foley's words hung in the air.

"She was brought in for protesting." Charlie forced himself to speak slowly. "How the hell does that have anything to do with someone chaining her to a wall?"

"It doesn't. Of course it doesn't." Foley at least had the decency to look embarrassed as he wiped a line of sweat from his forehead. He rolled up the sleeves of his button-down shirt to reveal light-brown freckles scattered across his forearm.

"And she left last night around 7:00 p.m.?" he confirmed.

"Eight o'clock. . . ." Charlie's mom, who'd had her fair share of alcohol, corrected him.

"Right. Sorry." He wrote something in his notepad, something that resembled scribbles more than actual words. "Eight o'clock."

"Do you want me to write that down for you?" Charlie said. At the rate Foley was moving, they'd never know what happened in that house, let alone why Jenny had been there. "Or maybe you could just try pretending to give a shit."

Foley closed his notepad and looked at Charlie, really looked at him. "What do you think happened to your sister?"

"I haven't figured that out yet. But she wouldn't have gone into that house, not if she knew about the danger inside. And if she had any idea about the women, she would've called the police for help. Maybe . . . maybe someone tricked her into going there."

"Earlier today, you said she took your dad's knife."

The knife she must've given to the surviving victim. "Yes."

"If she didn't know the house was dangerous, why bring it?"

Foley had a point. But Jenny could've been carrying the knife around all day, all week. A stretch, maybe, but they couldn't afford to make assumptions. And if Foley was right, then why did Jenny take their dad's knife to the house over another one? For convenience, or some other reason? "She also didn't have a car. Someone must've driven her there." Or taken her against her will.

"My team is looking into that now."

"And the homeowner died in the fire?" If Foley couldn't manage to remember their answers, Charlie would ask the questions.

"Tuco Alvarez, yes. From what we can tell, he wrote a note claiming responsibility for the fire. We're still looking for a writing sample to confirm his penmanship, and we're also analyzing matches found behind the house."

His phone rang. He checked the screen.

"I have to go," he said, standing up.

"That's it?" Charlie stood as well. Foley barely asked them anything, and he only took a few notes. He hadn't even written down Shevy's name—Jenny's friend who was with her on the night she disappeared. "There has to be more."

"What are you now, a police officer?" his dad said as he glared at him, a storm brewing in his eyes, a storm that Charlie knew all too well. "You couldn't even finish college, let alone find a real job. And now you think you can solve this case?"

"Not now, Dad." They'd had this argument before, different variations of the same words. Unlike Jenny, Charlie hadn't found a genuine interest in law, in the one-way track their dad laid out—a decision that his dad had yet to get over, that he likely never would. One that Charlie didn't feel like rehashing now.

He turned back to Foley. "How can I help?"

"I thought you were supposed to protect people," his dad jabbed.

"And I thought you were supposed to try cases," Charlie shot back.

Smith v. Kenton was the reason his dad had pushed Charlie and Jenny so hard to study law. Not because he'd had their best interests at heart, but because he was desperate for a second chance at his career, a chance he'd planned to take through his kids. "Too bad you can't use Jenny to get back into the courtroom now."

The words burned Charlie's throat, acid in his mouth.

His dad's jaw went slack, and he pointed at the door. "Get the hell out of here."

Charlie wasn't leaving, not yet. He faced Foley. "You'll keep us posted?"

"I will." Foley held Charlie's gaze, then regarded his parents. "I'll be in touch. Call me if you think of anything else." He slid his cell phone back into his pocket and walked out of the room, his notepad tucked under his arm.

"Show yourself out, Charlie," his dad said as he followed

Foley with Charlie's mom in tow, the purple mug clutched tightly in her grip undoubtedly due for a refill soon.

Charlie stood still and listened to their retreating footsteps, to the front door open only to slam closed. Silence enveloped the room, a silence thick in accusation. This was the first time he'd been alone since hearing the news about Jenny.

Since realizing that he let his sister burn.

CHAPTER 9

Jeff turned into the CPD's parking lot and pulled into a spot. He jerked his keys from the ignition, furious at the way he handled himself with the McMahons. The first interview was a chance to instill trust, to set a foundation for the days to come. That was standard with any case. And yet he'd been too distracted to even remember their answers. He all but lost his composure in front of them. Why?

Because his brother was on his mind.

His brother, who may or may not have smoked a cigar left at the scene of the crime. His brother, who was a grown man now, not a kid desperate for an extra buck on the street. Isaac had moved on with his life. Jeff had to believe that.

He had to do the same.

But he couldn't stop imagining the worst: that Isaac's name would be on the lab's analysis report. He had fingerprints in the database. Jeff did, too. They'd cleared themselves from a robbery or two as kids. And now, if Isaac's prints were on the cigar, he would be pulled in for questioning. He'd be thrust right back into Jeff's life.

He'd bring their past along with him.

Jeff would have to tell Lieutenant Reid that he and Isaac were related. He'd be switched to a new case. But still, the risk would be there. Proximity to Isaac was enough to threaten the life Jeff had created along with everyone he loved, his wife and daughter included. The Isaac that Jeff remembered was unpredictable, a loose cannon, and there was no telling what he'd do if backed into a corner.

There was no telling what he'd say.

Jeff refused to sit around and wait to see what happened next. He had to be proactive and give himself enough time to come up with a plan if needed, before the lab's analysis came back. He had to know if Isaac had been at that house.

And only one person would be able to tell him that.

He pulled out his phone and scrolled to Isaac's name. His number was still there despite the years of silence, years that would've continued had the fire never happened. Jeff didn't want to make the call, but he was curious at the same time. For all he knew, Isaac would be glad to hear from him. Maybe he would even apologize for what he'd done.

That, or he'd be exactly the same.

A car pulled into the spot next to Jeff's. Once the woman climbed out of her car and walked inside, Jeff selected Isaac's number. He put the phone to his ear, his pulse quickening with each ring.

The line clicked and the ringing stopped.

"Jeff." Isaac's raspy voice still had the same edge. Apparently, he still had Jeff's phone number, too. And that was potentially a good sign.

"Hi, Isaac." Jeff took a breath. "It's been a while."

"Why're you calling?" Isaac's words held no emotion, nothing to suggest that he and Jeff were brothers or that they'd grown up under the same roof.

"No reason," Jeff lied, wishing he had an excuse. Then again, judging by the silence on the other end of the line, he'd better get to the point. "Actually, I wanted to ask about the Adolfo Elon cigars you used to smoke." He held his breath, the truth sounding worse than the lie.

"What about them? I don't have all night."

"I was just wondering if you still smoked them."

Isaac used to accept the cigars on the street for a job well done, imitating the older men until he could take a controlled drag just like them. He'd wanted to fit in, to be accepted. And after some time, that's exactly what happened. The men started paying him in cash, and then he'd been able to afford the cigars on his own.

The memories made Jeff want to hang up the phone.

But running away wasn't an option. Not anymore.

"You're wasting my time, Jeff. It's getting late here. I have to go." Voices picked up in the background. People laughed and music blared.

"Wait." Jeff sat up straighter. "Where are you?"

"Saint Lucia."

The indifference in Isaac's voice was dangerous. But Jeff had one more question.

"How long have you been there?"

"Two weeks." The sounds grew louder. "Goodbye, Jeff. Don't call me again."

The line went dead.

Jeff dropped the phone to his lap. The cigar in the log's picture had looked fully intact. Surely, the shaft would've somewhat decomposed if left on the lawn for more than a week. Isaac had been gone for two. He couldn't have smoked that cigar.

There was a knock on the car window.

Jeff jumped and swore before turning around to find Keith Griffin bending over and staring at him through the glass. Jeff opened the door.

"Are you trying to give me a heart attack?" he said as he pushed his phone back into his pocket. Keith didn't know that Jeff had a brother. He didn't know anything about Jeff's past. And Jeff preferred to keep it that way. "What's going on?"

"I had a nice talk with Lieutenant Reid today." Keith's sarcasm was thick, their opinion of Reid shared. "Sounds like he's getting ready to wrap up your case."

"No surprise there."

Just as he thought, Reid wouldn't waste any time in pushing Jeff's investigation toward a close and moving them on to the next case.

"He wants my notes in the system tonight. I think I'll hold off until tomorrow," Keith said with mischief in his hooded eyes. "A few extra hours won't kill him."

"I wouldn't be so sure." Jeff laughed.

"You coming inside?"

"Soon." He needed time to collect his thoughts after his phone call with Isaac.

Keith's eyes narrowed. "You okay?"

"I'm fine. Really." Jeff did his best to sound convincing. "I'll see you in there."

"If you say so." Keith turned away and walked toward the building.

Jeff shut the door and leaned back in his seat. He closed his eyes and replayed his conversation with Isaac in his mind, over and over again. For years, he'd imagined the man his brother had become. He'd hoped that Isaac had changed.

And now he knew.

Isaac hadn't changed.

He never would. He wanted nothing to do with Jeff on top of that. And that was fine. The feeling was mutual. Jeff picked up his phone, scrolled to Isaac's name, and deleted the contact.

He wouldn't need the number again.

CHAPTER 10

Charlie didn't remember climbing the stairs, turning right at the bathroom, and continuing down the hall. He didn't remember walking into Jenny's room. Yet there he was, standing next to her bed, her turquoise comforter undisturbed from the night before. An open textbook lay on her desk, folded clothes on her chair. There was nothing to suggest that she wasn't coming home, that she'd never set foot in her room again.

That she was dead.

But she *was* dead, his sister who knew exactly what she wanted out of life, who lived with more purpose than he'd ever felt himself. She'd never open another textbook again, would never graduate and become a lawyer like she'd planned. She'd never protest for another cause. And that was just the beginning. There was everything else, too. She wouldn't move into her own place, get married, have kids.

She was gone. She wasn't coming back.

A creak came from downstairs.

Charlie ran a hand over his face. He had to leave. The last thing he needed was his dad coming into the room. He couldn't take another argument, not tonight.

He turned toward the door and bumped into the desk, just catching a stack of printed case studies and graded papers before they fell to the floor. A worn leather notebook with Jenny's name stamped into the cover was at the bottom of the pile.

He put the papers on the desk and opened the notebook.

No, not a notebook. A journal.

Jenny's journal.

He turned to the last entry.

Thursday, October 18

This week has been busy. The highlight? I got a new pen on Wednesday. What does that say about me? Pretty lame, right? Anyway, green ink isn't really my thing, but maybe it'll stick. We'll see. Aside from that, I'm meeting up with Shevy in a few.

That's all for now.

October 18 was the day before the fire, the day before Jenny died. He read the words a second time, hoping for something more, a clue into what happened later that night, but nothing came. He flipped through the other pages. She hadn't written every day, but her other entries had more detail, a purpose. He could all but see her writing the quote about law school on one day followed by the lentil soup recipe on the next. Compared to those, this last entry seemed random, pointless even. If nothing happened on Thursday, why had she bothered writing at all?

"What're you still doing here?"

Charlie spun around, tucking the journal into his back pocket.

His dad stepped into the room.

"I was just leaving," Charlie said.

"Good. We're tired." His dad's eyes were bloodshot.

"Right." His parents didn't want him in their house. And he didn't want to be there. He started walking toward the door. "Call me if you hear anything tomorrow."

A light flickered through the window.

"What's that?" Charlie opened the curtain.

A crowd had gathered on the street and was arranging flowers and candles along the curb in front of the house. He recognized a handful of faces, some Jenny's friends, some his friends, others acquaintances they hadn't spoken to in years.

"What're they doing here?" his dad asked.

"Paying their respects."

Jenny's family wasn't the only one in pain. She'd left her mark on everyone, friends included—friends who might have more insight into what happened. He didn't see Shevy in the crowd. He hadn't seen her in a few months, now that he thought about it, and he wanted to ask her about last night. But Andrew was there, Jenny and Shevy's friend from law school. He might know something, too.

"Will you close those?" His dad elbowed him aside to shut the blinds. "We're not some animals at the zoo." His hands shook, his voice, too. "Please, just get out."

"Okay." For once, Charlie did as his dad said. He rushed into the hall and took the stairs two at a time until he reached the first-floor landing. He went outside.

The crowd fell silent, motionless, as he stepped into the yard. A few of his friends came forward and patted his back, but he didn't listen to what they said. He moved toward Andrew instead. "Hey."

"I'm so sorry for your loss," Andrew offered as he shook Charlie's hand.

"Thanks." Charlie looked around. "I wanted to talk with Shevy. Is she coming?"

Andrew tensed, subtly, but there. "She already came by, actually."

"And left?"

Something about his tone didn't feel right. He seemed on edge.

"She felt a little awkward, everything considered."

"Everything considered?" He had no idea what Andrew was talking about. And he didn't have time to guess. "What happened?"

"Oh, well . . ." Andrew scratched his head and sighed, as if he'd said too much. "Look, I'm not sure what happened, but she and Jenny had a falling out."

"When was that?"

Jenny and Shevy had been inseparable since they were kids, best friends. He'd never heard of so much as an argument between them.

"A week ago. They hadn't spoken since."

"A week? Are you sure?" That couldn't be right. They were together last night. Jenny told their parents as much. She wrote the same in her journal.

"Pretty sure." He nodded. "Anyway, she brought that poster over there."

Charlie turned.

A blown-up photo of Jenny and Shevy leaned against the mailbox, surrounded by candles, flowers, and cards. They were young in the picture, smiling wide, both wearing pink tutus. He moved closer, drawn to the image, to Jenny's gray eyes staring back at him—just as piercing as they'd been on Wednesday night.

The lights in his parents' house turned off, casting the property in darkness.

Charlie stopped. A hush fell over the crowd.

The candles' flames around the poster flickered in the wind.

The flames danced around Jenny's face.

CHAPTER 11

Talia Griffin sat in the CPD's lobby, staring at Charlie McMahon's name in her phone, irked that she became flustered in front of him the other day. He was tall with light-blue eyes and a shadow of facial hair. Of course she thought he was handsome. His uniform hadn't hurt either, if she was being honest, and she admired his line of work. So yes, she felt a shock when their hands had touched. But so what? He was also persistent to the point of annoyance.

She didn't know Charlie, and she didn't want to get to know him. Dating certainly wasn't on her radar. She didn't have the time. Had Charlie not offered to help her patient, she wouldn't have even given him a second thought. She would've been content to never see him again. But he *had* offered to help.

And this wasn't about Talia. This was about the woman from the fire. She was completely alone in her hospital room. Until either she was identified by the CPD or someone came looking for her, that wouldn't change. She needed all of the support she could get right now. And if Charlie was willing to give her that, then Talia wouldn't be the one to stand in his way, breach in protocol or not.

If he could help her patient, she'd let him.

She typed a message into her phone and sent him a text.

She woke up.

Just that morning, the woman had opened her eyes. She had yet to speak and likely wouldn't for some time; she was still in critical condition and unimaginable pain. But she made progress. And at that stage in her recovery, they couldn't have asked for anything more.

"Talia?" the officer behind the CPD's front desk called as she hung up the phone. "Sorry about the wait. Are you here to see your dad?"

"Yes. Can I head up?" Talia stood, stuffing her cell into her purse.

"Go right ahead."

"Thanks." Talia went to the stairs and climbed to the second floor. She hadn't told her dad she was coming. He wouldn't appreciate her checking in on him unannounced. But she hadn't seen him in a week, and she'd barely heard from him, either. That meant long work hours, not enough food, and hardly any sleep. He was predictable that way. He used work as a distraction and promised that he was fine.

And she believed him.

She just preferred to confirm as much with her own eyes.

She cut across the second floor, stopping just outside of his office. He was sitting behind his desk, flipping between documents with a scowl on his face. His dark hair peppered with gray looked thin under the harsh florescent lighting.

"Hey, Dad." She walked into the room and pulled out the chair opposite him.

He glanced up, documents still in his hand. "I thought you were working this morning."

"I got off early." She sat, deciding not to mention that she'd worked twenty-four hours straight, that her charge nurse sent her home last night and told her not to come back until she had a proper night's sleep. Her dad would worry at that. He would realize he wasn't the only one in need of a distraction once the sun went down. And that wasn't a conversation for today or for any day.

"You should spend the morning with your friends. How're they?"

"They're great." Talia hadn't spoken with her friends in over a month. Things had changed since the accident. Even now, two years later, all she heard was worry in their voices and pity in their questions. A constant reminder. So she called when she could and they talked, avoiding anything personal. Then they hung up.

They'd all become used to the routine.

She pulled a paper-wrapped bagel from her purse and set it on the desk: toasted halves, egg and cheese in the middle. His favorite. "I picked this up on the way."

He put the documents down and reached across the desk, bringing the bagel over to his side. "I'm supposed to be looking after you, remember?"

"How could I forget?" He told her the same last week, and the week before that; he didn't like to be coddled. But she couldn't help herself. He was all she had left. "You can't look after me without a meal in your stomach."

His phone rang.

He reached for his cell and looked at the screen. "Dammit." He tossed the phone into his lap and sighed. "Did you happen to see Jeff out there?"

"No." She hadn't seen Jeff, his wife, Angela, or their daughter, Lucy, in weeks. And that was too much time, considering everything Jeff and Angela had done for Talia and her dad since the accident. She would find them at the CPD's Halloween potluck later and catch up with them then. "What're you working on?"

"A fire in Berwyn, three casualties." He leaned back in his seat. "One survivor."

"The survivor is one of my patients. Are you leading the case?"

"Jeff is. I'm just documenting the scene." He frowned and tapped his pen against the desk while his gaze drifted to the door over her shoulder, lingering there—a look she'd seen before, one she could read like a book.

"Dad, what's wrong?"

He attempted a smile. "Confidential, honey." He checked his watch. "Now, if you don't mind, I have some work to get back to."

She tilted her head, tempted to snub his dismissal. But she had to pick her battles. She'd learned as much over the years. She stood, walked around the desk, and kissed his cheek. "I'll see you at the potluck later this afternoon?"

"Yes." He grabbed his phone. "Shut the door on your way out, will you?"

"Sure." She walked to the door before stealing a backward glance. The phone was at his ear and the bagel was still wrapped, forgotten at the corner of his desk, likely to stay that way now. She'd make sure he ate something at the potluck later.

She went into the hallway and shut the door, stepping away from his office.

"Jeff?"

She could hear her dad's voice through the walls.

She stopped, listening.

"Call me back. I'm reviewing the files." He paused. "Something's missing."

CHAPTER 12

Charlie stepped into the CPD's lobby with Jenny's journal in his back pocket. He'd read each entry the night before. Yet he wasn't any closer to understanding what happened to his sister on Thursday night and Friday morning.

He still didn't understand why she'd been in that house.

Detective Foley might be able to find something Charlie had missed. He was privy to more information, so he may have a different perspective. If nothing else, the journal's entries would give Foley insight into Jenny—the Jenny that Charlie had known. And based on their interview last night, the sooner Foley had that, the better.

Charlie approached the officer who was typing at lightning speed behind the front desk. "Excuse me? I was hoping to speak with Detective Foley."

She glanced up at him, her fingers poised over the keyboard. "He's in an all-department meeting this morning. Would you like to wait?"

Charlie checked his watch, already 10:30 a.m. He didn't have time to wait, not if he wanted to visit the woman in the hospital that morning. And he did want to visit her, especially now that she was awake. He wanted to find Shevy, too.

"I'll stop back this afternoon."

She reached for a pen. "Do you want to leave your name?"

"Charlie?" someone called in the distance.

They turned toward the voice. A group of officers filed out of a room across the lobby, Foley included. His hair was disheveled compared to yesterday and the beginnings of bags were forming under his murky-hazel eyes, hopefully a sign that he had plenty of leads to follow related to Jenny's case and not the opposite.

He walked to the front desk, a mug of coffee in his hand.

"Are you here to see me?" he asked Charlie.

"Yes. Do you have a minute to talk?"

"Sure. I wanted to show you something, too."

Foley led Charlie up a flight of stairs and into his office on the second floor. The low ceiling made the space feel small and stuffy, cramped. Foley shut the door.

"Footage from a neighbor's security camera came in last night." He turned the computer on his desk toward Charlie and opened a video file on the screen.

Rewinding the footage until Thursday night, he stopped at 8:30 p.m., thirty minutes after Jenny left their parents' house.

"Watch this."

He hit play.

The neighbor's camera picked up the front of Tuco Alvarez's house, lights off and windows dark. The street was quiet, not a single person in sight. A cab came into the shot, ambling toward Tuco's house and parking across the street.

The cab's back door opened.

Jenny climbed out.

Charlie watched as she made her way to the front door, wearing dark clothes and her hair pulled back. He knew what would happen in the end, yet he willed her to turn around all the same, to get back into the cab and go home.

She reached the door and knocked.

The cab pulled away just before the house's front door opened, no one visible on the other side. Jenny stepped forward.

Then she stopped.

She looked over her shoulder, seemingly right at the camera, right at Charlie. She stared at him and he stared back, holding his breath. Seconds passed that felt like minutes. And then she turned back around and walked into the house.

The door shut.

She was gone.

Foley paused the video. "Now we know how she got there."

"I guess we do." Charlie pulled his eyes away from the screen, from the frozen frame of the house. He didn't know what he expected to see, but Jenny getting out of a cab alone didn't give them much. "Did you speak with the driver?"

"Yes," Foley said as he stuffed his hands into his pockets. "He didn't remember the ride."

"What else did the footage show?" There had to be more.

"Not much. Tuco was the only one in and out of that house's front door. There's a side door, but no camera coverage there."

"The neighbors didn't see anything?"

"Nothing. And the only prints we could pull from the knife belonged to Jenny and the surviving victim, still a Jane Doe." Foley leaned against the edge of his desk.

"What about the note?" Charlie asked. "Was Tuco's handwriting confirmed?"

"Unfortunately, no. We didn't find any other samples to use as a base. We also weren't able to pull any prints from the matches found behind the house, or to tell if they started the fire."

"So what happens next?"

Charlie needed something to go off of, anything. He felt Jenny fading away with each update Foley gave, one dead end after another.

"We're still waiting for the lab's report on a cigar left at the scene." Foley hesitated. "If nothing comes from that, the case will likely close."

Charlie didn't understand. "That's impossible. The investigation just started."

"Everything we've seen suggests that Tuco acted alone."

"But nothing has been confirmed." They still didn't know

why the women had been at that house or what happened inside of those walls. They didn't know anything, surely not enough to draw any conclusions. "You have to keep looking."

"Unfortunately, it's not my call."

"So this is coming from the top?" Three women had been chained to the wall, and two were dead. Yet the CPD was ready to move on to the next case? "Let me guess, bigger fish to fry? Tuco Alvarez didn't kill enough women for this to be a priority?"

Foley stiffened. "Listen, I'm sorry. I wish we could do more."

"Then do more."

Foley was the lead detective. He had to have some sway.

The door opened, no knock.

A man with graying hair stuck his head into the room. He scowled at Foley, but didn't acknowledge Charlie, and he didn't apologize for the interruption, either.

"We have a meeting with Chief Nelson in five minutes," the man said.

Foley sighed. "Lieutenant Reid, this is Charlie McMahon."

Reid gave no indication that he heard the introduction. He readjusted his wireframe glasses and pointed at Foley. "Meet me outside of Nelson's office in one minute." He stepped away from the room and shut the door.

"Always a pleasure," Foley muttered, tenser than he'd been before. He turned his attention back to Charlie and studied him. "Here, take this." He reached into his pocket and handed Charlie his card. "Call me if anything comes up, okay?"

"So that's it? You're done?" Charlie fumed.

"I'll be in touch soon." He walked to the door and turned back around. "I almost forgot. You came to see me. Was there something you wanted to talk about?"

"No." Charlie would be damned to give Foley Jenny's journal now. He knew exactly where the entries would end up: pushed to the side and ignored.

Foley stood there a second more before leaving the room.

He walked away, the lead detective on Jenny's case, the one who was supposed to be searching for answers, fighting for the truth, and investigating on her behalf. After everything she'd been through, Jenny deserved to have her story told. The full story, not bits and pieces here and there. And if Foley weren't willing to finish the job, Charlie would find the answers on his own.

He'd find out what happened inside of that house. He had a whole week of medical suspension to dig into the details, to find the truth.

And he knew exactly where to start.

He left the CPD and jumped into his truck.

He selected a number on his phone. The line rang and connected to voicemail. "Talia, it's Charlie McMahon." He shoved his keys in the ignition, starting his truck.

"I need your help."

CHAPTER 13

That year's CPD potluck had one of the best turnouts Talia had ever seen. The community center was filled. Kids ran around wearing all types of Halloween costumes, and even some of the adults had dressed up. There was an apple bobbing station in one corner and a line for face painting in the other. Talia added store-bought brownies to the folding table of food in the center of the room. Not the homemade pan de muerto she'd planned, but easier. No memories attached.

She didn't see her dad in the crowd. The officers without kids to entertain were all congregated together, but he wasn't with them. She wanted to find him and see if he got a hold of Jeff since that morning and if he ate a meal. But her dad wasn't the only one on her mind, not since Charlie called her earlier and asked for help. With what, she wasn't sure. But she would find out. She'd agreed to meet him at the hospital before her shift later tonight.

She made her way around the room, spotting Angela and Lucy along the far wall. Lucy was dressed as a ladybug, her costume complete with two wings and antennas pinned into her curly strawberry-blonde hair. She was blowing bubbles through a wand, her eyes wide as she watched them float away. Angela was smiling at her side, a mother's smile, one filled with love and pride. A smile that Talia hadn't seen on her own mom's face in two years, one she'd never see again.

She joined them. "I was hoping to see you two here."

"Well, hey there, stranger." Angela's blonde hair was in a bun at the nape of her neck and freckles spread over the arch of her nose. She pulled Talia into an embrace. "No costume this year?" she joked as she pulled away and resituated the red cape tied around her neck.

"Who, me?" Talia gestured to her scrubs. She'd never been one for dressing up, and her job just so happened to make that easier. "I'm a nurse. Can't you tell?"

Angela laughed. "A nurse I barely recognize anymore."

"It's been a while," Talia agreed. She and her parents used to get together with Angela and Jeff at least once a month, a friendship that stemmed from her dad and Jeff's work together at the CPD. In the months after the accident, she and her dad saw them even more often than that. Jeff and Angela were as good as family. But schedules had been hectic that fall and visits less frequent. "Great turnout today."

"Much better than last year," Angela commented as she tucked a loose strand of hair back into her bun. "I found myself searching for your mom's bread on the table."

Talia stiffened.

Angela's smile dropped. "I shouldn't have said that. I'm sorry."

"Don't be." Talia had to loosen up. She couldn't react every time someone mentioned her mom. She avoided Angela's concerned gaze and looked around the room, desperate for a change in subject. "Have you seen my dad?"

"He pulled Jeff over there a minute ago." She pointed toward an empty hall.

"Mommy?" Lucy held her bubbles into the air while pushing a loose antenna away from her eye. "Play with me. Bubbles!"

"Hang on, honey. Mommy's talking." Angela took Lucy's hand.

"It's okay. I have to head out." Talia had planned to stay at the potluck longer. But now, she felt more than ready to leave.

She gave Angela another hug and Lucy a high five. "Let's do dinner sometime soon."

"Next week," Angela promised.

Talia walked back through the crowd. She had a run-in with a dragon and a witch on a broom before she reached the hallway and started breathing easier from there, chatter from the potluck fading away with each step. She passed two offices and heard her dad's voice coming from a third, the door cracked open.

She slowed, knowing she shouldn't interrupt. But she'd been worried about him since visiting the CPD that morning. She would feel better if she saw him long enough to say goodbye. *I'll be quick,* she told herself as she approached the room.

"The documentation isn't there. I checked twice." Her dad spoke in a lowered voice. Talia stopped just outside of the door. She could feel the tension from the hall.

"The cigar's detail was in the system last night." Jeff's tone was defensive.

"Strum said the same." Her dad paused. "He also asked how you were doing. He said you acted strange when he showed you the cigar's picture in the log."

Silence.

Talia stood stock-still. She didn't dare peer around the door.

"Is something going on?" her dad probed.

"No." Jeff's response was short, pointed.

"That cigar could be a lead." Her dad's voice lowered even more. "If the detail isn't back in the files tonight, we'll have to tell Reid." His words hung in the air.

"Just let me look into things first," Jeff insisted, sounding agitated.

Feet shuffled and he barreled into the hallway, glancing her way. "Hi, Talia," he said as he stormed past.

"Dinner next week!" she called after him.

"Talia?" Her dad came into the hall, his mouth set in a straight line.

"Hi." She wasn't sure what to say, whether to acknowledge what she heard or not. Then again, she wasn't one to beat around the bush. "What was that about?"

"Nothing."

"It didn't sound like nothing." It sounded like files were missing, like her dad thought Jeff was involved. "I'm sure the cigar's documentation will turn up."

"Enough, Talia." He sighed as if exhausted, not from work, but from her.

"Enough of what?"

"Everything: you showing up at the department unannounced, clocking my meals, eavesdropping on my conversations. I'm a grown man. I don't need you checking up on me every second of every day."

She stepped back, feeling like she'd been slapped. She checked up on him, yes, but only because she was terrified of losing him. Besides, this was different.

"I was just coming to say goodbye," she said.

"It has to stop."

A vaguely familiar man wearing a pinstripe suit walked out of the office across the hall. He slid a mask over his face as he made his way toward the potluck.

Her dad's voice softened. "You don't talk to your friends anymore. You don't socialize, or go on dates, nothing. You're missing out on life. You have to move on."

"I have to move on? You can't be serious."

He was the one who couldn't talk about his wife's death, who worked around the clock as much as he could.

"I am serious."

His words hurt. Out of everyone, he was supposed to understand. She thought he had. She'd been wrong.

"And what about you?" she asked. "You're too busy distracting yourself from what happened to even remember that you have a daughter in the first place."

"Lower your voice, Talia."

"All you care about is work. All you've ever cared about is work."

"That's enough."

"Had you been home that night, Mom would still be alive!"

He flinched as if he'd been shocked.

She covered her mouth with her hand. She had no idea where the accusation came from. It wasn't even true. Her mom had been going to dinner with friends that night. She would've left home had Talia's dad been back from work or not. And yet Talia said the words all the same. Out loud, to his face.

"I didn't mean that."

"I should go." He looked away.

"No. I'll go." She waved her hands in front of her face as tears prickled her eyes. She'd hurt him, the one person she had left. "I'm so sorry." She ducked her head, not able to bear the pain etched into his face. "I'll call you later."

She turned around and hastened back the way she came.

CHAPTER 14

Charlie pulled onto Galder Avenue and rolled down his window. The neighborhood smelled of stale smoke. Aside from two pumpkins on a house's front porch, the pothole-lined street looked forgotten, with an empty tree swing on one lawn and a broken fence on another. He wondered if Jenny noticed the same in her cab ride on Thursday night, if she'd been afraid.

He wondered what she'd seen in the dark.

He parked across the street from Tuco Alvarez's house. Given that the roof was caved in and the structure completely burned, he wasn't sure what he'd find when he stepped outside of his truck, or if he'd find anything at all. But he had to look for answers somewhere. The house was the last place Jenny had been seen alive.

The house was a place to start.

He still had a few more hours until he would meet Talia at the hospital and talk to the surviving victim if he could. And he still wanted to ask Shevy about her and Jenny's supposed falling out, too. That and their plans on Thursday night.

He called Shevy, hanging up when her line went straight to voicemail.

He'd stop by her place later that night to try to catch her in person. In the meantime, he would see what else he could find.

He stepped onto the street and walked toward the house. The flames were long gone, but he could see them all the same. He could feel their heat on his skin. The memory now was worse than the actual flames had been on Friday morning. Now, he knew that Jenny had felt their heat as well. More than just their heat.

She'd felt their burn.

He forced himself to keep going and made his way around the right side of the house, over the dead grass covered by ash, splinters of wood, and glass. The side door was there, just as Detective Foley said. Charlie walked into the back alley.

The windows were farther apart than he remembered, all four shattered with three still covered by metal grilles. He peered through each one, looking for chains or handcuffs, anything to suggest where Jenny had been held. But each room was the same—nothing but scorched walls and blackened floors covered in debris.

A mark between the last two windows caught his eye.

He moved closer and took in the soot arranged in a V-like figure.

He'd seen similar markings before: indication of a fire's origin. He was trained to notice as much, and he shouldn't have been surprised to see it now. Detective Foley told him about Tuco's note claiming responsibility for the fire.

But he was surprised—not by the mark, but by the fact that Tuco started the fire outside. He risked being seen in the alley, a neighbor calling the fire department, or the flames being extinguished before they did their job, before they killed. Tuco could've started the fire inside of his bedroom or in his kitchen if he'd wanted. He could've had same results with more control. But he used the alley instead.

And that didn't make any sense.

"Who the hell are you?"

He turned around.

A man stood ten feet in the distance, his army-green jacket zipped up to his chin. Charlie hadn't heard him approach. He didn't know how long he'd been there. "I could ask you the same thing," he said.

"I live over there." He jerked his head toward the apartment building across the alley. "I saw you walking around back here. It's a crime scene."

"I know," Charlie responded. *And if he could see me from his apartment, then maybe he saw something else that could help. Something related to the fire.*

"Were you around on Thursday night or Friday morning?" he asked.

The man looked him up and down. "What are you, a cop?"

Charlie had a feeling he wouldn't be too keen on talking to the police or to one of the victim's brothers. "No, I'm just curious."

"Go be curious somewhere else."

"I think I'll stay here, thanks."

"Oh yeah?" He peered over his shoulder and scratched his head, his greasy hair pulled back into a ponytail. "Well then . . . I'll just call the cops."

"There's no need for that." Charlie couldn't have Detective Foley showing up and realizing that he started investigating on his own. But the man seemed defensive, like he had something to hide. And Charlie wanted answers. "Did you know Tuco?"

"That's it. I'm calling them." He pulled out his phone. "I'm dialing!"

"Okay." Charlie held up his hands. "I'll leave." He backed away, turned at the house's corner, and walked back to the street, unsure what to make of the exchange.

Detective Foley's team must've talked to the neighbors by now. They could've rubbed them the wrong way. But if that were the case, if the man didn't want to get involved, he wouldn't have threatened to call the police. He would've kept his distance. He came out of his apartment to drive Charlie away instead.

Charlie reached his truck and looked over his shoulder.

The man was nowhere in sight.

He felt eyes watching him all the same.

CHAPTER 15

Jeff walked through the crowd, looking for Angela and Lucy. He hadn't seen them since Keith pulled him away. They'd planned to stay at the potluck for a few hours and to make a Saturday afternoon of the event. But that afternoon was about to be cut short.

Jeff had to get back to work. He had to check the case's files. Keith's claim that the cigar's information disappeared was impossible, his suggestion that Jeff played a role in the disappearance insane. Jeff reacted when Strum showed him the cigar's picture, yes. He thought his brother could be involved with the case. But he would never tamper with files, no matter the circumstances.

Keith had to know that.

Regardless, Jeff would look through the files again and would talk to Strum if needed. If the cigar's information was still missing after that, he and Keith would go to Lieutenant Reid together. Jeff would prove he had nothing to hide.

"Jeff!" a faint voice called from the crowd.

Angela stepped around two officers and reached his side. She had picked a yellow shirt that morning, melted butter, not too bright. Beautiful, as always.

She smiled, her cheeks flushed.

"There you are," she said.

He kissed her cheek and looked away, afraid she'd read the unease in his eyes. She was like that—observant, aware. She cared about him, and that was more than he could say about most people in his life.

"Sorry, honey. I got caught up. Where's Lucy?"

"You won't believe this." She stepped closer to him and leaned forward, lowering her voice for added suspense. "She's with your brother."

"What?" Now he was leaning forward. He must've misheard. The voices around them were too loud, too close. He was distracted.

"Where is she?"

"With your brother."

"Seriously, Angela." He waited for her smile to break, for the joke to be over. Isaac had been in Saint Lucia the night before. He couldn't be back already.

"I'm serious."

She seemed pleased. And she would be. Ever since Jeff had told her that he and Isaac had merely grown distant over time, she held out hope that they would reconnect. She looked him up online every so often, and even introduced herself to him a few years back after running into him in the city.

She thought he'd seemed nice.

"He's making an effort," she said.

"Like hell."

She didn't know about Isaac's past. She didn't know what he'd done—what Jeff had done. Had she known, she wouldn't have left Lucy alone with Isaac for a second. She might not have left Lucy alone with Jeff, either. But she didn't know.

Because Jeff had never told her the truth.

"Which way did they go?" He looked around, but he didn't see them. He couldn't get a clear view through the crowd. For all he knew, they weren't even there. Isaac could've left. He could've taken Lucy with him.

"Jeff, what's wrong?" Angela asked.

"Which way?" He raised his voice and grabbed her shoulders. She flinched and he dropped his hands to his side, stepping back. "Just wait here."

He darted past her and through the crowd. "Lucy?" he shouted. He didn't see her or her ladybug costume anywhere. He didn't see anything but unfamiliar faces.

"Jeff," Angela called from behind, "wait!"

But Jeff didn't stop. This was his fault. This was all his fault.

"Lucy!"

"Hello, Jeff." A man stepped in front of him.

They collided.

The man was wearing a grim reaper mask with a white face and black eyes just above a mouth that gaped open into a long black hole.

Mask aside, Jeff would recognize Isaac's low, raspy voice anywhere.

"You bastard."

Jeff shoved Isaac's shoulder. Lucy stood at his brother's side. Her face was wet with tears, her hand stuck in his grip. She was missing one of her antennas and her wings were askew. Jeff picked her up and held her tight, the only thing preventing him from beating Isaac to a pulp.

"What the hell did you do?"

"Bubbles," Lucy sobbed into his shoulder.

"Jeff," Angela said as she caught up to him. Her face was red and her eyes were slits. "What's gotten into you?" She took Lucy from his arms. "You're acting like a crazy person."

"She lost her bubbles." Isaac took off his mask and patted Lucy on the back.

"Don't touch her," Jeff growled before shoving his finger into Isaac's chest.

"What are you doing? He's your brother," Angela scolded. She looked at him in alarm, like she didn't recognize him anymore, like he was the monster.

She turned to Isaac and shook her head at Jeff's expense. "I'm sorry, Isaac."

She doesn't know what he did, Jeff reminded himself while taking a deep breath. She saw the good in everyone. But there was no good in Isaac.

Jeff learned that the hard way growing up.

"Angela, can you please give us a minute?" he asked in a strained tone.

"I'll give you more than a minute." She adjusted Lucy on her hip and turned their daughter a fraction of an inch away from Jeff, a small movement, but one that hurt more than she could know. Isaac wasn't the problem, not in Angela's eyes. "I'll see you at home." She walked away, Lucy's tear-streaked face tucked into her neck.

Jeff turned back to Isaac. He hadn't stood this close to his brother in years. Isaac was a few pounds overweight and had a clean-shaven face. He wore a pinstripe suit, the opposite of the sweats and baggy T-shirts they wore as kids.

But his eyes were the same: dark, beady, and threatening.

Jeff stepped toward him. "If you so much as look at my daughter again, I'll tell your story," he warned in a hushed, leveled voice.

"*Our* story," Isaac corrected, a smirk on his face. "Remember?"

Jeff remembered better than anyone. "What're you doing here?"

"I never turn down a costume party. "

"Bullshit."

They'd both lived in Chicago for years now. Up until that point, they managed to avoid each other just fine, up until Isaac went out of his way to get Jeff's attention. "I'm not doing this with you. What do you really want?"

"Still a wet blanket, I see." Isaac dropped his mask to the floor and smoothed the lapels on his suit jacket. "We need to talk. Somewhere quiet."

"Fine." Jeff wanted him gone. If hearing him out would make him leave, he'd do exactly that. He led Isaac into the empty hall.

"Why're you here?" he asked again.

"You called me."

Jeff shouldn't have called. He should've let the case play out. But he couldn't change that now. He couldn't turn back time.

"That was a mistake. I won't be reaching out again," he said.

"You won't have to."

"What does that mean?"

Isaac was playing games, trying to get under Jeff's skin just like he did when they were kids. But things were different now. Jeff wasn't willing to play along. "You know what? I don't even care."

He stepped away.

"I wasn't in Saint Lucia."

Jeff turned back around. "What did you just say?"

"The cigar was mine."

"You're lying." He had to be. But how did he know about the cigar? Jeff had asked him if he still smoked Adolfo Elons on the phone last night, but he hadn't mentioned anything about the investigation.

"The sex ring on Galder Avenue is mine, too." He spoke matter-of-factly.

"The sex ring?" Jeff's team hadn't found any proof that Tuco Alvarez's house was used as a ring. They were about to close the investigation on the grounds that Tuco acted alone. And yet as much as Jeff wanted to dismiss Isaac's claim, he couldn't ignore his track record. "Let me guess—customers used the side door?"

"Good job, Detective."

"You're exactly the same." Twenty-five years later, and he was still desperate for power, thriving on others' pain. He was worse—running a sex ring, for Christ's sake. Jeff had no idea how many women were suffering at his hands, how big of a network he had. But he would find out. "Your prints will be on that cigar."

"That's been taken care of."

"Of course it has."

Keith might have been right about the missing information after all. But that didn't matter. Jeff had Isaac's confession now. He could turn him in that same day. Isaac must've known the same.

"Why're you telling me this?" Jeff asked.

"I need your help."

"No way. Not in a million years."

Isaac sighed. "I guess I'll just take care of Keith on my own."

"Keith?"

Isaac had never met Keith. He shouldn't have even known his name.

"He's digging too deep."

"Digging too deep into what?" Jeff asked.

But he already knew. Keith had asked about the cigar—a cigar that could very well connect Isaac to the crime scene. Isaac must've overhead their conversation and Keith's plan to inform Lieutenant Reid of the missing information. He would've perceived Keith as a threat. And he didn't respond well to threats.

He eliminated them.

"He's harmless," Jeff added.

"I wish I believed that." Isaac's eyes were pinpricks. He patted his pockets, then pulled out his keys and turned to leave. "He won't be a problem much longer."

"Leave him alone, or I'll put you behind bars myself." Jeff had seen Isaac hurt people in more ways than one. He wouldn't let him do that to Keith and Talia. They were like family. They'd been through enough already. And that was the difference between Jeff and Isaac. Jeff would never hurt someone like that again.

Isaac chuckled and turned back around. "You'll do exactly as I say, Jeff."

"And what makes you say that?" He squared his shoulders, standing taller.

Isaac pulled something out of his pocket and threw it Jeff's way.

Jeff caught it. A bottle.

A bottle of bubbles.

"You have your own family to worry about."

CHAPTER 16

Charlie parked across the street from the firehouse, cursing when he saw the first two garages empty, Truck 59 and Chief Freeman's car gone. He wanted to talk to Freeman about the fire's origin and the neighbor with the ponytail. He hadn't stopped thinking about either since leaving the scene of the fire. The house's remains.

He removed his keys from the ignition, hoping Freeman would show up before he had to leave to meet Talia at the hospital. He'd wait in his truck instead of going inside. The firehouse was a reminder now, more than anything. A reminder that the fire had won, that Charlie hadn't even put up a fight.

A reminder that he'd left Jenny to the flames.

He grabbed Jenny's journal from the back seat, needing a distraction, and turned to the last entry. The words were just as ambiguous as the night before—mention of the green pen and Shevy, nothing more. He flipped through the pages.

Something caught his eye.

He backtracked until he found the page. Last Tuesday's date had been erased at some point. But that wasn't what grabbed his attention. The date had been rewritten in green. The same green ink Jenny used in Thursday's entry. He wasn't sure how he missed that detail the night before.

He reread Tuesday's entry. It was short, just like her last one.

Tuesday, October 16

My Legal Writing class's research paper has been taking up all of my time. The good news? I'm almost done. The assignment is due by midnight.

After confirming a few details with my dad tonight, I'll turn the paper in. Here's to hoping I get my social life back after that . . .

Nothing about the entry jumped out at him.

Jenny had been in law school and their dad was a lawyer. Asking for his help would've made sense. Even so, according to her last entry, she didn't get the pen until Wednesday. The fact that she bothered to go back and change Tuesday's date to green after that, and to mention the pen in Thursday's post at all, made him wonder if she connected the days on purpose, if she'd wanted someone to notice.

A flash of red shot past his window.

Truck 59 and Chief Freeman's car pulled into the firehouse. Charlie's squad jumped out of the truck and Howell from the passenger seat—Charlie's seat. His promotion to lieutenant must've finally come in. Charlie was happy for him, and he knew that Howell was the best one for the job. After Friday morning's fire, Charlie didn't trust himself or his instincts. He wouldn't ask his squad to trust him, either.

He stepped out of his truck and walked halfway up the drive. Howell saw him first. He set down the equipment he was holding and came out to meet him. The others followed, Chief Freeman included.

Howell placed a hand on Charlie's shoulder. "We've been worried about you," he said as he nodded at the rest of the group. "We tried calling."

"I know."

Charlie had received their messages, the same with those from his family and friends. He hadn't read or listened to any yet. He already knew what they'd say—that he was in their thoughts, their prayers. But he didn't deserve their mind space, a second thought, and certainly not a prayer. "Can I talk to you, Chief?"

"Of course," Freeman answered, and the rest of the squad backed away. Some patted Charlie's back, others offered condolences. Charlie thanked them, but he didn't feel a thing. He was numb and preferred to stay that way.

"How're you holding up?" Freeman asked.

"I'm fine." Any more of an answer would be a waste of Freeman's time, of Charlie's time, too. "I wanted to ask you about the fire."

Freeman crossed his arms over his chest. "What do you want to know?"

"I went back to the house this morning."

"Alone? It's a crime scene." He frowned, not amused.

"I know that." The man with the ponytail had pointed out the same. Charlie didn't need a reminder then, and he didn't need one now. "I found the fire's origin."

"In the alley."

"Yes." He felt a sting of adrenaline talking to someone who'd been there, who could help. "I don't understand why Tuco Alvarez would've started the fire outside."

"That's not your job to understand."

Still, he had to know if Freeman agreed. "But it's strange, right? He could've used the accelerant inside of the house and had more cover with the same results."

"Okay . . . sure." Freeman went with that. "What're you getting at?"

Charlie had yet to share his hunch with anyone. But Freeman might be able to make sense of his suspicion.

"What if someone else started the fire? Someone who used the alley because they didn't have a way to get inside."

"Didn't Tuco leave a note?" Freeman asked.

"Yes, but the message could've been forged. And according to Detective Foley, the police haven't confirmed who actually wrote the note yet."

Freeman nodded slowly, as if finally understanding. He uncrossed his arms and slid his hands into his pockets. "Have you gotten much sleep since the fire?"

"Sleep?" Charlie pulled back. "What does that have to do with anything?"

"You just lost a sister. And you hit your head."

"I'm aware, thanks." He didn't come to the firehouse to talk about himself or his sleep schedule. He came to talk about the fire. And he wasn't done yet. "There was a neighbor, too. A man with a ponytail. Did you see him on Friday morning?"

"You have to let the CPD do their job."

"They're not doing anything. That's why I'm here. You know more about the fire than anyone, the CPD included. I need your help."

"I'm here for you. We all are." Freeman gestured toward the firehouse and the men still standing in the garage. "But we can't help you if you don't help yourself. You're hurting right now. Your emotions could be clouding your judgment."

"They're not." If anything, he was the only one keeping an open mind. "Please, just come back to the scene of the fire with me to see if anything stands out."

"Get some rest, Charlie. Take a break," Freeman said, his tone final. "Come back in a few days and we can talk more then."

"I don't have a few days."

He couldn't help but feel that his time was running out, that the truth was just within reach but slipping away with each second that passed. Yet Freeman didn't seem to care. And why would he? He had a firehouse to run, a group of men to protect. And for the next six days, that group of men didn't include Charlie.

He stepped away from Freeman, from the firehouse, from his squad.

Freeman sighed. "I'm sorry, Charlie."

That was the second apology he received that day.

First Detective Foley, now his own chief.

He hoped he wouldn't get a third.

CHAPTER 17

For the first time in as long as Talia could remember, work was failing to serve as a distraction. No matter how many patients' vitals she took or how many EKG monitors she scanned, the accusation she made against her dad reverberated through her mind. She wished she could take back the words more than anything. But she couldn't take them back. The accusation hadn't only been said, but heard.

The damage had been done.

"Did you get some sleep?"

Talia startled at Amy's voice. She and her charge nurse were not on the best of terms, not since Talia's overtime stunt the night before. She'd only stayed past her shift because one of her patients had declined suddenly and begged her not to leave. And yes, maybe also subconsciously because she wanted to avoid going home to an empty apartment, but she never would've stayed had she thought for even one second that she would be putting her patient at risk. She sat next to the woman's bed and held her hand. She kept her company, and that was it. No harm done.

But Amy didn't care about any of that. She cared about rules and time tracking, sticking to the schedule. If she sensed Talia's scattered mind now and realized that she started rounds thirty minutes early tonight, even if only because traffic had been light, she would send Talia home again, no questions asked. And Talia couldn't spend the night alone with her thoughts, not after what she said to her dad.

She turned around and forced a smile. "I did, thanks."

"I hope so." Amy inclined her head as if about to say more, but then her eyes settled over Talia's shoulder. She smiled. "Can we help you find something?"

"I'm here to see Talia, actually."

Talia turned.

Charlie stood a few feet away. He looked paler than he had the day before, thinner, worn out. Still, he was handsome, more handsome than she remembered. His charcoal shirt complemented his blue eyes.

"Do you still have time to talk?"

"Yes." Her pitch was off, too high, too loud. She cleared her throat, had to get a grip. She took a breath and tried again. "I still have time. Let's go over here."

She led him to an empty room across the floor, pretending not to notice the amused glint in Amy's eye as they passed.

"Thanks for meeting me."

"You said you needed help with something?" All afternoon, she'd been curious to hear what he had to say. Now that he was here, now that she felt flustered all over again, she wanted him to leave. She wanted to get back to work and her familiar routine.

"I need to ask the woman from the fire some questions."

"She's still restricted to family visitation."

The police had gone into her room earlier that day to take a fingerprint from her unburned hand. But that was different; it was cleared by the doctor.

"Besides," she added, "she hasn't spoken since she woke up."

"That's fine. I'll do the talking."

"No, you won't," Talia said.

He wasn't listening. She should've expected as much. He was the same as yesterday. Only tonight, she didn't have the patience to repeat herself.

"Like I said, she's restricted to family visitation. I'll let you know when that changes. But until then, I have work to do."

She walked toward the door without another word, relieved at having nothing more to say.

"My sister died in that fire."

That made Talia stop and turn back around. "Your sister?"

"Jenny. She was in the house. She didn't survive."

"I'm so sorry."

Talia didn't have siblings. She couldn't imagine what he was going through. But she had lost a loved one, so she was more than familiar with the pain.

"I need to know what happened that night," Charlie told her.

"Can't you ask the police?"

"They're closing the case." His words had a bite. He didn't offer anything else.

And neither would she. She wouldn't mention that her dad helped with the investigation and that the lead detective was like family. She wouldn't mention the cigar. If she learned anything from the potluck earlier that day, it was that she was better off minding her own business.

"I'm sorry," she said. "I can't help you."

"Please, Talia. I only need a few minutes with her, that's it."

She looked away, the rawness of his ask too familiar. She'd been there herself, begging nurses for updates and doctors for details, searching for closure she'd never find. But again, this wasn't about Talia. It wasn't about Charlie, either.

This was about her patient.

If Talia let Charlie into that room, what was the worst that could happen? The woman could become upset at his presence, in which case, they'd leave. Talia could also be caught, and based on her current standing with Amy, she would most certainly get in trouble. The best that could happen? In a case like this, one where the mental trauma may outweigh the physical damage, feeling less alone could be the difference between life and death. "How do I know I can trust you?"

"You don't."

Handsome and honest. Talia kicked herself for the thought.

"But you can trust me," he added. "I promise."

As simple as that.

"And you'll be there for her? Not just tonight, but through her recovery?"

"I'll be here as long as she needs me."

Talia believed him. And for her, that was enough. "Okay. I'll help."

"Thank you. Thank you so much."

"You'll need a guest pass." She'd never smuggled someone into a restricted patient's room before, but she walked to the front desk as if she had, before she lost her nerve. Plenty of her burn patients were stable and open to visitors. She just had to take her pick. "This is Charlie McMahon. He's here to visit Spencer Abbott."

"Spencer?" The receptionist behind the desk typed into her computer while chomping on a piece of gum. She squinted at Charlie, then back at the screen.

Talia held her breath.

"Here you go." She handed Charlie the pass.

"Thank you." Talia started for the woman's room, much more aware of Charlie's presence by her side than she would've liked. He had that effect on her, apparently. One she wanted nothing to do with, not with Charlie, not with anyone.

They stopped in front of the woman's room.

He looked over his shoulder at the empty hallway. "What's next?"

"We go inside."

Or not. She still had time to change her mind. But Charlie could give the woman a fighting chance. And Talia's job was to make sure her patient had just that.

She opened the door.

"Two minutes," she said. Less, if things went south.

"That's all I need."

He walked into the room and she followed him inside, shutting the door and closing the observation window's blinds. Light filtered in from under the door, the room otherwise cast in shadows. He sat in the chair next to the hospital bed, next to the woman lying on her back with her eyes closed.

He didn't waste any time. "You probably don't remember me." He spoke in a soft and gentle voice. "My name is Charlie. I was at the fire. My teammate and I pulled you from the flames."

The woman opened her eyes.

She turned her head toward him.

Talia's breath caught. Her patient hadn't so much as made eye contact since waking up that morning. Now she was staring at Charlie. She was listening.

"My sister died in that fire." He held the woman's gaze. "The police are giving up. But I'm not. I'll find whoever did this to you and make sure they pay," he said as he reached into his back pocket and pulled out his phone. "But to do that, I need your help."

He scrolled on his cell and turned the screen to the woman. "This is my sister, Jenny. She was at Tuco Alvarez's house Thursday night. Did she give you the knife?"

Two seconds passed in silence, three, four.

The woman nodded, barely a fraction of an inch, but a nod all the same.

The door opened.

Amy stepped into the room, a clipboard in her hand. She glanced at Talia, then at Charlie. "What the hell is going on in here?"

"Nothing. We were just leaving." Talia went over to Charlie and put a hand on his shoulder, his muscles tense beneath her touch. "Let's go."

He didn't budge. "Did Tuco Alvarez start the fire?" he asked the woman.

"Talia!" Amy scolded. "Get him out of here."

"The owner of the house." Charlie spoke with more urgency than Talia had heard him use before. He was begging the woman. "Did Tuco start the fire?"

The woman blinked. A single tear rolled down her cheek. She shook her head no.

CHAPTER 18

Charlie's mind was anywhere but on the road. His thoughts were back at the hospital, back with Talia and her patient, the woman who shattered the CPD's investigation with just one shake of her head. Given the fire's origin in the back alley, Charlie believed her. Tuco Alvarez didn't start the fire. And if he didn't start the fire, then he didn't kill the women or leave the note behind.

Someone else did.

Thanks to Talia, Charlie's hunch had been confirmed. He'd tried calling her after leaving the hospital but had yet to hear back. He couldn't help but take that as a bad sign. She risked her job sneaking him into that room. She helped him when no one else had. He trusted her for that and wanted to make things right. If he didn't hear from her by tomorrow night, he'd go back to the hospital and explain that everything was his fault.

He'd get Talia out of whatever mess he put her in.

He turned onto West Thomas Street and parked by the curb. Shevy's sublet hadn't changed much in the months since he'd dropped Jenny off there last. A slightly tilted frame added character to the white paint, and burgundy flowers were arranged in a pot out front. He should've driven to the police department first and told Detective Foley what he learned about the fire. But based on how the CPD was handling Jenny's case, Charlie didn't trust them. Besides, they had their chance to find answers.

Now it was his turn.

He stepped out of his truck and climbed the steps up to Shevy's slanted front porch. No one answered when he knocked or when he rang the doorbell. Sitting down on the front steps, he pulled out his phone and dialed Shevy's number.

The line rang three times.

"Charlie?" Shevy answered in a tentative voice, one he'd never heard from her before. "I've been meaning to call you . . . I'm so sorry for your loss."

"I'm sorry for yours. How are you holding up?"

"I just don't understand what happened."

"That makes two of us." He stood and walked toward the other side of the porch. "That's why I called, actually. I wanted to ask you about your plans with Jenny last Thursday night."

"Last Thursday? We didn't have any plans."

"She told my parents that you did." He read the same in Jenny's journal.

Shevy was quiet for some time. "I hadn't seen her in over a week, Charlie."

"Why is that?"

According to Andrew, they had a falling out. But again, Charlie wasn't sure how much truth that could possibly hold. Shevy and Jenny had been in the same classes. They had the same group of friends, study groups, everything. Avoiding each other would've been nearly impossible.

"Were you two fighting?" he asked.

"Listen . . . Charlie, I'm at the airport. I can't really talk right now."

"The airport?"

She was leaving town two days after her best friend was murdered?

"Where're you going?"

"Minnesota. I'm visiting my grandma. I'll be back for the funeral, though."

"The funeral. Right."

In the haze of the past few days, he hadn't even thought about Jenny's funeral. His parents would be making arrangements by now, the service likely to take place that coming weekend. But Charlie refused to bury his sister without knowing her killer had been found and locked away. So while Shevy may not have had the time to talk, his questions couldn't wait.

"I just need five minutes, maybe less," he said. "Please, Shevy."

"We're boarding. I have to go."

She ended the call.

"Dammit." She had answers; he knew she did. Answers she didn't seem too keen on sharing. But she wouldn't be able to avoid his questions forever. He'd call her again tomorrow and swing by her house later that week to try to talk then.

He strode down the porch's front steps.

A woman walking down the sidewalk turned into Shevy's front yard. She was wearing a hoodie, jeans, and tennis shoes. Her hair was piled on top of her head.

She stopped when she saw Charlie. "Are you here to see Shevy?"

"I was, yes. She's not home."

She pulled a set of keys from her bag. "She told me you might come by."

"She did?"

"She tried to reach you this afternoon, but she had the wrong number." She walked past him, climbed the porch steps, and stuck her key into the door. "Come back tomorrow night around this same time. She'll have her portion of the case study done by then."

"Tomorrow? Isn't she visiting her grandma in Minnesota?"

She turned around and looked at him as if he were more of an annoyance than anything else. "Visiting her grandma? A week before the mock trial?"

Obviously, the answer was no. "I'll come back tomorrow, then."

"You do that." She stepped into the house and slammed the door shut behind her.

Charlie didn't move. Shevy had lied about Minnesota. She made up the trip when he asked her if she and Jenny had been fighting. Why, he didn't know.

But he'd find out.

He'd see what she had to say tomorrow night.

CHAPTER 19

Talia stood on one side of the conference room and wished Amy would stop pacing at the other, or at least that she'd say something. She was angry, and Talia understood that. But she also hadn't been inside of that room. She hadn't seen the good that Charlie's visit did. Talia had.

"Her eyes were glued to his face, Amy. She was listening."

"That doesn't matter." Amy stepped toward Talia and lowered her voice to a whisper. "What matters is that you let him in there in the first place."

"But he helped her," she replied. "Before he went into that room, the woman hadn't acknowledged anything, let alone anyone. The second he started talking, that changed. She became perceptive, aware. That has to count for something."

"That's not the point."

"Then what *is* the point?" Talia countered. "We're nurses. We help patients in need. Bringing him into the woman's room was a risk, yes. But that risk paid off."

"And what if someone asks me about tonight?"

"You tell them the truth. I let Charlie into a restricted patient's room. I broke the rules. But the patient's condition improved as a result, dramatically so."

"It's not that easy. This happened under my watch."

"I know."

Amy may not have let Charlie into the room, but she managed the nurse who did. She'd be associated with the breach in protocol, positive results or not.

"This was my doing, not yours. I fully accept the blame," Talia assured her.

"It's too late for that." Amy dropped her eyes to the floor, shaking her head. "You worked too many hours yesterday, now this. What's next?" She sounded defeated, like she needed a way out. And if giving her one would help, then Talia would do just that.

"Nothing." She promised. "You don't have to worry about me anymore."

"I do worry about you. And I can't keep letting you off the hook. It's not fair." Amy looked up with resolve in her eyes. "I'm sorry, Talia. I have to suspend you."

"Suspend me?"

Talia had known she could get in trouble for this, that Amy would be upset. But upset enough to keep her away from her patients? That wouldn't do anyone any good. There had to be another option.

"I'm already here. I'm ready to work."

"It'll only be a week."

"That's too much time." Way too much time. Talia had barely missed a shift since joining the hospital. "Please, just give me one more chance."

Something beeped.

Talia checked her pager. "It's the front desk."

"Give me your pager. And your badge." Amy held out her hand.

"Come on, Amy," Talia begged, desperate for a sign of uncertainty, a sign that she could be swayed. But there was nothing there. Nothing but Amy's hard stare.

Talia waited, holding her breath.

Amy didn't so much as blink. "I've made up my mind."

Talia sighed. "Fine." She unclipped her pager and her badge.

Another beep.

Amy looked down at her own pager, her brow furrowed.

"The front desk."

She walked to the room's landline and dialed. "It's Amy." Silence. "What?" She dropped her voice and glanced back at Talia. "Are you sure?" She waited, listening.

"What is it?" Talia asked as she stepped closer.

"Thanks." Amy hung up the phone and turned back to Talia. Her face had lost some color. Her hard stare had softened. "You need to go to the second floor."

"The second floor? Why? What's happened?" Amy suspended Talia seconds before. Now she wanted her to go to the surgical unit?

"Your dad is here."

"My dad?" She hadn't spoken to him since the potluck that afternoon. *He must've come by to talk,* she realized. *I can apologize for what I said. I can make things right.* She'd promise to relax, to give him more space. "Thanks. I'll head down now."

"Talia." Amy blocked her path. "He's in surgery. There's been an accident."

"An accident?" That couldn't be right. Talia had just seen him that afternoon. He was fine. Upset with her, but fine. "That's impossible."

"He was in a car accident. They found his ID."

"No."

She shook her head. The room started to spin. This couldn't be happening. Not another car accident. Not so soon. Her dad was a careful driver. He'd never been in an accident. And yet he was here now, at the hospital—just like her mom had been two years before.

He hadn't come to talk. He was on the second floor.

He was in surgery.

She dropped her badge and her pager. She reached for the wall.

"Easy," Amy said, grabbing her shoulder.

"I have to go."

Talia stumbled to the doorway and took off running down the hall, shoving the exit doors open and tearing up a flight of stairs onto the second floor. The OR schedule was filled. She found her dad's name, ran to the third room, and scrubbed her hands. A nurse was waiting for her by the sink. "Talia, right? Let me fill you in."

Talia secured her mask over her face and pushed past the nurse.

"Wait!" the nurse called.

Talia burst through the surgery doors.

She stopped short.

The top of her dad's head was visible on the operating table, covered in blood. Two doctors and four nurses had scrubbed in for the procedure.

A big team.

"What happened?" Talia whispered. It was all she could manage.

The surgery doors opened and the nurse who tried to stop her came into the room. "You can't be here, Talia. You need to leave."

Talia ignored the order and moved toward the side of the table, her feet heavy, her breathing slow. The metallic scent of blood filled her nose—not just another patient's blood this time. Her dad's. She reached the edge of the table and couldn't look away. He was unconscious, his face slick with blood. He had a gash across his forehead and a breathing tube down his throat. His shirt was already cut open.

"You need to leave," one of the doctors repeated.

"What happened?" Her voice was raised and raw, unfamiliar.

The doctors looked at each other. One of them spoke up. "Pneumothorax, broken bones, and possible head trauma. We have to start surgery, now."

Talia wiped her tears and grabbed her dad's hand. The doctor was right. They had to start. They'd been too late with Talia's mom.

She leaned forward. "I'm here, Dad," she whispered into his ear. Then she stepped back and took her place against the wall.

The doctors glanced at each other again. She wasn't supposed to be there. They all knew that. But she wasn't leaving. Maybe they knew that, too.

The doctor reached for a scalpel. "Let's get started."

CHAPTER 20

Jeff shut his office door and sat down at his desk. He turned on his computer and scrolled through the case's files. There was no mention of the cigar, just as Keith had said. He paged through the inventory log next, only he didn't see the cigar's photograph there either, as if he imagined the picture in the first place. But he hadn't imagined a thing—not the details in the system, not the picture in the log.

They'd been there. Now they were gone.

And Jeff knew exactly who to blame. Isaac didn't only know about the cigar; he boasted that his prints were no longer a concern. He was behind the missing information. He had to be. But deleting the files wouldn't change the fact that the lab still had the cigar. Isaac's prints could still be found.

Jeff grabbed his cell and dialed the lab. He asked for an update on the cigar's analysis. The technician put him on hold for some time, then came back onto the line.

"I'm sorry, Detective. We never received a cigar," she said.

"Are you sure?"

Strum sent the cigar for testing yesterday. Jeff had seen the status in the system. "My team didn't send anything yesterday morning?"

"They sent plenty: matches, a pocketknife, and more. Just not a cigar."

"Check again, will you? It's important."

She sighed and put him back on hold. After a few minutes, she picked up the line. "Like I said, it's not here."

Jeff hung up. He stood and racked his mind. Strum could've misplaced the cigar before sending the evidence to the lab. But he wouldn't have deleted the files to cover up the mistake, not after showing Jeff the cigar's picture the day before.

No. This wasn't Strum.

This was Isaac.

He found a way to delete the files and intercept the cigar, all to protect his name. Jeff was sure of it. Isaac must've thought he was in the clear. But that'd been before the potluck, before he overheard Keith mention going to Lieutenant Reid. Now, he seemed to think he still had one more person standing in his way.

Jeff called Keith for the third time that night.

His line went straight to voicemail, yet again.

Jeff hung up. Had Isaac not threatened Keith that afternoon, Jeff wouldn't give the missed calls a second thought. But Isaac *had* threatened Keith. Jeff should've found him by now and confirmed that he was okay. He should've reported Isaac. But he hadn't reported a thing. Why? Because Isaac was clear at the potluck. If Jeff didn't fall in line, Angela and Lucy would pay.

Then again, Jeff's family would be at risk whether he followed Isaac's command or not. No matter what Jeff did, Isaac couldn't be trusted. Angela and Lucy wouldn't be safe unless Isaac was locked behind bars.

And Jeff would keep his family safe no matter the cost. He couldn't turn Isaac in for what he did twenty-five years back. Too much time had passed. But he could find a way to connect Isaac to the sex ring, to the women. And he would.

Even so, he had to be careful. He couldn't pull in the CPD too early and risk word of his plan reaching Isaac before the arrest was made. Jeff would find evidence against Isaac first. He'd engage the CPD only when an arrest was inevitable.

Then he'd put Isaac in handcuffs himself.

And once Isaac was locked away, Jeff would tell Angela everything about his past. Not because he had to, but because she deserved to hear the truth. Because the time had come for him to stop lying to the people he loved, for him to live up to the oath he took to protect. And that oath didn't just apply to Angela and Lucy, but to the city of Chicago as well, to everyone suffering at his brother's hands—to Keith.

Assuming Isaac didn't get to him first.

Jeff jogged to the parking lot. He jumped into his car and pulled onto the street, accelerating as he went. There was hardly any traffic at 9:00 p.m. and Keith lived close. As long as he was home and safe, Jeff's trip would be short.

He turned onto Doreen Street only to slam on the brakes. The car in front of him had come to a complete stop. A line of cars was clogging the street.

"You've got to be kidding me."

He honked his horn as he inched forward at a snail's pace.

A police cruiser was parked up ahead, half a block away from Keith's house, headlights on. A closed-off three-way intersection explained the hold up. Jeff spotted a bumper in the middle of the road and a car's hood wrapped around a telephone pole: a silver Honda.

Keith drove a silver Honda.

Jeff's grip tightened on the wheel. The car could belong to anyone. Plenty of people drove Hondas and silver was a popular color. Besides, Keith was a safe driver. Talia had hung a Saint Christopher medallion from his rearview mirror, for Christ's sake. His car couldn't be wrapped around that pole, not after what happened to his wife.

But an accident would explain why he hadn't called Jeff back.

Jeff pulled over and parked. He climbed out of his car and walked to the scene of the accident, the police cruiser's headlights illuminating skid marks across the intersection. From what he could tell, the Honda had been rear-ended, the trunk smashed inward and the hood forced straight into the pole. Whoever hit the car must've been distracted.

Or not.

Sweat gathered on Jeff's forehead and his hands grew clammy. The Honda was the only damaged car in sight. The windows were shattered and something dark pooled just outside of the driver's side door.

Something that looked a lot like blood.

"Hey!" A young officer trotted over. He was new to the job, if the bounce in his step was any indication—a bounce that would disappear with enough shifts under his belt. "You can't come any closer." He stepped in front of Jeff and put hands in the air. "It's a crime scene."

"I work for the CPD," Jeff said as he showed his badge and tried not to react to the officer's choice of words. A "crime scene," not the scene of an accident, but a crime scene. He dropped his eyes back to the pool of blood. "What happened?"

The officer lowered his arms. "Looks like a hit-and-run."

Jeff motioned toward the Honda and forced the question out of his mouth.

"And the driver?"

"The guy didn't look too good. They took him to the hospital."

A guy—could've been anyone.

"Did you find any ID?"

"No. The ambulance came before we could search him. We can't get into the car to look for registration, either. Too much damage." He gestured toward a cop leaning against the cruiser with a phone to her ear. "We're running his plates now."

"Good." Jeff wiped a line of sweat from his brow. He wished he knew Keith's license plate number, but he didn't. And for now, he couldn't jump to any conclusions. He'd wait in his car until they knew more. He would call the hospital, too, and ask if Keith had been brought in. He'd find him, one way or another.

When he turned to leave, he felt something under his shoe. He lifted his foot. A pendant lay on the ground, cracked down the middle.

A Saint Christopher medallion.

CHAPTER 21

Talia sat down next to her dad's hospital bed and watched the early-morning light filter through the blinds. She held his hand while taking inventory of his black eyes and cracked ribs, his broken leg suspended above his waist, and the gauze wrapped around his head. A ventilator was helping him breathe. Everything considered, he barely survived the crash. But he was alive.

That's all that mattered.

He was alive.

And yet there was no guarantee he'd ever open his eyes. Talia had seen her fair share of loss on the job. But she'd seen miracles, too, patients who held on despite the odds, who heard their family's voices through the fog.

"I'm here, Dad," she whispered with tears in her eyes. "Stay with me."

The door opened.

Jeff stepped into the room.

"Jeff." Talia stood. "I was going to call you this morning." The surgery had taken hours the night before and ended late. She hadn't managed to call anyone yet, but Jeff was at the top of her list. "I'm so glad you're here."

"How is he?"

He walked past the bed and wrapped Talia in an embrace. Judging by the deep creases around his eyes; his wrinkled, untucked shirt; and his unkempt hair, she hadn't been the only one up all night. He pulled back and glanced at her dad.

"Jesus Christ."

"He's in an induced coma."

She kept the rest of the doctor's explanation to herself—that the extent of brain trauma was still unknown. She couldn't go through the details, not again.

"An induced coma . . . right." He was holding her dad's briefcase in one hand and fidgeting with something else in his other.

"What's that?" she asked.

"I picked these up at the crime scene." He set the briefcase down and took her hand. "I thought this might be more useful here." He placed two pieces of metal into her palm: a broken Saint Christopher medallion, the one she'd given her dad days after her mom died. She'd even snuck her mom's La Virgen De Guadalupe prayer card into his center console. She thought the medallion and the card would protect him.

She knew better now.

She closed her hand around the broken halves. "What happened?"

"A hit-and-run." He walked to the other side of the room and started pacing, his hands behind his head. He didn't just look tired now but nervous, too, wired.

"It was across the field by his house," he added.

"On Doreen?" The speed limit couldn't be more than thirty on that street. Her dad's injuries looked as if he'd been driving seventy. He or the other driver, at least. The driver who left him bleeding on the street. "Do you know who hit him?"

Jeff avoided her gaze. "Not yet."

"Were any other cars involved?"

Her dad would be devastated if that were the case, if the collision caused injuries on top of his own.

"No one else."

"Just my dad."

The safest driver she knew. But being cautious on the road wasn't always enough. It didn't protect her mom from the drunk driver who ran the red light. This time, Talia couldn't help but feel responsible for her dad's accident. She couldn't help but wonder if his mind had been on the accusation she made at the potluck, if he'd been distracted from the road.

"We got into an argument today, a bad one," she told Jeff.

"This isn't your fault."

"I shouldn't have mentioned the cigar."

Jeff stopped pacing. "The cigar?"

"I was standing outside of the office at the potluck, remember?"

"You overheard our conversation?"

"Yes." And she didn't need a lecture from Jeff on minding her own business now, too. "The next time you want privacy, why don't you try shutting the door?"

"Did anyone see you in the hallway?" he asked with panic in his voice.

"I have no idea. Why?"

He came to her side of the bed. "I need you to forget what you heard, okay?"

"What's gotten into you?" She didn't recognize the intensity in his gaze. "Are the files still missing? Is that it?"

"What? No." He shook his head. "You have to stop asking questions."

"I'll ask whatever I want, thanks."

"Then you'll end up in the same position as your dad," he snapped.

A beat passed. His words settled, his warning. "What does that mean?"

"Nothing." He stepped back and raked a hand through his red hair. "Just forget it."

"You said asking questions would put me in the same position as my dad." Her dad, who'd been hit by another car. "Are you saying this wasn't an accident?"

"I didn't say that."

"You insinuated as much." Her dad was a private man. Ever since her mom's accident, he kept to himself. If he asked questions, they would've been about a case. And as of that morning, he only mentioned one. "Is this about the fire?"

"Of course not." Jeff turned away.

"He asked you about the cigar, and suggested you go to Lieutenant Reid." She spoke slowly, piecing the timeline together. "He was hit hours later, half a block from his house."

"That's a coincidence."

"Is it? Why was the cigar deleted from the files in the first place?" That didn't sound like something that'd happen by chance. "Who did this, Jeff?"

"We don't know that yet."

"You're the case's lead detective." He had to know something. Her mere mention of the cigar minutes before had set him off. *He knows more than he's letting on.*

"You're hiding something."

"Just drop it, will you?"

"No." She didn't know what happened, what Jeff was keeping to himself. But there was something. She was sure of it. He was lying, all while her dad was hanging on by a thread. And she didn't need that, not from him.

"You should leave."

"Talia . . ."

"Now." She pointed at the door, her arm shaking. If he didn't understand that she needed the truth, then he didn't know her at all and she didn't want him here.

"Get out."

Jeff hesitated. "I'll fix this, okay? Just sit tight."

He left the room.

Talia sat down in the chair by the bed. The hit-and-run couldn't be a coincidence, not given Jeff's warning. And if someone had felt threatened by her dad, what would happen when that same person realized he was still alive?

The driver would come after him again.

CHAPTER 22

Charlie stood outside of his parents' front door. They weren't expecting him, and they wouldn't be happy to see him, either. But he had to talk to his dad. Jenny's journal entry from last Tuesday and the date in green were still on his mind. He couldn't help but think she rewrote the date for a reason. What that reason was, he had no idea. But she mentioned their dad and her research paper in the entry.

And that's why Charlie was there. To find out more.

He rang the doorbell, knocked, and waited. He rang the bell again. No one answered. His parents weren't home. That, or they stopped answering the door, every knock a neighbor with a casserole, avoiding visitors now part of their routine.

He hadn't let himself into his parents' house since before he moved out. After that, he only visited when Jenny asked him to come. And even then, she was always the one to open the door and welcome him inside. Now, he was on his own.

She'd never open that door again.

He unlocked the door with his set of keys and stepped inside.

The house was quiet. His parents' shoes were discarded in the entryway and his mom's coat was heaped on the ground. Jenny's jacket still hung from the coatrack, the cherry-red fabric worn thin from use over the years.

He shut the door. "Hello?"

Something shattered.

He stepped over the shoes and the coat and strode down the hall.

His mom was standing in the middle of the kitchen, reaching for a broken plate's fragments scattered across the brown-tiled floor. She leaned too far forward and toppled to the ground, her nightgown's hem tearing in the process.

"Mom, are you okay?"

He moved around the broken plate and helped her stand, the stench of vodka there as always. "Here, sit down." He led her to the table and pulled out a chair.

"I'm fine," she mumbled as she shrugged away from his touch and fell back into the seat.

"You're not fine." He poured her a glass of water and set it in front of her unsteady hands. "Drink this. You'll feel better."

She pushed the glass aside and stared at the table with glazed-over eyes.

"Where's Dad?" If things were anything like they'd been growing up, he'd be sitting in his study with the door shut, ignoring the dishes in the sink, the crumbs scattered across the counter, and the empty milk carton next to the toaster.

He'd be ignoring his drunk wife. "Is he home?"

"I said I'm fine."

"Right." Whether or not his dad was hiding from his life didn't matter. What mattered was that Charlie's mom needed help. And he was the only child she had left. He grabbed the broom and swept up the broken plate before opening the cabinet under the sink to throw the pieces away. "Have you eaten today?"

He stopped.

A bottle of vodka sat behind the trash, half full.

His mom's hiding places hadn't changed. Apparently, her preference for cheap vodka hadn't, either. He dropped the plate's fragments into the trash, then held the bottle up in the air. "You can't live like this, Mom."

Her gaze settled on the vodka.

Her eyes became clear. "Put that down."

"You have to stop."

She wouldn't stop, especially now that Jenny was gone. She'd drink whatever she wanted, whenever she wanted. And why wouldn't she? Her husband didn't care. Charlie did, but he couldn't be there every second.

I'm here now.

He unscrewed the cap and poured the vodka down the drain.

"Stop!" She jumped up, lunging forward, and tried to reach around him to grab the bottle. She came up short and resorted to small, weak punches on his back. "Please!"

The last drop fell into the sink.

He put the bottle down and took hold of her flailing arms, trying to catch her eye. "You need help. It's killing you, Mom. Do you understand that? It's killing you."

"I hope it does," she sobbed, breaking away from his hold. She grabbed the empty bottle and stumbled out of the room. Seconds later, a door slammed shut.

"What's going on in here?"

Charlie turned as his dad walked into the kitchen. He had dark circles under his eyes and pallid, taut skin. He looked terrible, like a more angular version of himself. He looked worse than Charlie's mom. But that didn't stop Charlie's anger from boiling over. "I should be asking you that question."

"Excuse me?"

"She's drunk. But you wouldn't know that, would you?"

"You watch your tongue," his dad warned.

"She needs help."

"You have no idea what she needs."

"You just lost a daughter. Do you really want to lose your wife, too?"

Silence settled.

His dad stepped closer. His voice was hoarse, low. "Get out of my house."

"I'm not leaving." Charlie didn't want to stay, not for one more second. But he couldn't forget why he came in the first place. "I need to talk to you about Jenny."

"No." His dad held up his hand. "Not tonight."

"Five minutes, then I'm gone."

If anything would convince his dad to open up, the promise of Charlie leaving would do the trick. "Otherwise, I'll stick around."

They glared at each other. The vein in his dad's neck pulsed. "Five minutes. That's all."

He led Charlie into his study. The same pictures as always sat on the dark, paneled shelves: one of Charlie's parents on their wedding day, another of Jenny graduating from high school, and one of Charlie and Jenny running around outside as kids. His dad turned to face him, glancing at his watch.

"So?"

Charlie's time started now. "Did you and Jenny meet up last Tuesday?"

"How do you know about that?" His dad frowned.

"She told me you were helping her with a paper," Charlie lied. He didn't plan on mentioning the journal—not yet and maybe not ever. "How did she seem that night? Different? Distracted?" He cast a wide net, hoping for something, anything.

His dad walked to his desk and sank into the seat. "I wouldn't know. She was supposed to meet me at my North Avenue office on Tuesday night, but she never showed."

"Why not?"

"She and Shevy apparently lost track of time."

"Shevy?" Yet again, Jenny's supposed plans contradicted Shevy's claim that they hadn't seen each other in a week. "Are you sure that's what she said?"

"Yes." He narrowed his eyes. "Why're you asking?"

"I'm trying to make sense of everything."

Aside from meeting their dad, Jenny hadn't offered any other plans in her journal. "Did she mention anything about her paper?" Charlie asked next.

"What does that have to do with anything?"

"Probably nothing." But given the date rewritten in green, he wasn't sure. "Did she tell you what the research paper was about, anything like that?"

"No." He checked his watch again. "You're down to two minutes."

"I'm done." He had what he needed. Jenny's Tuesday-night plans were something to look into further, something to ask Shevy about. Now, he just had to check Jenny's room for the paper. Then he'd be on his way.

"I need to grab something from my room before I leave."

"Fine."

Charlie walked back to the entryway. The staircase's first step creaked under his weight as he climbed to the second floor. He went straight for Jenny's room.

The stack of papers was still on her desk.

He heard his dad leave the study and walk toward the kitchen.

He paged through the documents, but he had no idea what he was looking for. Nothing stood out. And maybe nothing would. Maybe the paper was irrelevant.

A creak sounded, the first step on the staircase.

His dad was coming up.

Charlie rushed, flipping to the last document.

The assignment was typed, everything aside from Jenny's name, which was hand-written in the paper's header. She'd used tight, neat letters—cursive.

She'd used the green pen.

CHAPTER 23

Jeff's knuckles were white on the steering wheel. Keith's bandages were yet another reminder that Isaac was capable of inflicting pain, or worse. One day had passed since Isaac came back into Jeff's life. One day, and Keith was already in the hospital, badly injured, and Talia's life had been turned upside down. Jeff had no doubt in his mind that his brother was responsible and that this was only the beginning.

He had no doubt in his mind that things would only get worse.

He made a mistake at the hospital, hinting at a connection between the crash and the case to Talia. She wasn't about to let that go. Sooner rather than later, she'd report what he said, and Lieutenant Reid would likely be her first call. After that, her claim that the hit had been on purpose would spread. Isaac would find out. He always did.

He'd come after Talia next.

Jeff wouldn't let that happen. He could tell Talia everything he knew and hope she listened to him after that. But even then, she was strong-willed and stubborn. She wouldn't wait around while he searched for evidence on his own. She would want to help get Isaac behind bars. She'd put herself in danger. And because of that, he couldn't tell her a thing. The less she knew, the safer she'd be.

Jeff had planned to build a case on Isaac first and pull in the CPD only when an arrest was inevitable. But now, he didn't have any time to waste. He had to talk to Lieutenant Reid today and tell him about his and Isaac's past. He had to warn him that Talia would likely reach out, that the investigation had to stay under wraps. Hell, he'd ask for Reid's help in finding proof against Isaac and in protecting Talia, Keith, and Jeff's family. He'd ask for any help he could get.

He pulled out his phone and selected Reid's number. The line rang, then clicked.

"Lieutenant Reid," he answered.

"Lieutenant, it's Foley. Have you heard about Keith?"

"The car accident? Yes."

"It wasn't an accident." Jeff switched lanes. "Can we talk in your office?"

"Sure. I'm here now."

"See you soon." Jeff hung up and stepped on the gas. He'd barely said a thing, but he felt a weight lift from his shoulders all the same. After all of these years, he was finally doing what he should've done from the beginning. He was making sure Isaac never hurt anyone again.

He pulled into the CPD's parking lot and headed straight inside, straight to Reid's office. The door was open and he stepped into the room.

"Hi, Lieutenant."

Reid was sitting at his desk, filling out some kind of a report. He peered up at Jeff over his glasses and pushed the document aside.

"Foley. What's going on?"

"I have to tell you something." Jeff sat down, then stood. He shook his hands at his side, too wired to be still. "You might think I'm crazy, but just hear me out."

Reid leaned back in his chair. "Okay . . . shoot."

Jeff took a breath, no good place to start. "A sex ring was operating out of the house on Galder."

He checked for Reid's reaction and didn't see one, at least not yet.

"My brother, Isaac, owned the ring," he continued. "He also planned the hit-and-run against Keith to stop him from digging too deep into the case."

Reid didn't say anything. His face was blank. He must've been in shock, and rightly so. Jeff was dumping this on him all at once. "I know it's a lot to take in."

"I already know about Isaac. And the sex ring."

"You do? Since when?"

"Since the beginning."

"Why didn't you say anything?" Had Reid shared what he knew up front, they could've avoided the missing files and Keith's attack—everything. But Reid hadn't said a thing. Regardless, Jeff couldn't get caught up in the past. They had to move forward and make a plan. "More importantly, what do we do about Isaac now?"

"We make sure the crash doesn't lead back to him."

"What do you mean?" Jeff wasn't following.

Reid studied him. "Why do you think I assigned you to this case?"

"To close the investigation." The same reason he assigned anyone to any case.

Reid shook his head. "Because Isaac asked me to."

"What the hell are you talking about?" Jeff couldn't help but raise his voice. Reid wasn't making any sense. He wasn't listening. "Isaac has to be stopped before he hurts anyone else, okay? I need your help putting him behind bars."

"Shut up, Foley." Reid's voice was cool and flat, dead.

Jeff had never heard him speak like that before, not to him, not to anyone. He treaded lightly. "I don't think you understand what I'm saying. He's dangerous."

Reid stood and walked around the desk, behind Jeff. He shut the door. "Isaac needs our help."

"Are you insane?" Jeff turned around to face him, the beginnings of a pit forming in his gut. Reid knew about the sex ring and the hit-and-run. And despite all of that, he still wanted to protect Isaac. That could only mean one thing.

"What does he have on you?"

Reid chuckled. "Nothing."

"Then why are you helping him?" Jeff was missing something.

"We have an arrangement."

"An arrangement?" Jeff couldn't believe they were having this conversation. "What kind of an arrangement? You protect him and he does something for you?"

"He makes sure I'm comfortable." The corner of Reid's mouth rose.

"That's impossible."

The one man Jeff reported to every day couldn't be crooked. Jeff would've known. He would've sensed something off about the case. He hadn't sensed a thing.

But Keith had.

Reid had access to the notes and the system, the lab schedule, everything. Jeff had been too focused on Isaac to even consider that the manipulation had been an inside job. "You deleted the files, didn't you? You took the cigar."

"I did what I had to do." Reid spoke in a detached, casual tone like it was just another day. "Isaac did, too. And now, we can't let the crash point back to him."

"Keith could've died." Jeff spoke through clenched teeth.

Reid brushed his comment aside. "I have two witnesses ready to claim they saw Keith at Ronan's bar. That he was drunk, got into his car, and drove away."

"You son of a bitch."

Ronan's was a hole in the wall, a dive, usually empty. There wouldn't be anyone around, let alone any security cameras, to prove the witnesses wrong.

Even so, no matter how many false testimonies Reid lined up, Keith's blood would've tested negative for alcohol. "The reports will tell a different story."

"Reports can be changed. Haven't you learned that by now?"

"No one will believe you." Changed reports or not, Keith didn't drink. He hadn't since his wife's accident. Everyone knew that.

"Maybe not." Reid agreed. "But they'll believe you."

Jeff's sweat turned cold. "What does that mean?"

Reid stepped away from the door and walked toward Jeff. "We can agree that Keith has been drinking lately, can't we? Showing up at work smelling of booze?"

"Like hell we can."

Reid knew as well as Jeff that the witnesses' testimonies wouldn't stand on their own. He needed a statement from Jeff, too. But the rumor would ruin Keith and Talia. And Jeff refused to hurt them any more than he already had. "I'll turn you in to Chief Nelson long before I ever consider helping you."

"With what proof? Besides, Nelson enjoys Isaac's perks just as much as I do." A smug look settled on his face. "This goes all the way to the top."

"You're lying." He had to be.

Yet Jeff couldn't help but believe him. Isaac could've been making connections at the CPD this whole time. Jeff wouldn't put that past him. And if Nelson were involved, there was no way to know where Isaac's alliances ended and where they began.

There was no way to know who Jeff could trust.

"This arrangement has been working for years now. If anything changes that, anything at all, we'll know exactly who to blame." Reid jabbed a finger in Jeff's direction. "If I were you, I'd fall into line and keep your mouth shut."

"And if I don't?"

Reid shrugged. "Angela and Lucy will pay."

"Touch them and I'll kill you." Jeff stepped toward him.

Reid held his phone into the air. "Don't make me tell Isaac why you came here today."

Jeff stopped. Reid smiled.

"So, Foley, what'll it be?"

Jeff knew what Reid wanted to hear. He wouldn't help him, no chance in hell. But Reid didn't need to know that, not yet. "I'll do whatever you want."

"I thought you would." He clapped Jeff's shoulder. "I'll be in touch when it's time to give your statement." He opened the door. "Now get the hell out of my office."

Jeff stepped into the hall, his heart hammering against his chest. Reid would tell Isaac about Jeff's visit. And that gave Jeff more reason to build his case against Isaac now, fast. But first, he had to make sure Angela and Lucy were safe.

He had to get them out of the city. Today.

CHAPTER 24

Talia walked around the hospital room, still shocked over what Jeff had said . . . and what he hadn't said. He insinuated that the hit-and-run had been on purpose and that her dad had been asking too many questions. Then he refused to say anything more. He had the nerve to ask that she sit tight while he fixed things. But sitting tight wasn't an option, not when her dad had nearly been killed and was still in danger.

For that reason alone, she needed information, enough to keep her dad safe. If Jeff wasn't willing to answer her questions, she'd find someone who would.

She grabbed her phone and called the police department. After asking to be transferred to Lieutenant Reid's line, she waited to be connected.

"This is Reid," he answered.

"Lieutenant, it's Talia Griffin."

"Talia . . . ?" He cleared his throat. "How's your dad?"

"He's hanging in there. But that isn't why I called. Do you have any updates on the hit-and-run?"

At that point, anything he could share would help.

"The hit-and-run?" he asked, sounding confused.

She tried not to take that as a bad sign. "Yes. Did they find the other driver?"

Reid took his time responding. "It wasn't a hit-and-run, Talia."

"What do you mean?" She stopped in place. "Jeff told me what happened."

Another pause, a long one. "He may have been trying to protect you."

"Protect me? Protect me from what?"

She didn't need any protection. Her dad did, and the sooner the better. Reid didn't seem to understand that.

"I'm sorry to be the one telling you this, but your dad had been at a bar."

She flinched. "Excuse me?"

"He drove home drunk and swerved into a pole."

"That's impossible." Her voice rose. The accusation threw her off guard. Just that morning, Jeff told her that her dad had been hit. And he wouldn't have lied about that, certainly not to spare Talia's feelings, not after everything she and her dad had been through. He would've known the truth would surface eventually.

"Unfortunately, we have witnesses."

"Witnesses? Who are they?" she asked. "I want to talk to them."

Reid was her dad's boss. He knew her dad didn't drink, and he should've been giving him the benefit of the doubt. This wasn't just any other case.

"That's confidential," he responded just before a muffled voice spoke in the background on his end of the line. "One second, Talia," he said.

Half a minute passed before he came back onto the call. "I have to run."

"He wasn't drinking. You have to know that."

"You focus on his recovery. I'll take care of the rest."

He ended the call.

Talia dropped her arm to her side. Her body shook. Her dad had been sober. He was hit, just like Jeff had said. She'd never been so sure of anything in her life. He would never drink and drive. She knew him better than anyone.

And yet Reid was sticking to his story.

Why, she couldn't imagine. How he and Jeff were on such different pages, she didn't understand. But if Reid wasn't acknowledging the hit-and-run, she had a feeling the rest of the department wasn't, either. If that were the case, then no one aside from Jeff would be looking for the other driver. She had to change that, fast.

Reid refused to listen. Jeff wanted to work alone. Fine. Talia would prove that her dad had been a victim of a hit-and-run on her own, that he hadn't been drinking. The CPD would have to listen to her after that. Reid, too. They'd have to give her dad protection. And until then, she'd make sure no one got close enough to her dad to hurt him. She would request security outside of his room.

By the time he woke up, he'd be safe.

Her dad's briefcase was as good a place to start looking for answers as any. Sitting down in the chair by his hospital bed, she thumbed the worn leather handles and the frayed stitching along the seams. She inhaled the leather scent. Everything about the bag was familiar—everything aside from the stain of dried blood across the center.

She looked inside of the bag.

A manila folder was tucked into one side and a notebook on the other. She took out the folder, *Galder Fire* written across the cover, and opened the front flap.

The first page contained a list of names. Jenny McMahon's was first, with her parents and Charlie listed to the right. The other two women were documented as Jane Does. Tuco Alvarez was last and alone, apparently, no family left behind.

She turned to the next page and found a picture of Tuco's note. *They deserved to burn.* If her patient had been right, Tuco didn't author the note or start the fire. Someone else did. Maybe the same person who hit her dad.

Someone knocked on the door.

She hurriedly stuffed the folder back into the briefcase just as Amy stepped into the room, holding a clipboard against her chest. She glanced at Talia's dad.

"How's he doing?" she asked.

Talia stood. She wasn't sure if Amy was still upset about the other night. But she was about to find out.

"He's okay. Could you request security for his room? With the other driver still out there, I'd feel better if someone were here."

"Sure," Amy answered. "And listen . . . about the other night. Let's just forget about the suspension. You can take some time off to be with your dad instead, as much time as you need."

"That would be great. Thanks, Amy." Talia appreciated the gesture more than Amy would ever know.

"I don't want to add any additional stress," Amy continued, "but the woman from the fire passed away this morning. I thought you would want to know."

"This morning?"

The woman had been making strides just the day before. She turned a corner with Charlie. Or, at least, Talia had thought she did. The woman had been through hell. She deserved a better life, so much more. "I thought she would pull through."

Amy didn't respond. She didn't leave, either.

"Is there more?" Talia probed.

Amy sighed and handed Talia a folded piece of paper. "Given what happened yesterday, I'm not sure I should even be giving this to you," she said. "The woman was holding this when she passed away. No one else had been in her room."

Talia unfolded the paper.

The hospital's logo was in the corner. The woman had written a note using the standard notepad on every patient's bedside table. Her letters were loopy and hard to read.

Charlie—1564 Lonemill Avenue. 6:00 p.m.

She'd written a note to Charlie.

"Any idea what it means?" Amy shifted the clipboard to her other arm.

Talia shook her head.

But she'd find out at 6:00 p.m. tonight.

CHAPTER 25

Charlie parked in an alley between two rundown buildings across the street from 1564 Lonemill Avenue. He had a straight view of the beige one-story house's façade and the dead shrub out front. The curtains were closed. He couldn't imagine why Talia wanted to meet him there, but her text was the only response he received since reaching out to her the night before. Because of that, he hadn't asked any questions.

And now, he had some time to spare until she showed.

He pulled Jenny's research paper out of his coat pocket. Everything was typed except her name written in green. She could've printed the assignment to edit, maybe preferring to mark up an actual piece of paper to a Word document. Or maybe she left the hard copy for someone to find. Either way, after his conversation with his dad, he was starting to think she really had used the green pen to grab his attention, to point him in the right direction. Why she left clues instead of writing what she'd actually wanted him to know, he had no idea.

Maybe she'd been scared of the information falling into the wrong hands.

Or maybe he was losing his mind.

He focused in on the paper's prompt, directing students to research a trial from the past twenty years and detail an argument on how the prosecution could've better presented the case. He flipped to the next page, the title front and center.

Smith v. Kenton: An Examination of Justice

He stared at the words. *Smith v. Kenton* was the case their dad had lost, the case that changed everything. Jenny's plan to review the paper with their dad on Tuesday night made even more sense now. He would've known all of the details.

The first paragraph summarized what Charlie already knew. Caroline Smith sued Patrick Kenton for sexual assault and their dad failed to convince the jury of Kenton's offense. In the end, Kenton walked away a free man and Caroline Smith was forever labeled a liar. For an outsider looking in, it was just another case.

But Charlie wasn't an outsider looking in.

He lived the ramifications of that verdict, of Caroline Smith's suicide two weeks after the trial. That's when his dad stopped caring about anything and started retiring to his study earlier and earlier each night, when their mom started drinking and stopped being a mom. Charlie and Jenny had been left to pick up the pieces.

Of course, Jenny's paper didn't mention any of that.

She focused on the facts, on what she would've done differently to win the case. A better presentation of evidence was at the top of her list, followed by a more pointed cross-examination. But that only skimmed the surface. Her list went on and on, long enough to suggest their dad hadn't been prepared for the trial. And Charlie couldn't help but wonder why. What else had been going on?

The passenger side door opened.

Charlie jumped and swore under his breath.

Talia climbed into the front seat and shut the door. She was still wearing scrubs, light blue this time. Her hair was loose over her shoulders and her eyes were puffy. She looked as if she'd been crying or she hadn't slept in the last few days.

Maybe both.

"Sorry to scare you," she said.

He set Jenny's paper down and studied her face. "Are you okay?"

"Yes." She didn't sound okay.

After last night, he had a feeling he knew why. "They fired you."

She shook her head. "Really, everything is fine."

He didn't believe her. Her silence earlier had been clue enough that something wasn't right. And that was Charlie's fault. He'd asked for her help. She didn't deserve to be punished because of him.

"I'll call your boss right now and explain everything," he said. "Charlie."

"What's her name?" He reached for his cell.

"My dad was in a car accident last night." She spoke softly.

"An accident?" He faced her again. "How bad is it?"

"Bad. But I won't know how bad until tomorrow." She let out a breath and pressed her palms to her eyes. She dropped her hands. "He'll be fine. He has to be."

"Of course."

She was tough; he'd known that since they first met. But now, she was also hurting. And she helped him last night when he felt the same. Tonight was his turn.

"How can I help?"

"You can read this." She handed him a piece of paper she pulled from her bag. "The woman from the fire passed away this morning. She left this note behind."

"She died?" He was jolted by the news. She was the only real connection he had to Tuco Alvarez's house and the fire. He just saw her last night. He talked to her and she listened to him; she helped him. And now she was dead. Just like Jenny.

He read the note, the address, the time. "She wanted me to come here."

"Yes, and we're about to find out why." Talia pointed to a set of headlights bouncing down the road. She ducked and peered over the dashboard.

He did the same.

A Lexus pulled into the house's driveway. After parking, a tall man wearing fitted clothes stepped out of the car. He smoothed back his comb-over before turning toward the street and scanning the area.

His gaze flashed over Charlie's truck.

Charlie dropped lower. Talia, too.

"Did he see us?" Her eyes were wide.

"I'm not sure."

They stayed hunched over, eyes locked, heads close—close enough for Charlie to notice the light-brown rim around the edge of Talia's dark-brown eyes.

She blushed and pulled back, looking away. "Did you recognize him?"

"No." He cleared his throat, then stole another glance outside. The man was walking to the house's front door, waving at an SUV pulling into the driveway.

The newcomer parked and stepped out of the car.

Charlie blinked and squinted. *What the hell?* "That's Lieutenant Reid." The man who interrupted Charlie's conversation with Detective Foley just the day before.

"What's he doing here?" Talia leaned closer to the windshield.

Reid joined the man at the front door and loosened the tie under his suit jacket. They shook hands before Reid took out a set of keys and opened the door.

They stepped inside and closed the door behind them.

Charlie and Talia sat there, eyes glued to the house. Charlie waited for a twitch of the curtains, a flicker of the lights, something, anything. Nothing happened. Ten minutes passed. He reached for the driver's side door.

"I have to get closer," he told Talia.

Just then, the house's front door opened.

Lieutenant Reid came back outside and walked to the SUV. His jacket was slung over his arm and his tie was gone. They watched as he fiddled with the zipper of his pants, climbed into his SUV, and reversed out of the drive.

He passed Charlie's truck and turned out of sight.

Talia looked at Charlie. "Do you think more women are inside?"

"Yes." He did. And if women were inside of that house, if they were in handcuffs, chained to a wall, then Charlie would bring the whole CPD down with Lieutenant Reid. If women were inside, he'd get them out. "I'll come back tonight."

"I'll come with you," Talia offered.

He'd already gotten her into trouble at work. He wouldn't involve her in something where she could get hurt on top of that. "No. It's too dangerous."

"Too dangerous for me, but not for you?"

"Yes." He was the one with a case to solve, not Talia. And yet she was here all the same. *She could've sent me a picture of the note,* he realized. But she came to the house instead, all while her dad was recovering from an accident.

Something about that didn't add up.

"Why do you care so much, anyway?" he asked.

She stiffened. "I grew attached to the woman from the fire."

"In one day?"

"Yes."

"Right." There was more. He could feel it. There was something she wasn't ready to share. And that was fine. He wouldn't push, not tonight. "Still, you're not coming back with me. I'll call you tomorrow and let you know if I find anything."

"Fine." She gave a tight smile, opened the door, and jumped out of his truck. "I'll wait to hear from you then." She shut the door and walked back up the street.

He watched her go.

Something told him she wasn't the waiting type.

CHAPTER 26

Jeff carried two suitcases down the stairs, packed and ready to go. The airline tickets had been purchased: one for Angela, one for Lucy. He'd surprise them with the trip when they came home and would somehow convince Angela that a visit to see her parents was long overdue. They'd be out of the city later that night, safe in Florida for a week.

He set the luggage at the bottom of the stairs by the front door and slipped a note into Angela's suitcase, a note that'd tell her the truth about Jeff's childhood, Isaac, and the Galder case. The conversation was meant to be in person. But sharing details before she was out of the city could put her in danger. And by the time she and Lucy arrived in Florida, Jeff would have to be fully focused on Isaac's case.

He heard someone outside on the other side of the door, walking across the front porch, and he reached for the doorknob. His best bet at getting Angela and Lucy straight back into the car would be to catch them before they came inside.

He opened the door. "Welcome home. I have a surprise."

Angela and Lucy weren't there.

Isaac's beady eyes stared back at him instead. "Ooh, I love surprises."

Jeff let go of the doorknob. "What're you doing here?"

"I was in the neighborhood."

"You expect me to believe that?"

Isaac had never stopped by Jeff's house before. Lieutenant Reid must've told him about Jeff's visit earlier that day.

His timing couldn't have been worse. "I'm in the middle of something. You need to leave."

"I don't think so." Isaac stepped toward the door.

Jeff blocked his path. "You're not coming inside."

No way in hell.

Isaac lifted the edge of his argyle sweater, just enough to show the outline of a gun tucked into his jeans. He glanced pointedly over his shoulder at an SUV idling outside of the driveway. He brought backup. "Are you sure about that?" he asked, a condescending smirk spreading across his face. "Your call."

Jeff's gun was in the safe upstairs. Not only that, but Angela and Lucy would be home any minute. He couldn't risk them being around Isaac. He had to get them to the airport. But Isaac wasn't about to walk away. The sooner Jeff let him in, the sooner he'd leave.

"Fine. But it has to be quick," he said as he backed away from the door.

Isaac stepped into the entryway. "So, this is where my little brother lives?" He shut the door and scanned the space. His gaze settled on the suitcases. "Going somewhere?"

Jeff's muscles clenched. He should've taken the suitcases out to his car. He had to think, fast. "Those are mine from a trip last week."

"We'll see about that." Isaac stepped toward the luggage.

If he opened Angela's suitcase, he'd find Jeff's note. That would ruin everything. Jeff would be better off telling him the truth and feigning nonchalance.

"Okay. You win," he blurted. "Not that it's any of your business, but the girls are visiting Angela's parents in Florida for a week."

Isaac sighed and turned around. "No, Jeff. They're not."

"They go every year."

"And yet you waited until tonight to buy their tickets."

How the hell does he know that? Jeff could think of only one explanation. And Lieutenant Reid would've had to help him access the information.

"Are you tracking my credit card?"

"Of course, I am." Isaac pulled the gun out of his jeans and made a show of polishing the gun's barrel with his sweater. "You continue to underestimate me, Jeff. Just like this morning when you couldn't keep your mouth shut."

Jeff's eyes followed the gun. He spoke slowly, carefully. "I made a mistake."

"You seem to be making a lot of those these days."

"It won't happen again." He'd be more careful now. He had to be.

"You're right about that."

A car door slammed outside, then another.

Angela and Lucy were home. No telling what Isaac would do now. Jeff didn't plan to find out. He stepped toward him. "You've made yourself clear. Now leave."

Isaac's jaw set. He walked to the door and locked the chain.

"What're you doing?"

He stepped back, aiming his gun's barrel at the door.

"Are you out of your mind?"

Jeff moved in front of the gun. He reached for the chain, needing to tell Angela to grab Lucy and get back into the car, to drive away.

"One more inch and you'll be sorry," Isaac warned.

Jeff stopped. He held his hands in the air and turned back to face Isaac. He had to do something—rush him, tackle him to the ground. But if he did that, Isaac would shoot. Jeff had no doubt in his mind that he'd shoot.

And he wouldn't be aiming at Jeff.

"Just put the gun down."

He heard Angela and Lucy walk across the front porch. The doorknob twisted and the door pushed inward, halting when the chain's slack ran out. "What in the world?" Angela knocked on the door, calling into the house, "Jeff? Are you home?"

Her voice ripped through Jeff's core. He stood there, the gun pointed at his chest, and willed Angela to sense that something wasn't right and leave.

The front door closed.

Jeff released his breath. They'd be moving to the garage, but that still didn't give him much time. They'd be inside of the house in seconds.

"What the hell do you want? Just tell me," he all but begged.

"Pick up the suitcases." Isaac spoke quietly.

Jeff did as he was told, grabbing both handles.

He heard the garage door open and Lucy and Angela climbing the stairs to the main floor, laughing about something.

"Now what?"

"Get rid of them." Isaac inclined his head toward the closet under the stairs.

Jeff bolted that way and whipped open the door. He threw the suitcases inside, slammed the door shut, and turned back around. "Put the gun away," he demanded.

Lucy's footsteps bounded down the hall.

"Now!"

Isaac slid the gun into the waist of his jeans.

Lucy rounded the corner, the train of her favorite yellow princess dress dragging behind her on the hardwood floor. She came to a halt when she saw Isaac. Ducking her head, she skirted toward Jeff and reached for him.

"Hi, Superman," she whispered as he picked her up.

He flinched, the nickname mocking him now more than ever. His family was in danger because of him, because of Isaac. Lucy deserved Superman as a dad, someone who would never ever let anyone hurt his little girl. She had Jeff instead.

She pulled back with an expectant expression, waiting.

He forced a smile. "Hi, Ladybug."

Angela joined them in the entryway. She paused and took them in.

"Well, isn't this a surprise." She set down a bag of groceries and looked at the door, at Jeff and Isaac. "Why is the chain locked? Did you hear us trying to get inside?"

"We didn't hear you." Jeff answered before Isaac had a chance.

Her eyebrow arched. She didn't press the topic. "Sorry we took so long." She took off her coat. "We got a flat tire at the grocery store. Can you imagine that?"

"A flat tire?" Isaac asked. "Such a shame."

Jeff recognized his brother's tone; he was basking in a job well done. The flat tire hadn't been an accident. Someone had been following his wife and his daughter.

"Are you staying for dinner, Isaac?" Angela took Lucy from Jeff's arms.

"No, he's not." Jeff unlocked the chain and opened the door. He stepped onto the porch, avoiding Angela's gaze, blood pounding in his ears. "He's leaving."

"Maybe next time." Isaac patted Lucy's head and joined Jeff outside.

Jeff shut the door and followed Isaac back to the road, tempted to forget about putting him behind bars. He could shoot him instead. But in that moment, Isaac had the gun. Jeff had a family waiting for him to come back inside.

They reached the SUV.

Jeff stepped in front of Isaac. "You're trailing my family now?"

Isaac spit on the ground. "We were low on groceries."

"You low-life piece of shit." Jeff reached for him.

The SUV's front door opened. The driver had a gun in his lap and wore a hood over his head. He sat there, saying nothing, his presence warning enough.

Jeff stepped closer to Isaac. "If I see you here again, I'll shoot you before you reach the front door. Do you understand me?"

He meant every word.

Isaac chuckled as he turned and walked to the SUV's back door. His driver joined him and opened the door for him, then waited. Isaac didn't get inside.

"Do you like baseball, Jeff?" He tilted his head, his smirk back. "I have to admit, I'm a fan."

"Go to hell." Jeff spoke through clenched teeth.

"Is that a no?" Isaac mocked surprise, his performance met with a snicker from his driver. "Let me make this easy for you, then. Your call to Lieutenant Reid this morning was your first strike. The suitcases were your second."

His smile was gone and he held Jeff's gaze. "One more strike and you're out."

He tossed an invisible ball into the air, swung an invisible bat.

He followed through toward the house.

"You're all out."

CHAPTER 27

Charlie parked across the street from Shevy's house. The shades were drawn and the lights were on. If her roommate had been right the night before, Shevy would be home. Given her made-up trip to Minnesota, he wasn't sure how she'd react to seeing him there. But he had to know the truth—if she really hadn't spoken to Jenny in a week or if they saw each other as Jenny mentioned in her journal and to their dad.

He stepped outside of his truck and made his way to her front porch. After knocking on the door, he heard quick steps coming from inside of the house.

The door swung open.

Shevy stood in the entryway. She wore sweatpants and a baggy orange sweatshirt. Her hair was parted down the middle and braided into tiny black braids that started at her scalp and extended all the way down to her ribs.

"Charlie." Her mouth opened, then snapped back shut. "I was going to call you," she said, fumbling over her words. "My flight was cancelled—weather, I think."

"I need to talk to you about Jenny. Can I come in?" He didn't care to hear any more of her excuses or to waste any more time than she already had.

"Tonight won't work, actually." She checked her watch before scanning the front yard. "I'm meeting someone from school."

"He's not coming."

Unless Shevy or her roommate had spoken to Shevy's class-mate since Charlie had been there last night, he wouldn't have known to show up.

"How would you know that?" She looked back at him with a creased brow. "You know what? It doesn't matter." She rubbed her swollen eyes, the motion making her seem more exhausted than anything else. "I know you want answers about Jenny. But I'm not supposed to talk about the case, not until the police investigate a potential lead I gave them."

"A lead?" Apparently, one that Detective Foley hadn't felt a need to share with Charlie and his parents. No surprise there. "What was the lead?"

"Didn't you hear me? I can't tell you."

"And I can't leave until you do."

She'd spent more time with Jenny than possibly anyone. Whatever lead she had was worth following. "Please, just tell me."

"No. And this is exactly why I didn't want to talk to you, Charlie. I knew you wouldn't listen, and that you'd pester me for information."

She started shutting the door.

"Is that why you lied about Minnesota?"

She paused, staring at him, and sighed. "You asked questions I wasn't supposed to answer. I panicked and said the first thing that came to mind."

"Apparently."

"Look, you can judge me all you want, but I'm just trying to follow orders so the police can do their job."

"Do their job?" He stepped forward. "Shevy, they're closing the case."

She stiffened. "Already? Did they make an arrest?"

"No."

"Nothing?" A series of emotions played out on her face: disbelief, anger, relief, confusion. "I guess that means they didn't find anything then."

He wouldn't mention that Detective Foley hadn't done much of anything at all, that the CPD cared more about closing the case than actually uncovering the truth.

"Exactly," he said. "So what's the harm in telling me what you told the police?"

"Nothing, I guess . . ."

"I'm her brother, Shevy. I just want to know what happened."

She glanced over her shoulder, then back at him. "Okay. Come in."

He stepped inside and followed her down a narrow hallway leading into a living room with small windows, a TV stand, and built-in cabinets. Trinkets and sea shells were arranged on top of the cabinets, along with a framed picture of Shevy and a woman holding hands at the beach, stretched smiles on both of their faces.

Charlie sat on the couch.

She ducked out of the room and returned with two glasses of water, setting one on the side table by Charlie before sitting in the chair across from the couch. She clutched her glass with both hands. "I don't know where to start."

He did. "You said you hadn't spoken to Jenny in over a week?"

She nodded.

"Are you sure you didn't see her on Tuesday or Thursday?"

"I'm positive."

"Do you know where she could've been? Or who she was with?"

"Where, I'm not sure." She transferred her gaze to the window, as if the shades were open and she had a view. "Who she was with, I may have an idea."

"Okay." He waited, sensing her hesitation. "Shevy?"

She took a deep breath. "Flynn Maccabee."

"Who's that?"

"Jenny's boyfriend."

"Boyfriend? But she wasn't in a relationship."

At least nothing that was serious. Surely, Charlie would have known. His parents would've known. They would have told Detective Foley.

"Yes, she was." Shevy set her glass of water on the floor. "They'd been dating for just over five months. She made me promise not to tell anyone."

"Why would she keep him a secret?" He didn't understand. Jenny had told them about boyfriends before, only a few, but none that'd lasted that long.

"He has a record, so she was afraid your family would judge him."

"A record? What kind?" That didn't sound right, didn't sound like Jenny.

There had to be more to the story.

"I'm not sure." She raised her shoulders. "She never told me."

"Do you know Flynn well?"

"Now? No. He's a math major at Loyola, so I only crossed paths with him when he was with Jenny. But I did know him during our sophomore year of college. He was dating one of my good girlfriends at the time."

"And?" Charlie asked.

Her tone didn't sound promising.

"Let's just say he was too high to remember he had a girlfriend." She crossed her legs. "Jenny deserved someone better. I told her that more than once. In hindsight, I may have pushed my opinion of him a little too hard."

"Is that why you two weren't talking?"

"Yes. And if it turns out that he had anything to do with that house, that I walked away instead of doing more . . ." Tears and guilt filled her eyes. "But you said they didn't arrest anyone, right? So he must not be involved."

Charlie wasn't sure about that. "Who did you talk to at the CPD?"

"A guy with glasses and gray hair. He was kind of a dick."

"Lieutenant Reid?"

"Yes, that's him."

The same man who'd been at the Lonemill house.

Charlie leaned forward, a bad feeling in his gut. "What exactly did he say?"

"He said they would look into Flynn and I couldn't tell anyone about him, or I'd compromise the case." She shifted in her seat. "That's all, really."

"And he hasn't reached out since then?"

"No one has."

He stood, unsure what to make of the new information. Detective Foley had never mentioned Jenny's boyfriend. Lieutenant Reid could've kept the lead to himself. That, or he and Foley decided Flynn wasn't worth exploring.

"I have one more question," he said. "Do you know anything about a research paper Jenny had been writing?"

"Our Legal Writing assignment? Yes. We were in that class together. But I don't know anything about her paper's actual topic." She eyed him. "Why?"

"No reason." He glanced at the door. "I should get going."

He now had a secret boyfriend to find. Not tonight—he still had to go back to the house on Lonemill and look around—but tomorrow.

"Call me if you think of anything else, will you?"

"There is one more thing," she said as she stood. "After I heard about Jenny, I went to find Flynn. I wanted to talk to him myself."

"Did you find him?" He'd take any head start he could get.

"No." She frowned. "No one has seen Flynn since Jenny died."

CHAPTER 28

Jeff stood at the end of his driveway as darkness settled over the street. He had yet to go back inside, to face the fact that his plan had failed, that Angela and Lucy wouldn't be going to Florida after all. The trip was too risky now that Isaac knew about the flight. One more strike and Jeff was out, his family was out.

Isaac was a man to be taken at his word.

But that didn't mean Jeff would give up. He was a detective, for Christ's sake. He could figure out another way to keep Angela and Lucy safe, to protect them while he brought his brother down. He'd create a different plan. A better plan.

And this time, he wouldn't get caught.

Something moved in his peripheral vision.

He turned, scanning his next-door neighbor's front yard. They left for Arizona the week before but a car he didn't recognize was in their driveway. He didn't see anyone in the front seat; he couldn't see much of anything in the dark. Yet years on the job had taught him how to read the prickle down his spine and the chill spreading through his limbs.

He was being watched.

He walked down his driveway and across his neighbor's strip of grass, pulling out his phone. With his flashlight on, he approached the car from the driver's side.

There was someone in the front seat. A man with a buff build wearing a red shirt glowered straight back at Jeff, his hands on the wheel.

Jeff motioned for him to roll the window down.

The man considered him, then cracked the window halfway. "What do you want?" he asked.

"I want to know why you're watching my house." Jeff swept his eyes over the inside of the car. Empty food wrappers were scattered about alongside bottles of soda and clothes.

A gun was in the man's lap.

"I think you know why." His lower lip bulged. He spit a line of brown out of the window, barely missing Jeff. "Now get the hell out of my sight."

He started rolling the window up.

"Get the hell out of your sight?"

Jeff was done. He was done taking orders at his own house and at the CPD. And he was done being threatened, letting Isaac think he had any control over Jeff and his family. He put his phone into his pocket and banged on the window. "Hey, jackass, you're in my neighborhood. *You* get the hell out of *my* sight."

The window stopped rolling. "Do that again," the man dared.

"What, this?" Jeff hit the window a second time, then a third. "How's that?"

The door opened.

The man stepped onto the driveway. "Did you enjoy yourself?"

"Not as much as I'll enjoy this."

He punched the man in his face. Pulling his arm back, he swung again, but the man dodged. Jeff's knuckles connected with the car just as the man grabbed Jeff's forearm and yanked it behind his back.

He threw Jeff against the car's hood. "You'll regret that, Detective."

"Is that the best you can do?" Jeff seethed through clenched teeth.

"Jeff? Is that you?"

The man dropped Jeff's arm, the release almost as painful as the hold.

Jeff grabbed his throbbing shoulder and spun toward the voice. His neighbor stood in his driveway across the street, the belt of his robe tied tight around his large waist and his terrier alert at his feet.

"Is everything okay over there?"

"Robert." Jeff stepped toward him, needing a witness.

Something hard jabbed into his back: the gun's barrel. "One more step, and I shoot the fatty and his dog," the man whispered from behind. "Try me."

Jeff stood stock-still. Robert had a wife and three kids of his own. Jeff couldn't involve them in this. Besides, Robert would call the police. And Jeff couldn't risk that, not when he didn't know who else at the CPD was connected to Isaac.

Jeff was on his own. He had to accept that.

"Everything is fine, Robert," he said as he forced a wave.

"If you say so." Robert looked between Jeff and the man. He shrugged. "Have a good night, then." He picked up his dog and moseyed back into his house.

The man grabbed Jeff's shoulder roughly and turned him around. He held the gun to Jeff's stomach. "I think it's about time you went back inside, too," he said, his eyes blazing.

"Is that your plan? Keep us in the house all day every day?"

"No. Tomorrow you'll go to work and your family will go to school."

"And pretend that everything's normal?" They didn't have a choice. Calling in sick would only last so long. People would start asking questions and poking around.

"Exactly. Now get back in your house before I decide to come in with you. I'm sure your pretty little wife wouldn't mind adding an extra dinner plate at the table."

Jeff wanted to swing at him again, to swipe the smug look off of his face. But Angela and Lucy would call for him soon. And if he went inside now, the man would assume he'd given up. He would report as much to Isaac and they'd leave Jeff alone after that, at least for tonight. That would give him enough time to come up with another plan.

He started walking backward. "No dinner for you, then."

The man cocked his gun. "Feel free to bring me out a plate."

"And distract you from all of this?" Jeff held up his hands and looked around the neighborhood, nothing but dark and quiet. "I wouldn't dare."

Turning his back, he continued up the driveway toward his house, sarcasm left in his wake. He stepped into the entryway and shut the door.

The house was quiet—too quiet—and the air too heavy. Something wasn't right.

"Angela?" He moved down the hallway, picking up his pace. "Lucy?"

He rounded the corner into the kitchen.

Angela was sitting at the table, a piece of paper in her hands.

"Ange?" He stepped forward.

The edge of her suitcase was visible just behind the kitchen island, the top unzipped. She'd found the luggage and the note he tucked into her bag.

The note that explained everything.

She looked up at him, her face ghostly white.

"What've you done?"

CHAPTER 29

The Lonemill house appeared more menacing than it had at dusk. Charlie was parked in the same alley as before, across the street from the front yard. He'd been there for thirty minutes. So far, the house's lights had yet to turn on. He hadn't seen anyone come or go through the front door. He hadn't seen any movement at all.

And for him, that was enough to get started.

He reached into the back seat and grabbed supplies he'd taken from the firehouse: a flashlight and his Halligan bar that would help him force his way inside. Breaking and entering was illegal. He knew that. But reporting the address to the police wasn't an option, not after seeing Lieutenant Reid leave the house earlier that night.

Besides, the woman left the note for Charlie, not the CPD.

He stepped out of his car and shut the door as quietly as he could. Pulling the collar of his jacket higher against the wind, he walked toward the street.

Something wheezed behind him.

He spun around.

A bearded man wearing a torn purple coat was sitting on the ground at the far end the alley, his back leaning against the brick wall and his legs stretched out before him. His eyes were closed and he was holding a half-empty beer bottle in his hand. More bottles were scattered around him.

He was snoring, loudly.

Charlie turned back toward the house.

The lack of a fence around the property made for easy access. But approaching from the front would increase his chances of being seen. He'd be better off going to the backyard and finding a point of entry there.

He crossed the street, hearing nothing but his own footsteps on the cement and the rustling of a paper skeleton attached to a neighbor's front door as it jostled in the wind. He reached the driveway and looked around, seeing nothing. Hopefully, he and the man in the alley were the only ones out at that time of night.

He strode up the driveway and leaned against the house's siding. Edging forward, he peered into the backyard. A line of windows spanned the back of the house, and a door was situated between them.

A door that just might be his way inside.

He dropped down and crawled under the windows to the back door, the leaves on the ground sending a chill through his sweatpants to his knees. Rising to a crouched position, he tried the knob—locked. He wedged the Halligan bar's fork between the door and the frame. Praying that he wasn't about to trigger an alarm, he forced the bar forward. The wood began to bend.

A dog barked.

Charlie froze.

The dog barked again, louder.

The neighbor's upstairs light turned on.

"Shit." Charlie put more pressure on the bar. The door bent farther away from the frame, but still not enough. The barking continued, then stopped.

The neighbor's back door creaked open.

A shadow hovered over the back stoop. "Who's out there?"

Charlie gave one last push.

The door popped open. He stepped inside and quickly closed the door behind him, pushing his back against the wall. The sound of his breathing was loud in his eardrums.

That was close. Too close.

The room was darker than outside. He waited for his eyes to adjust. The outline of a stove appeared first, then the cabinets lining the wall. He turned his flashlight on. Plates were stacked in the sink, and empty beer bottles and cans of chew were scattered on the counter.

He stepped forward, tensing when the floorboard creaked under his weight. His movements had to be soundless, light. He bent down and took off his shoes. After tucking them along the wall, he continued in his socks past the stove.

He left the kitchen and moved down a hallway leading to the front door.

A thud sounded.

He punched off his flashlight and stood still. A scratching noise came next, as far as he could tell, from the same place as the thud: a closet halfway down the hall.

He followed the sound and pressed his ear against the closet door.

The scratching carried through the walls. He grabbed the doorknob and hesitated, having no idea what could be waiting for him on the other side of that door. But he came to look around. And he wouldn't leave until he did exactly that.

He took a breath and opened the door. His eyes had adjusted enough by now to tell that the closet wasn't a closet after all, but a room.

That's when he saw her.

She was sitting in the corner, glaring at him with her short ash-blonde hair covering half of her face. She couldn't be more than twenty years old.

He stepped into the room, shut the door, and crouched down to make himself less threatening. Moving slowly, he set the Halligan bar and flashlight on the ground and held up his hands so she could see them.

"My name is Charlie. I'm here to help," he whispered.

She pulled her feet closer to her body and raised her right hand into the air, a butter knife clutched in her grip.

"Get away from me," she said in a weak voice while her arm shook. A chain extended from the wall and connected to a handcuff around her wrist—just like the women from the fire.

Just like Jenny.

He inched closer. "I'm a firefighter. I can get you out of here."

She held her head higher and jutted her chin into the air. Her hair fell away from her face, revealing a bruise under her eye and a cut on her swollen lip.

"What's your name?" he asked.

She didn't answer. She didn't trust him, not yet. And why would she? He had to give her something to judge him by, first—something real.

"My sister was in a house like this. She was chained to a wall just like you. Her name was Jenny McMahon."

She twitched at the name.

He lowered his hands. "Did you know Jenny?"

She studied him, a growing distrust in her eyes. "Yes."

"Okay, then." His heart beat faster. He was desperate to hear what she knew, what she could tell him about his sister. But they didn't have time for that now. He had to get her out of here.

"If you put the knife down, I can help you."

She didn't lower the knife.

"You can trust me. I won't hurt you," he tried again.

Still, she didn't move. But she seemed to consider his proposal.

Seconds passed.

She dropped her arm and the knife.

"I'm Dani."

"Let's get you out of here, Dani." He crawled to where she sat.

Scratches were etched into the chain and the handcuff. She must've been using the knife to try to cut her way out. An impossible feat, but proof that she hadn't yet lost all hope.

A metal ring secured the end of the chain to a square base on the wall. He wedged his Halligan bar into the ring; it was just small enough that he could leverage his weight. Pushing down on the bar, he felt the metal flex.

"Almost there," he said.

He pushed harder.

The ring cracked and fell away from the base, clattering to the floor.

He helped Dani stand and picked up the chain. He'd break the handcuff off of her wrist once they were out of the house and somewhere safe.

"Are more women here?" he asked.

She shook her head.

A key sounded in the front door.

Charlie spun around.

A squeak came from the other side of the room's closed door.

Someone stepped into the house.

CHAPTER 30

Talia leaned closer to the windshield and held her breath, staring at the man's back—the man now standing in 1564 Lonemill's entryway. She didn't know who he was, but the fact that he used a key to get inside couldn't be a good sign. She willed him to turn back around, to go back the way he came, to go anywhere but inside of that house. But he didn't turn around.

He shut the door instead.

"Shit, shit, shit." She shoved the files she'd been reading back into her dad's briefcase and twisted in her seat. Charlie was nowhere in sight. She saw him sneak around the house minutes before, with some sort of crowbar in his hand. Whether he broke in or not, she had no idea. Either way, he'd be fine. He'd come running out of the backyard at any second and get back into his truck.

But the house was still, eerily so.

"Hurry up." She tapped the wheel, anxiety mounting. She should've told him she was still here, demanded that he let her help, at the very least keep watch while he went inside. But she hid in her car to avoid an argument instead, him demanding she leave and her refusing. And now he could be in trouble, hurt.

She reached for her phone to call the police. And tell them what? That Charlie may have broken into a house? She couldn't do that. Besides, not only had Jeff told her to stay away, she wasn't sure if the CPD could be trusted—not after her call with Lieutenant Reid that morning and seeing him at the Lonemill house that night. And if she couldn't call Jeff or the police, she'd have to find Charlie herself.

She could knock on the house's front door and pretend to be lost. She might be able to distract the man long enough for Charlie to run. It wasn't much, but it was the best plan she had. The only plan she had. And that would have to do.

She stepped out of her car. Locking the door and throwing her keys and phone into her bag, she walked toward the house, ready to cross the street.

Light bounced off of the house's mailbox as a car turned onto Lonemill Avenue and ambled her way. She stepped back over the curb. The driver would see her if she crossed. Given the circumstances, the fewer people who saw her that night, the better.

She turned back around and ran into the alley, ducking behind Charlie's truck and peering around the side. The car approached and slowed, stalled.

She moved deeper into the alley. She must've been seen.

The car continued down the road.

She exhaled.

Something yanked at her bag.

"Hey!" She spun around and fumbled for a grip on the strap. A man in a purple coat was standing behind her, pulling her bag toward him and grunting from the effort.

"Let go of that!" she yelled.

He burped and the smell of day-old beer filled her nose.

She recoiled just as he jerked the bag out of her grip.

"Aha!" Purse now in his hand, he picked up a beer bottle from the ground and stumbled toward the alley's opening, his upper body swaying.

"Give that back!" Talia followed at a careful distance.

"Yahoo, yahoo, a sailor's life for me!" he sang and took a swig of beer before throwing the bottle against the alley's brick wall.

The glass shattered and fell to the ground.

He reached the alley's opening and turned to face her,

scratching his unkempt, scraggly beard. "What's in here?" he asked, fishing around in her bag. A drunken grin spread across his weathered face as he opened her wallet.

"Talia Griffin. 1004 East Righten Avenue," he said with a slur and a salute to no one, then shoved her wallet back into the bag.

"What do you want?" Her voice shook. He wasn't after her money. He would've taken that by now. But if not that, then what? She didn't want to find out.

He licked his lips. "What's a pretty lady like you doing here?"

A shiver traveled down her spine. She had to get out of there. She glanced over her shoulder: a dead end. There was only one way out. She would have to pass him. It'd be easy enough anywhere else, considering his intoxicated state. But the alley was so narrow that avoiding contact would be nearly impossible.

He could have a weapon, a knife.

Even if she did get past him, her keys were in her purse. She wouldn't be able to get into her car. She'd have to take her chances and find a neighbor, a gas station, a grocery store. She would have to find someone who could help. And that didn't sound promising, not that late at night.

"Give me my bag," she demanded. "Now."

"If you say so." He placed the purse around his shoulder and mock sauntered her way, his hand against the wall for support.

"What're you doing?" She moved back.

He stepped on the beer bottle's broken glass with his worn shoes, sending a crunch into the quiet night. "Here I come, pretty lady!"

"Stay away from me," she warned.

He was getting too close. She had to get away from him, bag or not. She had to go, now. She jolted forward and hugged the alley's wall opposite the one keeping him upright.

"What's the rush?" He dove and wrapped his arms around her torso.

"No!" She fell to the cement. Her palms broke her fall and her lower body tangled with his. She tried to push herself away but he grabbed her wrist.

He pulled her toward him. "You're a feisty one, huh?"

"Let go of me!" She kicked as hard as she could and felt her foot connect with his stomach.

He grunted and hunched over. His grip around her wrist slackened.

"You'll pay for that, you bitch," he wheezed.

She pulled free, shot to her feet, and grabbed her bag.

She sprinted out of the alley and into the street.

"I'll see you again, Talia Griffin!" he hollered from behind.

She unlocked her car and jumped into the driver's seat. After locking the door again, she placed a shaking hand over her racing heart.

He hadn't followed her out of the alley.

The street was empty, mockingly so.

Her palms were scraped and bleeding. And for what? She was no better off than she'd been before. Charlie was still inside of the house, and she still had to get to the front door. She refused to let the man win, to just sit in her car and give up.

So she took a deep, steadying breath, then another.

She opened the door again.

CHAPTER 31

Charlie didn't dare move. He barely even breathed. Someone was on the other side of the door, in the hallway. And based on Dani's rigid stance and wide eyes glued to the door, it was someone he wouldn't want to meet. They had to get out of that room. But that was easier said than done. There was only one door and no windows.

There was only one way out.

A phone rang from the hallway.

"What do you want, Gus?" a man answered. Charlie recognized his voice, but he couldn't place him. Dani seemed to know him. Her fists clenched.

"A woman? Outside?" the man said as he walked past the room. "Where's she now?"

The hallway light turned on.

He continued toward the kitchen—a good sign. The more distance between him and the room, the better chance Charlie and Dani would have at making a break for the door, for Charlie's truck. He touched Dani's arm, trying to get her attention and warn her that they had to be ready to move. Her skin was burning up.

She didn't react to his touch.

The man's footsteps stopped. "Is someone else in the house?" he asked.

Silence.

Charlie's heart thumped against his chest.

"Then whose shoes are in the kitchen?"

Charlie glanced at his feet, in nothing but socks. Dani ripped her eyes away from the door and looked down before glaring up at him, accusation written across her face. She knew as well as he did that he made a mistake, one that could cost them everything.

"You fell asleep?" the man accused, a question that would buy them seconds, nothing more. He'd check on Dani soon enough. And when he did, he would realize she wasn't still chained to the wall. Charlie doubted he'd let her go after that, not without a fight. Unless, of course, he didn't notice that she'd been freed.

Charlie motioned for Dani to sit back down.

He angled her back over the chain's broken base on the wall. Then he placed her handcuffed wrist in her lap, and the chain's free end along with the metal ring behind her back. It was all he could do to erase his tracks.

"Like hell you're still getting paid. You took a nap, you stupid idiot!" the man seethed, followed by nothing, likely an argument from the other end of the line.

"What?" he asked. "You want me to call you 'Captain Gus'? Are you drunk?" he asked incredulously. "I tried to tell the boss you're good for nothing. Just wait until he hears about this!"

His footsteps picked up again, growing louder, faster.

He was coming back.

Charlie bolted across the room and flattened himself against the wall next to the door's hinges, his Halligan bar at the ready. The door flew open and swung in front of him. He grabbed the knob before the door hit his body.

The man strode into the room.

Charlie risked a glance around the door. He saw the man's back, his ponytail—the same man who'd been at Tuco Alvarez's house the day before, who found Charlie snooping around and claimed to live across the alley. He'd threatened to call the police. And now, he was here. He used a key to get inside.

The man moved toward Dani. "Has anyone been in the house?"

"I have no idea." Her voice cracked. Her throat sounded dry. And yet there was something else in her tone, too, a smugness. "If you wanted me to keep watch over the house, maybe you shouldn't have chained me to a wall."

"You think you're funny?"

"You and your greasy-ass ponytail are the only jokes around here." All humor from her voice was gone, replaced with a razor-sharp edge, a flipped switch. The man touched his hair. She rolled her eyes. "Go cry to the boss like you always do."

"I do not cry to the boss!" He advanced toward her.

"Not so fast." Charlie pushed himself away from the wall.

The man turned. He had a cut on his forehead, one that hadn't been there yesterday. He took Charlie in with squinted eyes.

"You again?" He reached for his back pocket.

Someone knocked on the front door.

The man turned that way.

Charlie lunged, wrapped his arms around the man, and tackled him to the floor. They hit the ground, hard, the Halligan bar falling out of Charlie's grip. He rolled over and got to his knees, but the man was already back on his feet. He was holding a gun, the barrel in front of Charlie's eyes.

"Who the hell are you?" he shouted as he sucked in air.

Charlie ducked under the gun and rammed into the man.

He propelled him into the wall.

A shot rang out, exploding in Charlie's ears.

He fell to his knees and grabbed his head. His hearing was distorted from the sound, his ears ringing. The man stumbled away from him, toward Dani.

"Run!" Charlie yelled. "Now, Dani! Run!"

"She's not going anywhere." The man turned to Charlie, Dani now behind him. He swayed on his feet and aimed the gun at Charlie's head. "And neither are you."

"Are you sure about that?" Charlie shot up from the floor and ran straight for the man, for the gun. Dani jumped to her feet, too. She raised her hand—the butter knife clenched in her fist. She brought the blade down into the man's back.

He cried out, dropping his arm and turning toward Dani.

"You slut!" he screamed.

Charlie grabbed the Halligan bar and struck the man in the back of the head.

He fell to the ground with a sickening thunk.

His body went limp.

Charlie pocketed the man's gun and went to Dani. He grabbed her hands, burning up just like her arm. Her eyes were trained on the unconscious man, her face expressionless and detached, her skin flushed. She must've been in shock.

"Are you okay?" he asked.

She didn't offer a reply. He didn't need one.

"We have to move." He reached an arm under her legs and the other around her back, lifting her from the floor. She was light, like a child.

He carried her into the hallway.

A door from the kitchen slammed shut.

Charlie spun around, dropping Dani's legs, and reached for the gun.

Talia stepped into the hallway. "Charlie!"

"Talia? What the hell are you doing here?" he yelled, a combination of adrenaline, anger, and fear. He could've shot her, killed her on the spot. She shouldn't have been there. She knew that. "You were supposed to go home."

"Relax. The back door was open," she offered, as if that explained everything.

"We need to leave, now." He didn't have time to ask any more questions. Someone could've heard the gunshot and called the police. He grabbed his shoes from the kitchen and led Dani out the front door and across the street.

Talia followed.

She opened his truck's passenger side door and Charlie

helped Dani climb into the seat. "She needs to go to the hospital, Charlie," Talia said.

"The hospital? No way." Dani made to climb back out again.

"She's right. They'll ask too many questions." The doctors would likely call the CPD, too. And Charlie wanted to talk to Dani before Detective Foley had a chance. Besides, she needed rest, a place to feel safe. "We can go to my apartment. Dani, how's that?"

"Fine by me." She leaned back in the seat.

Talia nodded. "I'll meet you there."

"No, you won't," Charlie said. She had to be kidding. She wasn't even supposed to be here with them now, let alone continue to involve herself in the case. "Go home."

"I'm a nurse. Hospital or not, she needs one."

He couldn't argue with that. Besides, if tonight had been any indication, Talia would follow them to his apartment either way, invited or not. If she came with them now, at least he'd be able to keep an eye on her, to know that she was safe.

"Okay," he relented. But that was as close as she'd get. He wouldn't sit by and watch while she risked her life, no matter her reasons. "But then you're done."

"Then I'm done," she agreed.

A siren rang out in the distance.

Charlie turned toward the house, tempted to go back inside and grab the man, to make him tell Charlie everything he knew. But he had Dani to think about now, and Talia, too. Crossing paths with the CPD wouldn't do any of them any good.

Another siren blared, closer than the first.

Their time had run out.

"Let's go."

CHAPTER 32

Talia followed Charlie and Dani up the apartment building's staircase, desperate to find out what happened inside of that house. She wanted to ask Dani about the handcuff on her wrist, to ask Charlie about the gun tucked into his back pocket and the steel bar in his grip. But she didn't ask. Not yet, at least. Now wasn't the time.

"This one's mine," Charlie said as he ushered them into his apartment. The setup was simple, refreshingly so. He had a kitchen that extended into a living room with a small wood-burning fireplace, a couch, and a TV.

He took off his jacket before rummaging through a kitchen drawer.

"Here we go." He uncoiled a paperclip. "Let's take care of that handcuff."

He went to Dani and turned her wrist toward the ceiling.

He hesitated.

Talia stepped closer, close enough to see the track marks covering Dani's forearm. Some were red and raised, and others were white pinpricks with bruises to match. They needed to be cleaned, all of them, a handful potentially infected already.

Dani shook her wrist. "Hello? Are you just going to stand there?"

"Right. Sorry." Charlie jammed the end of the paperclip into the handcuff and maneuvered the wire back and forth. After a few attempts, the lock clicked and the cuff fell away.

He gathered the chain and the cuff and tossed the bundle into the trash.

"How're you feeling?" Talia felt Dani's forehead. Her skin was on fire.

Dani pulled away. "You're a nurse. You tell me."

"I'm a nurse, not a psychic." Talia held back a further retort, reminding herself that Dani had been through hell. She was likely feeling vulnerable, afraid. And Talia wanted to help. She'd start with her fever. "Is there a shower we can use?"

"Yes." Charlie walked to a door across from the kitchen and led them into his room, a space that smelled comforting, of soap and a firefighter's hint of smoke—of Charlie.

"The bathroom is in there." He pointed to a door by the bed as he pulled sweatpants and a sweatshirt out of his dresser and handed them to Dani. "You can wear these if you want," he offered. "They might be more comfortable."

Dani looked down at her own outfit: a ripped tank top and a mini jean-skirt.

She crinkled her nose at Charlie's sweats. "They're huge."

Talia passed the books stacked under the windowsill and went into the bathroom. She pulled open the shower curtain and ran the water. "Keep the temperature lukewarm, okay? And put soap on those cuts." She'd bring disinfectant back tomorrow to treat Dani's track marks more thoroughly then.

Dani joined her in the bathroom and studied her reflection in the mirror.

Talia paused by the door. "Do you need anything else?"

"Yeah. Privacy."

"Right." Talia took the hint, stepped out of the bathroom, and shut the door.

She left Charlie's bedroom and went into the living room.

Charlie was waiting for her there. "How is she?"

"She'll be okay."

Dani's injuries would take some time to heal. But they would heal. The drug use was another story. Depending on the timing of Dani's last fix, withdrawal could be right around the corner. Talia had treated addicts before, enough to know the extent of the pain to come, the way every muscle would scream for another hit.

"I'm assuming you have a plan?" she asked as she sat down on the couch.

"Not really, no. Unless you call figuring it out as I go a plan." He walked from one end of the room to the other, then over to the fireplace. "Is it cold in here?" he asked as he grabbed a red box of matches on the mantel, only to set the box right back down. He ran a hand over his face.

"I just have to know what happened to Jenny."

"You will." She felt surprisingly sure.

Their eyes locked, a hint of humor in his. "So you are a psychic, then," he said.

She laughed. "No. But you deserve the truth."

The truth about everything, she reminded herself. And that included Talia's dad and her connection to the CPD. But she couldn't tell him about that now. He wouldn't trust her after that. He certainly wouldn't let her stay and talk to Dani. Talia would be back at square one, her dad in just as much danger as before.

She looked away, his gaze threatening to melt her reserves.

"So, what was Jenny like?" she asked.

"Amazing," he said with a shrug. "Smart, studious. Stubborn as hell."

"Sounds familiar," she teased.

"The stubborn part, yes." The corner of his mouth twitched. "But everything else was just . . . Jenny. She knew exactly what she wanted out of life and how to get there." He sighed, looking past Talia. "That's why none of this makes any sense."

They sat in silence for a while, the quiet welcome.

"I'm done." Dani walked out of the bedroom. Her hair was wet and tangled. She looked smaller in Charlie's clothes, younger by years. She had an innocence that Talia hadn't noticed before.

"I'm tired. Where can I go to sleep?"

"The bed is all yours."

Charlie stood and guided Dani back into his room. Talia followed, watching as he pulled back the covers for Dani to climb
under. He left the room and returned with a glass of water for
the bedside table.

"You'll be safe here," he said.

"Yeah. Sure." She took a sip of the water. "I'll only be here
for a few days, just long enough for the boss to realize he wants
me back."

"You can stay as long as you want." Charlie sat down on the
edge of the bed and didn't push the topic any further. He took his
time before speaking again. "So, you knew Jenny." A statement,
not a question.

Talia moved closer.

"I knew of her," Dani corrected, dislike clear in her voice.
Her eyes settled on Charlie's face, not an ounce of sympathy in
her gaze. "Your sister was a real bitch."

His jaw clenched. "What happened?"

"I was the boss's favorite." Her words were sharp, possessive.
"Then rumors started spreading that the new girl would take my
spot. And guess what? The rumors were true. Your stupid-ass
slut-of-a-sister spent one night with him before she died. And
where did I end up after that? Chained to the wall."

Charlie stood. "Who's the boss?"

"We don't know his name." Dani shrugged, unfazed.

"Are you sure?" Talia asked, not believing her.

If Dani were planning to go back to the boss in just a few short
days, she'd be more likely to lie to Talia and Charlie now than to
give up his name.

"Was the boss the one with the ponytail at the house?" she
tried.

"God, no." Dani laughed. "That's Marco, the recruiter."

"How does he recruit?" Charlie asked.

Dani yawned. "I'm tired, remember? What's with all of the questions?"

"I'm sorry. It's a lot. I know." Charlie sat back down on the edge of the bed. "I just really need your help. You're the only one who can answer these questions."

Dani tilted her head. Her eyebrows knitted together. "You need me?"

"Yes," he admitted, "more than you know."

Dani studied him, her facial expression shifting from one of indifference to interest. She leaned forward, closer to Charlie, apparently having caught a second wind. "Marco recruits through the drug trade. He targets kids who are using."

"Is that how he found you?" Talia was curious.

"Yeah. He heard I had a deadbeat mom and no dad." Her eyes remained on Charlie. "He invited me to his house, and I went. The boss was there. He talked me into working for him. Once you start, there's no way out. He makes sure of that." She coughed. "Before I knew it, five years had passed, and nothing had changed."

"What about the police? Don't they look for the kids?" Talia had to know. Certainly, they wouldn't ignore a missing persons report, not when children were involved.

"Who would report them missing? Their drugged-out parents? Their low-life boyfriends?" Dani shot Talia a look, one she couldn't help but read as a warning. "They have no one. Besides, the cops will do just about anything for a freebie."

"Do you know the officers' names?" Talia asked, ignoring Dani's pointed glare and trying to keep a level tone.

Based on what they'd seen earlier that night, Lieutenant Reid was in on the sex ring. But Talia's dad and Jeff wouldn't have known about the ring, the police corruption, or the victims. She was sure about that.

"Nope. And we're blindfolded with the police."

"I just don't understand." Charlie was looking out the window. "Jenny didn't do drugs. She had family. Uninvolved parents, sure, but they would've noticed if she went missing. She had a brother, friends. She wouldn't have fit Marco's mold."

Dani coughed again and pulled the covers higher.

Talia placed a hand on Charlie's shoulder, noticing a thin chain around the back of his neck—a necklace.

"She needs rest," Talia said. She still wanted to ask Dani about the cigar, but that could wait until tomorrow, until she could grab a minute with her alone.

Dani's eyes settled on Talia's hand and narrowed.

"Right. Get some rest, Dani." Charlie stood. "I'll be right out there if you need anything." He walked to the door, oblivious of Dani's eyes on him as he left the room.

Talia followed and shut the door. She glanced at her watch. It was just past midnight and time for her to get back to the hospital, to get back to her dad.

"I'll stop by tomorrow morning and check on Dani, if that's okay," she said as she made her way to the door.

"Did you fall?"

"No. Why?"

She turned to face him. He pointed to her hands, her scraped palms.

"Oh, that." She tucked them into her pockets. "Yes, actually. A man grabbed my bag in the alley outside of the Lonemill house. He knocked me over."

His face dropped.

"He didn't take anything. He just looked at my ID." She backtracked; she didn't need another scolding. And the way he was looking at her—with concern in his eyes, as if he actually cared, as if he actually cared about *her*—she had to go.

"I'll see you later."

She turned to leave.

"Was he wearing a purple coat?"

She froze. "Yes." She turned back around. "Why?"

He held her gaze, something more than just concern in his eyes. Something that looked a lot like fear.

CHAPTER 33

Details from Marco's phone call came rushing back to Charlie—details that meant nothing to him then, but everything to him now. Marco had asked the caller about a woman outside. He yelled at someone wanting to be called Captain Gus for falling asleep. The man with the purple coat must've been on the other end of that line. He'd been sleeping in the alley when Charlie had first arrived. That couldn't be a coincidence. Charlie had been lucky to sneak by.

Talia had not.

"Why're you looking at me like that?" Talia took a step back.

"The man in the alley was working for Marco. He was keeping watch over the house."

"That's impossible," she dismissed. "He just happened to be there at the same time."

"He called Marco with a report and told him about a woman." Charlie spoke carefully when he said, "I think he looked at your ID for a reason."

"The man was drunk. He probably doesn't even remember my name."

"But what if he does?"

She didn't respond to that.

Marco would be desperate to find Dani as soon as possible, to keep her quiet. She was a liability to the business now. And if the man from the alley had given Marco Talia's name, then she could very well be the only lead Marco had. One he'd use. "Marco will start looking for Dani tonight," he added.

"He can look all he wants. He'll never find her here."

"Not here, no . . . "

He wanted to tell her she had nothing to worry about, that everything would be okay. But he didn't know that yet. And until he did, he wouldn't downplay the risk, not when her safety hung in the balance. "But if he knows you were there tonight, he'll think you know where Dani was taken."

She didn't move. "You think he'll try and find me."

"Yes, I think he might." And if Marco found Talia, Charlie didn't want to consider how he'd go about getting information. But Marco wouldn't find Talia. Charlie would make sure of that. "You should stay here tonight."

"What? No." Her voice was pitched. "I can't do that."

"Marco might have your address. You can't go home."

"I'll sleep at the hospital."

"He could know where you work by now. For all we know, he's already at the hospital waiting for you. We can't afford to underestimate him."

"He can't be at the hospital." A look of panic crossed her face. "My dad is there."

She pulled out her phone and quickly dialed a number. "Amy?" She turned her back to Charlie and spoke in a hushed voice. "Is everything okay with my dad?" She listened. "Good." She nodded, walking around. "Great. Thank you."

She hung up.

"Everything okay?" he asked.

"Yes." Her face told a different story, one of uncertainty. "But I can't risk leading Marco back there." She took a breath and looked around. "I'll stay for the night."

"Great."

They stood there, staring at each other.

"You take the couch, then," Charlie offered.

He grabbed two blankets from a closet by the TV and handed one to Talia, taking the other for himself on the floor.

Her movements were slow as she settled into the couch, her mind seemingly somewhere else. But she was there all the same, hair loose over her shoulders, eyes tired.

"So"—she pulled the blanket over her lap—"what's your story?"

He laughed. "It's the middle of the night, and you want to know my story?"

"Please." She smiled softly, dimples hinting again on her cheeks. "I need a distraction."

"What do you want to know?"

She thought about that. "What's the necklace you're wearing?"

"This?" He grabbed the chain around his neck and showed her the pendant on the other end. "It's the McMahon crest. Everyone in the family has one."

"Tell me about your family."

"My family is . . . complicated."

He tucked the crest back under his shirt, accustomed to redirecting conversations about his parents by now. Even in his past relationships, he hadn't talked about his family, let alone his childhood. He hadn't seen a point. But something about tonight felt different. Something about Talia.

"Complicated how?" she asked like she wanted to know him.

And maybe he wanted that, too.

"My dad had plans for me to become a lawyer. He's still not over the fact that I took a different path." A sugar-coated version of the truth for now.

"What did you study instead?"

"I didn't graduate." He waited for the shift, for the point when she realized he wasn't who she thought he'd been.

She nestled deeper into the cushions instead. "Why not?"

He smiled. "You ask a lot of questions."

He didn't remember the last time he told anyone his story, his and Jenny's story. He didn't remember the last time anyone had asked, and had really listened.

But Talia was good at that. At asking, and listening.

"If you don't talk, my mind will run wild," she warned.

So he talked. He told her about the *Smith v. Kenton* case, how the verdict changed everything. He told her about his parents, Jenny, Jenny's studies, everything he could think of. He talked because she asked him to, because he wanted to. And when he finished, she looked at him not with pity but with interest.

"You were right." She arched her eyebrow. "That is complicated."

He laughed. "I told you. But enough about me. What about your parents?"

She stiffened, subtly enough that he almost missed the reaction. But the tension was there. She tucked a piece of hair behind her ear.

"My mom passed away."

"I'm sorry. What happened?" He could hear the pain, the ache, still fresh in her voice. Apparently, they had more in common than he knew.

"Car accident. Two years ago."

"And your dad? What does he do?"

"My dad?" Their eyes met and held, hers more vulnerable than he'd seen them before, more open. And then she blinked, and that openness disappeared. "My dad works in real estate." She yawned. "I think it's time for bed."

"Sure," he said. "Water?"

He could sense that her guard was up, so he'd wait until she was ready to tell him more. After filling them both a glass of water, he walked back and set his by the blanket on the floor. He went to place hers on the end table by the couch.

She reached for the glass at the same time.

Their fingers brushed.

Heat shot up his arm. She yanked her hand back and looked up at him, her brown eyes wide, a current pulling him closer. He put the glass on the table and sat down next to her on the couch. He placed his hand over hers.

She didn't move away.

He kissed her, softly at first—a shot of electricity through his limbs. She responded, kissed him back. They leaned into each other, her hand on his chest.

She pulled away.

She shot to her feet and brought her hand to her mouth. "I'm sorry." She shook her head. "I can't do this." She grabbed her bag and ran to the door, into the hallway.

The door slammed shut behind her.

"Dammit." He stood, kicking himself for not having left things alone. He darted after her, running into the hall and down the stairs. He burst through the building's front doors and caught up with her just outside of her car.

"Talia, wait. I misread the situation. You don't have to leave."

She opened her car's door.

"It's too dangerous for you to go home."

"I'll crash with a friend." She climbed into the driver's seat.

"It's late. Just stay here. I'll leave."

"I'll come back tomorrow morning and check on Dani." She reached for the door and paused, finally looking at him, her dark-brown gaze lingering on his face.

She closed her eyes. "I'm sorry."

She shut the door.

"You don't have to do this."

He wasn't sure if she even heard him. She reversed out of the parking spot and drove through the lot. Her brake lights turned on before her blinker signaled left. She pulled onto the empty road.

Then she was gone.

CHAPTER 34

Jeff paced in Lucy's playroom. He hadn't spoken with Angela since she read his letter. She'd busied herself with Lucy instead. She made dinner, ran a bath, read bedtime stories . . . anything to avoid talking to him and hearing him explain what he wrote in his note. But Lucy had been asleep for hours now, and Angela wasn't one to shy away from the truth. She'd find him soon enough.

He knew this day would come. He knew that for a while now. But he hadn't expected the conversation to happen tonight. He wrote the note for Angela to read in Florida, not here. And he still had to find something that would incriminate Isaac. He had nothing to reassure her that everything would be okay.

All he had was deceit—a lifetime of lies.

The door opened.

Angela came into the room and shut the door behind her. She'd changed into sweatpants and a long-sleeved Chicago Blackhawks T-shirt. Her arms were straight at her sides, as if bracing for what was to come. "Tell me everything."

"I'm sorry, Angela."

He moved toward her. She stepped away from him.

"Start from the beginning," she said.

"Okay."

He didn't want to start from the beginning. He didn't want to start at all because he couldn't predict how she'd react, if she'd still love him, if she would be willing to give him another chance.

That was the sole reason he hadn't told her about his past in the first place.

But if I don't talk, she'll leave. She'd walk out of his life forever with Lucy balanced neatly on her hip. And he wasn't about to lose them.

So he'd do what she wanted him to do. He'd talk.

He would start from the beginning. "You already know about my parents."

"Yes."

She knew his mom had been addicted to cocaine and heroin, anything she'd been able to get her hands on, and that his dad left when Jeff was only a few days old. He told Angela those details when they'd been dating.

But he hadn't told her everything.

"My mom wasn't exactly unemployed." His face burned, but there was no time left for shame, for anything but the truth. "She invited men over to our house and asked them for a twenty on their way out."

"She was a prostitute," Angela said.

"Yes." There was no stopping now.

"Isaac and I tried to steer clear of the men. And we did, for the most part. They went into her room. They left. But then one of them hired Isaac." The same man who gave Isaac his first box of cigars, his second, his third. "He was a sex trafficker. He used Isaac for help."

"Help with what?"

"Recruiting." Jeff started to pace again, blood pulsing in his ears. "He wanted Isaac to scout out girls, to lure them somewhere with a promise of money, love, whatever they wanted to hear. And just like that, the girls would be taken, gone."

The weight on his shoulders was still there. He hadn't gotten to the worst part yet—the part he'd been terrified to admit for the last twenty-five years.

"And I helped him."

Seconds passed before Angela spoke again. "How?"

"I stood watch on street corners while he led girls into an alley." He sucked in air. Tears prickled his eyes, emotion that'd been fighting for the surface for too many years. "I didn't understand that when they got into the van, they'd never come back. I was so young, just a kid." But his age wasn't an excuse. It never would be.

And his naïvety didn't last for long.

"Then there was Ruby." He could still picture her small rosy cheeks and the skepticism in her thirteen-year-old eyes, the trust when she looked at him. "She was my best friend, my only friend. She lived on our street. She . . ."

He sobbed, a violent, unexpected sound.

"Jeff . . ."

He wanted to stop, to forget everything from that time altogether. But the words poured out of his mouth.

"Isaac told me to invite her to our house. So I did. One minute, we were hanging out, just the two of us. The next, the men were there. They grabbed her, pulled her away, and stuffed her into their van."

Angela brought her hand to her throat.

"She was screaming," he choked out. "And the way she looked at me . . . God, I can still see the way she looked at me, like I betrayed her. I tried to help, to stop them. But they just pushed me away. They laughed." He balled his fists. "I lured her there."

"You didn't know," Angela whispered. She didn't understand. Not yet, anyway.

But she would.

"Her body was found a week later, thrown in a dumpster."

"You didn't know," she repeated. "You were just a kid."

"I should've known!" he yelled, slamming his fist against the wall. Even at a young age, he recognized that something wasn't right with Isaac, that his brother was cruel, that he hurt people. Hell, he knew Isaac better than anyone at that point. And still, he failed to stop him, to protect Ruby.

"Did you tell the police?"

"No." He pushed away from the wall, his knuckles smarting. "Isaac's boss threatened to kill me and my mom if I talked. Eventually, the threats started coming from Isaac, too." He spoke through gritted teeth. "After a few years went by, I convinced myself that there wouldn't be any evidence left, that even if I did report what happened, even if I told the truth, no one would believe me."

He'd been a coward, nothing less.

"So no one reported the crime? What about her parents?"

"They barely even knew they had a daughter."

Ruby had invited Jeff to her house only once when they were kids. Her drugged-out parents had sat on the couch, shooting up. They didn't so much as glance at the open door when she led Jeff inside. Isaac was with them that day, too. "She had me, and no one else."

"Then what happened?"

"Nothing. I didn't talk to Isaac after that day. He won a scholarship to college a few years later and I graduated high school three years after him. Our mom died that same year. He didn't come to her funeral. That was it."

"Until now. Until this case."

"Yes."

Until he recognized the cigar cataloged as evidence. And ever since then, his past had been his present. Only now, Jeff wasn't a thirteen-year-old boy. He was a grown man with a family of his own. And Isaac wasn't just involved in recruiting.

"He ran a sex ring out of the house that burned down on Friday morning. He wants my help covering his tracks."

She stepped closer and spoke as if she still had hope in him, as if he could possibly have the answers. "You have to tell someone. You have to report him."

"It's not that easy." He looked away. "I've tried. I'm still trying."

"Try harder. You have a family now."

"Don't you think I know that?" he snapped.

"Then turn him in!"

"If I do that, you and Lucy will be in danger. Is that what you want?"

"Don't you dare put this on us," she warned.

"Listen to me, okay?"

She was right. He couldn't turn the tables, not now. But he needed her to understand the severity of the situation, the consequences of stepping out of line. "Isaac planned the hit-and-run against Keith."

"What're you talking about?"

"Keith was digging into the case. He was hit that same night."

"You're wrong. The crash was an accident." Her tone edged on hysterical.

"I'm not wrong, Angela. Isaac has the police in his back pocket. If I report him, he'll know. He'll punish me by hurting you and Lucy, just like he did to Keith."

"That's crazy. You can't let that happen. No one will hurt our daughter, Jeff."

"I know." He crossed the room and took her hands. "I know, okay? No one will hurt Lucy or you. Isaac will be arrested. I just have to find a way to incriminate him."

"And if you don't?"

"I will." He tightened his hold. "I promise."

"That's not good enough." She broke away from him. "I won't sit here and wait for something to happen to Lucy. We need to leave, tonight, all of us."

"We can't."

"Why the hell not?"

"There's a man watching our house." He held her gaze. As hard as it was, he held her gaze. "He's armed, Angela."

His phone rang.

"Don't answer that. We're not done yet." Her voice was raw.

He pulled out his cell and glanced at the screen. He didn't recognize the number. Now wasn't the time to take calls. But no one ever called him this late.

He looked at Angela. "Please. Just give me one second."

He answered the call without waiting for her response. "Jeff Foley."

Silence.

"Hello?"

"Why was Talia Griffin loitering in front of one of my houses?" Isaac rasped.

"What?" Jeff turned away from Angela. He had no idea why Talia had been outside of Isaac's house. Then the reason hit him all at once. She'd asked questions at the hospital about the hit-and-run. He warned her to stay away.

She didn't listen.

"She doesn't know anything." He closed his eyes and held his breath. In truth, she knew too much. She'd connected the dots back to Isaac. Jeff couldn't imagine how. But he couldn't afford to have Isaac realize as much. "It's a coincidence."

"I wish that were true."

The line cut.

"Shit."

Jeff had to call Talia. He had to warn her before he was too late, before she was hurt just like her dad. Or worse. Like Ruby. He turned around to fill Angela in.

She wasn't there.

CHAPTER 35

Charlie was awake when the morning's first light peeked through the blinds. He hadn't slept all night, hadn't been able to quiet his mind. Dani was still asleep in his room. At least she was out of harm's way for now. But Talia had yet to return his call or his text from the night before. She had yet to confirm that she found a place to stay, that she was safe. Maybe she hadn't checked her phone.

Or maybe she had.

She could still be upset about the kiss. The kiss he hadn't wanted to end. He didn't know how she felt, only that she pulled away. She left. But with Marco potentially looking for her, now wasn't the time to disappear. She'd offered to come back and check on Dani. If she didn't show up that morning, and if he didn't hear from her soon, then he'd find her himself—whether she wanted him to or not.

His phone buzzed on the end table. He turned over on the couch and reached for his cell, hoping to see Talia's name on the screen. Shevy's appeared instead.

He bolted upright and answered. "Shevy?"

"Did I wake you?"

"No," he said as he rubbed the lack of sleep from his face and eyes. He hadn't expected to hear from her again so soon. "Is everything okay?"

"You asked me about Jenny's assignment yesterday."

"Yes." The research paper she wrote about their dad's case,

Smith v. Kenton, the paper she marked with the green pen. "What about it?"

"The assignment was due on Tuesday. Jenny never turned hers in."

"How do you know?"

"Our teacher posted scores on Friday morning. I just checked the results now. Jenny's code is marked as incomplete."

"Okay." He waited for more. Nothing came. Surely, she didn't call that early only to tell him about an incomplete grade. "Is there anything else?"

"No. It just seemed strange. She always turned assignments in on time."

"She probably just didn't finish." Based on Tuesday's journal entry, she'd still needed to confirm a few details with their dad in a meeting that never took place.

"I guess." She paused. "That could explain Wednesday."

"Wednesday?" Charlie stood, heading to make a pot of coffee.

"She was supposed to go to the protest with a group of our friends. But she called last minute and cancelled. She said something else came up. I assumed she was with Flynn. But she could've just been trying to finish her paper."

Charlie set the coffee down. "The anti-violence protest?"

"Yes."

"Jenny went." He would know. He'd picked her up from the jail himself.

"No. She wasn't there. Trust me." A car horn blared in the background. "Shoot. I have to run. I'll call you back tomorrow. Bye, Charlie."

She ended the call.

He pulled the phone away from his ear, trying to remember everything the jail's probationary officer had said on Wednesday night. According to him, Jenny had been arrested in a riot on

Michigan and Randolph. Then again, if Charlie remembered correctly, Jenny had also claimed she hadn't done anything wrong.

Maybe Shevy was right.

But if Jenny didn't go to the protest, if she came across the riot by chance, then she would've told that to the officer. Unless, for whatever reason, she didn't want him to know where she'd really been. But still, she would have told Charlie.

Maybe she tried to tell him outside of the jail.

He opened Google Maps on his phone and found the corner of Michigan and Randolph. He scanned the area, looking for somewhere else that Jenny could've been. He stopped just after State Street. His thumb hovered over a courthouse—the courthouse where *Smith v. Kenton* had been tried.

She could've gone there to do more research for her paper. But if the assignment had already been due the night before, she would've visited the courthouse earlier in the week. Besides, checking facts for a paper wasn't exactly something to hide from the police. If she'd been there, what had she been doing?

He went to his bedroom and glanced into the room to see Dani sleeping under the covers, one arm sprawled over her head and track marks stark against the white sheets. Her breathing was slow and light. He had more questions for her about the sex ring. But she needed rest and time to recover. If he left for the courthouse now, he'd be back in a few hours. They could talk when she woke up.

He just might hear from Talia by then, too.

Without waking Dani, he grabbed jeans and a hooded sweatshirt from his room and then changed in the living room. After writing a note in the kitchen that he'd be back soon, and including his personal cell number, he set his work phone on the counter in case Dani needed to reach him. No one from the department would call him while he was on medical leave.

Then he sent Talia a text letting her know he put his keys under the mat, and he left.

Thirty minutes later, he parked in a metered spot across the street from the courthouse. He walked through the building's entryway and spotted a receptionist on the other side of the lobby. Her gray hair was pulled back into a tight bun.

He walked her way. "Good morning." He waited for her to look up.

She didn't. "Can I help you?"

"Yes. Do you keep track of who comes and goes from the building?"

She clicked around on her computer. "We keep a visitor's log."

"Can I see the log?" His request was vague, odd. He knew that. But he didn't have time to waste explaining any details. "It's important."

"I'm sure it is." Her tone was brisk. "But that's confidential information."

"I understand. I just need to know if my sister was here last week."

"Ask your sister, then."

"I would if she were still alive."

She glanced at him, her eyes tired behind tortoiseshell glasses balanced perfectly on her thinly pointed nose. "I'm sorry about your sister, really. But still, my hands are tied. Now have a good day." She resumed her typing.

But he stayed put. He wasn't giving up yet. "That's a beautiful dog." He gestured to the picture of a black, shaggy dog by her computer. He'd never had one himself. He and Jenny knew better than to ask their parents for a pet growing up. But their neighbor's dog had been almost identical. "A Newfoundland?"

"Yes." Her fingers slowed on the keyboard. "That's Bear. He died."

"I'm sorry." He grimaced. Couldn't catch a break. Maybe she was in the market for another one. "The firehouse has an animal adoption event, you know."

"Your point?"

"A lot of dogs need a good home," he baited. "I could help you find one."

"I don't want your help. I want you to leave."

Even so, her tone had softened. She eyed him with a hint of interest. "I have always wanted to adopt."

"One look at the visitor's log, and I'll make sure you get your first pick."

She scanned the lobby behind him, left to right. "One look, nothing more. And I want a puppy, a cute one that'll follow me around the house. Got it?"

"The cutest puppy there." He held his hands up in mock surrender.

She gave a subtle smile—with any luck, a sign that she was warming to him. She grabbed the notebook behind the phone. "When was she here?"

"Last Wednesday." He had to stop himself from leaning over the desk.

She opened the log, flipped through the pages, and turned the book toward him. A whole list of visitors had been recorded that day. Jenny was the second.

She'd been there.

Not only that, but she wrote Judge Johnson's name in the Reason for Visit column; he was the judge who presided over the *Smith v. Kenton* trial. And if she spoke with him, then Charlie wouldn't leave until he did, too.

"Is Judge Johnson in?"

"Yes . . ." the woman said, watching him over her glasses.

"I need to meet with him. He may recognize my name: Charlie McMahon." Associating himself with Jenny might make the judge more inclined to meet. Then again, Charlie's last name could also remind him of the *Smith v. Kenton* trial, of Charlie's dad. And Charlie had a feeling that connection would hurt his chances more than help.

She tucked her chin. "I'm guessing you won't leave me alone until you do?"

"What gave you that impression?" he joked.

She rolled her eyes and shook her head. "The cutest puppy there," she reminded him before picking up the phone and dialing, the receiver pressed against her ear.

"Sara? Charlie McMahon is downstairs. He'd like to meet with Judge Johnson." She listened. "I understand, but they're old friends." She winked at Charlie.

He held his breath.

"Judge Johnson has twenty minutes before his trial?" She looked at Charlie, her brows raised. She covered the mouthpiece with her hand. "Take it or leave it."

"I'll take it." Twenty minutes wasn't much.

But it would have to be enough.

CHAPTER 36

The key was under the mat, just as Charlie had said. He wasn't home, which was a relief as far as Talia was concerned. She wasn't ready to see him yet. She didn't know what to say after leaving his apartment in a panic the night before. She'd wanted to kiss him again. Of course she had, and she still did. But she was lying to him about her dad and Jeff, and her connection to the CPD. She was lying to him about his sister's case.

And he deserved better than that.

So no, she wouldn't kiss him again. She wouldn't risk getting any closer to him than she already had, hurting him in the process. She'd stay away. After today, she wouldn't be back at his apartment again.

Using his key to open the door, she stepped inside and walked into the kitchen. She set her bag next to Charlie's note and a cell phone on the counter. Charlie's black sweats were on the couch. Aside from that, there was nothing to suggest he'd been there that morning. There was nothing to suggest they'd been there last night.

"Charlie?" Dani called as she emerged from the bedroom. She wore one of Charlie's shirts, the hem down to her knees, and an expectant smile on her face. A smile that disappeared the second she saw Talia. She crossed her arms.

"Where's Charlie?"

Talia held his note into the air. "Running errands."

"Why're you here?" Dani's face was flushed, her cheeks red.

"I came to check on you." Talia pulled gauze and disinfectant ointment out of her bag. "We can use these to clean your cuts."

"I don't want help. Not from you."

"Suit yourself." Talia set the supplies on the counter. Dani's health wasn't the only reason she stopped by. She came to get more information on the sex ring and the cigar, as much as she could before the doctors took her dad out of his induced coma that afternoon. "I wanted to ask you a few more questions, if that's okay."

"You're the last person I want to talk to."

"Why's that?"

Dani didn't seem to care much for Talia last night. But something today felt different. More personal.

"I have my reasons." She wiped her brow with her shaking hand.

"I'm sure you do." Reasons Talia didn't have time to worry about now. She had to convince Dani to talk, to answer her questions. "What if we make a deal?"

Dani eyed her skeptically. "What kind of a deal?"

"If you answer my questions, I'll get you medicine for your withdrawal."

Based on Dani's perspiration and hand tremors, she'd be desperate for help soon. Talia would get her the medicine either way. But Dani didn't need to know that.

Dani shook her head. "Medicine isn't enough."

"What more do you want?"

"Your word that you'll never kiss Charlie again."

Talia stiffened, taken off guard—not only by the fact that Dani knew about her and Charlie's kiss, but by the smug look on her face.

"You were watching?"

"I'm always watching." Dani sat down on the couch. "Anyway, that's my offer. I'll talk if you agree to bring me medicine and leave Charlie alone after that."

"I thought you weren't staying here long."

"Charlie needs me." She tilted her head. "He said so last night."

"I see."

Talia remembered the conversation differently. Dani's interpretation was unnerving at best. Talia would have to warn Charlie to be careful around her. But challenging Dani now wouldn't do Talia any good; it would ruin her chance at getting answers. Besides, she already decided to keep her distance from Charlie.

"So, do we have a deal?" Dani asked.

Talia ignored the unease building in her core, the feeling that Dani couldn't be trusted. Talia wanted this. She wanted answers. And this was her chance to get them. She would call Charlie and warn him about Dani. Then she'd stay away.

"Yes," she answered.

Dani smirked. "Good. Now, what do you want to know?"

Talia joined her on the couch. "Does anyone in the business smoke cigars?"

"The boss." The air of reverence Dani used when speaking about the boss last night was gone. "And before you ask again, no, I don't know his name."

"What does he look like?" He could've been responsible for the hit against her dad. There had to be something Talia could use.

"He's big, has black hair, wears nice things."

Dani's description was too vague.

"What else do you know about him?"

"I know he likes breaking girls in."

"Breaking them in?" The detached tone of Dani's voice made the hair on Talia's arms stand on edge. "What does that mean?"

"If any of the girls act up, he takes them to his warehouse. He reminds them of their place and pumps them with drugs until they're not a problem anymore."

"My god . . . someone has to stop him." Talia could hear the desperation and anger in her own voice. "Do you know where the warehouse is located?"

"No idea. And that's not really my concern anymore." Dani spoke as if they were discussing the weather, as if breaking women in was the norm. "What else?"

Talia didn't want to ask anything else. She didn't want to hear another word about the sex ring, the abuse, the suffering. But she couldn't stop now. She had to keep going, to focus back in on the cigar. "Does Marco smoke? Or anyone else?"

"Not that I know of." Dani wiped her forehead again. "But Marco is in love with the boss. I wouldn't be surprised if he took up smoking to get his attention."

"He's in love with him?"

"Yes. Marco had a falling out with his parents after high school. The boss took him in from the street and hired him for random jobs." She snorted. "He fell in love with the first man to show him any attention. Pathetic."

"Is the boss interested in Marco?"

"No." She picked at a scab on her arm. "And that drives Marco crazy. He must've been thrilled after the fire. Four less women for him to worry about."

"Wait a minute." Talia leaned forward. "Four women?"

"That's what I said."

"Only three women were found at the house." The files mentioned Jenny and two Jane Does. Aside from Tuco, no one else. "Are you sure four women died?"

"Yes. Jenny, Abigail, Matilda, and Beth."

"You're positive?"

Dani glared at her. "Why would I make that up?"

"I have no idea."

But if four women died, why had only three been found? If four women died, where was the other body?

CHAPTER 37

Charlie had no idea what to expect from his meeting with Judge Johnson. In spite of the years he'd spent resenting the *Smith v. Kenton* case growing up, he'd never actually given the judge much thought. And yet he was about to meet the man all the same—the man Jenny met with two days before she was killed.

The elevator dinged on the tenth floor and the door opened. A woman was waiting for him there. "Charlie? I'm Sara." She shook his hand. "This way."

He followed her down a narrow hall to a door marked with a nameplate as belonging to Judge I. Johnson. She adjusted her fitted blouse, knocked, and cracked open the door.

"Excuse me, Judge Johnson, Mr. McMahon is here."

"Send him in," Johnson said, his voice hoarse, gravelly. Sara opened the door for Charlie to enter and he walked into the office. She shut the door behind him.

Johnson was sitting at a large mahogany desk on the other side of the room. His suit was tight over his broad shoulders and his blue tie was one of the few pops of color in the space. He was typing on his computer, a crease between his eyebrows.

Charlie walked toward his desk. "Thanks for meeting me on such short notice, Judge Johnson." He extended his hand. "I'm Charlie McMahon."

"So I've heard. According to Sara, we're old friends." Johnson looked up at Charlie with his mouth set in a straight line, no smile. They shook hands.

"Right. Sorry about that." Charlie wasn't sorry, not at all. The lie got him into Johnson's office. An opportunity he wasn't about to waste. He dropped his hand to his side. "I was hoping I could ask you some questions."

"Fine. But I have a trial starting soon, so if you don't mind getting to the point . . ." Johnson gestured toward the empty chair across from him.

"Of course." Charlie sat.

A Loyola law diploma hung from the wall behind Johnson's desk, class of '85. That was one year after Charlie's dad graduated from the same law school. Maybe the courtroom hadn't been the first time they met. But Charlie wasn't there to talk about his dad. He was there to talk about Jenny.

"My sister was here last week. Jenny McMahon."

Johnson didn't react to the name. "Go on."

"She met with you, maybe about a research paper she was writing."

He wouldn't mention *Smith v. Kenton*, not until he knew whether Jenny had been there for her paper or not. Eighteen years had passed since the trial. But Caroline Smith's suicide after the verdict made everything that much more sensitive, complicated. Charlie just met the judge. He wouldn't risk alienating him right off the bat.

"Do you remember meeting her?" he asked.

"Jenny McMahon . . . It's not ringing any bells." Johnson pulled a box of mints from his desk's top drawer and popped one into his mouth. He didn't offer any to Charlie.

"She was twenty-four years old, a law student. She had long black hair and gray eyes." He was fishing desperately. At that point, he'd take anything Johnson had to offer about that day, about why Jenny had been there.

"I'm sorry. I don't remember her." The mint in Johnson's mouth traveled from one cheek to the other. "She must've met with someone else."

"She wrote your name in the visitor's log."

"She made a mistake." Johnson shrugged.

"I don't think so."

Jenny wouldn't have written his name in error. She met with him. Charlie was sure. Either Johnson really didn't remember, or he was lying.

Johnson's phone rang.

He checked the ID and answered. "Judge Johnson." He reached for a notepad and a pen. "Okay." He jotted down information and nodded along with the conversation. "Great. Talk later." He hung up. "Sorry about that. Where were we?"

Charlie didn't answer. He didn't even look at Johnson. His eyes were glued to Johnson's note instead, to the pen still clutched in his grip.

"Where did you get that?"

"This?" Johnson held up the pen, his name etched into the side. "Sara bought these. How she managed to order green when I asked for black is still beyond me."

Charlie barely heard him. The ink on the notepad matched the green date in Jenny's journal and her name written at the top of her law school paper.

"My sister had that pen." Or at least one with the same color ink. And what were the chances of that?

"That's impossible," Johnson dismissed.

"She must've taken one."

She could've, easily. The pens were in a pencil holder on Johnson's desk. More were lying in the middle of a round table by the door.

She could've been leading Charlie to Johnson all along. "She was here."

"No, she wasn't." Johnson's tone was firm. "There are plenty of green pens in the world. Don't you think you're being a little dramatic?"

"My sister was murdered last week." Everything about Johnson was rubbing Charlie the wrong way, his condescending tone and nonchalance included. "So, no, I don't think I'm being a little dramatic."

Johnson sighed and glanced at his watch without offering any condolences. "I'll send an email to the rest of the building and ask if anyone met with Jenny last Wednesday, okay?" He stood. "Now, I have a trial to get to."

Charlie stayed seated, Johnson's words echoing in his mind.

"How did you know Jenny was here on Wednesday?"

Johnson's eye twitched—just enough for Charlie to glimpse the man behind the façade, a man with something to hide. He shrugged, again.

"You told me."

"No, I didn't." Charlie stood. He hadn't mentioned the day. He was sure of it. Johnson met with Jenny. He was lying. "What the hell are you hiding?"

The office door opened.

A bald man in a suit strode into the room. He stopped when he saw Charlie. "Sorry, Judge, I didn't realize you were in a meeting."

"We just finished."

Johnson started walking around his desk, but Charlie blocked his path.

"Like hell we did."

"Don't make me call security," Johnson warned.

"Security?" The man looked between them. "What's going on?"

"What'll it be, Charlie?" Johnson picked up the phone, his eyebrows raised.

Charlie's jaw locked. He wanted nothing more than to slam the phone back down on the receiver, to force Johnson to answer every last one of his questions. But doing that would only cause a scene. Security would be called and they would escort Charlie from the building. He could be banned from coming back inside.

And he needed to come back inside. If Johnson wouldn't tell

him the truth about Jenny, then Charlie would have to find answers on his own. "I'll leave."

"Wonderful." Johnson smiled. "Hang in there, kid." He
walked him to the door and guided him into the hallway. "And
don't let me see you back here again."

He shut the door in Charlie's face.

Charlie stood there, rigid, his fists clenched. He resisted the
urge to pound on the door and force his way back inside. Johnson knew something about Jenny.

The lying son of a bitch.

He turned and ran into a janitor pushing a trash barrel down
the hall.

"Sorry," Charlie said.

"Excuse me," the janitor spoke at the same time. He peered
at Charlie from under his messy black hair. "Is everything okay?"

"No."

Jenny had visited the judge. That much was clear. And if
she went there to ask him about her research paper, then why
wouldn't Johnson tell Charlie as much? Why did he refuse to
admit that she'd been there at all?

He was hiding something, that's why. And Charlie wasn't
about to let that go.

"But it will be."

CHAPTER 38

Jeff peered out of his bedroom window. The car in the neighbor's driveway was gone, the man with the gun nowhere in sight. Even so, his instructions the night before had been clear. Jeff and his family were to go about their normal routines.

And they would: Jeff to the CPD, and Angela and Lucy to school.

They'd be safe at school. Angela's sixth-grade classroom was only a few doors down from Lucy's preschool room, and teachers were around every corner, students in the halls. Isaac wouldn't bother them there—too many potential witnesses.

If anything, he'd wait until they came back home.

He'd stop by their house uninvited again and would use Angela and Lucy to get under Jeff's skin, to control him. Someone could get hurt. And because of that, Jeff wouldn't let Isaac near his family again. So, yes, they'd placate him for today. They'd go about their normal routines. But they wouldn't come back home after that.

"Jeff?"

He turned around.

Angela was standing in the doorway. Her hair was in a messy braid and she had bags under her red-rimmed eyes. He hadn't seen her since last night, since she went into Lucy's room after his phone call with Isaac and locked the door.

He wanted to go to her now, to pull her into his arms. But something in her eyes told him to stay away, an edge he'd never seen before, one that shouldn't have surprised him. She'd had time to process what he said last night, what he'd done. She saw him differently now. Of course she did. She always would.

"Are you okay?" he asked.

"Do you have a plan?"

"Yes." He forced himself to focus on the logistics, to push all other feelings aside. "The Thompsons offered us their guest-house this week."

He'd been up half of the night looking for places where Angela and Lucy could stay. Then he remembered the guesthouse and the couple they hadn't spoken to in years. He called first thing that morning, mentioning broken pipes, and they offered the space, no questions asked.

"The Thompsons' guesthouse?" She didn't sound convinced.

"It's remote. Isaac will never find you and Lucy there. I'll pick you both up after school and drive you there myself. You can stay until it's safe to come back."

"And what about you?"

"I'll be taking care of Isaac."

He'd spend the day searching for a way to connect Isaac to the sex ring. If nothing came up, he would write a confession about the recruiting they did as kids, about Ruby. Twenty-five years had passed, yes. But Jeff was done using that as an excuse. Once Angela and Lucy were out of harm's way, he'd turn whatever he had into the CPD. He'd go to the media, too. And if protecting Angela and Lucy came down to implicating himself, then so be it. "I'll be fine."

She stared at him, her hard eyes transforming into the ones he knew, the ones he loved: soft, open, vulnerable. And today, afraid.

"I'm scared, Jeff."

"I know." He strode over to where she stood and wrapped his arms around her, holding her tight. "Everything will be okay. You just have to trust me."

"How? You've been lying to me since we first met. For the past *nine* years." She pulled away from him with tears in her eyes.

"I made a mistake." He took her hand and held on when she tried to pull away. "But you know me, Ange. I'm still the same person. Listen, I know I don't deserve forgiveness. But I'm ready to fight for another chance. Just please, don't give up on me yet."

She held his eye for a second more before looking down. "If things aren't better by tonight, Jeff, we're leaving." She softened her voice. "Me and Lucy."

"They'll be better," he promised. Losing his family wasn't an option.

"Okay." Angela nodded and stepped away. "We'll see you tonight, then."

She turned and walked out of the room.

Jeff watched her go, tempted to forget the plan, to grab her and Lucy and run away instead. But that wouldn't solve the problem. Isaac would still come after them.

Jeff's cell phone rang and Talia's name flashed across the screen. He answered, his tone harsher than he'd planned. "Where the hell have you been?"

"It doesn't matter."

"Like hell it doesn't matter." He'd been trying to reach her since Isaac called him last night to ask why she'd been hanging around one of his houses. She was frustrated, hurt. He understood that. But her recklessness was making things worse. "You have to get somewhere safe. Are you at the hospital?"

"No. But I have to tell you something."

"You can tell me later. Get to the hospital and stay there."

"There's another body, Jeff."

He could barely hear her over the line. "A what? Speak up."

"A body. Four women were in the house that burned down on Friday morning."

"No, three women were in the house. Two Jane Does and Jenny McMahon." He would know. He'd been there. He saw the women with his own eyes.

"Four." She sounded sure. "Abigail, Jenny, Matilda, and Beth."

"Who the hell are they?"

She had no idea what she was saying. *I don't have time for this,* he reminded himself. Not with everything else going on. He had to focus on Angela and Lucy, on locking Isaac up.

"Just send me a text when you get to the hospital, okay?" he said.

"The boss smokes cigars. Did you know that? He must've been behind the hit-and-run. The fourth woman's body could lead us back to him. This could blow the case wide open."

"You have to drop this, Talia, now."

She knew too much. She was in over her head, way over her head, and she was putting herself in danger. "You should be at the hospital with your dad, not messing around with this case."

Seconds passed. "Are you going to listen to me?"

"No, but you're going to listen to me."

She ended the call.

"Dammit!"

He threw his phone onto the bed. She'd lost her mind, acting like she knew more about the case than he did. And the names. Where the hell had she gotten those names? Jeff's team searched the entire crime scene. If another woman died in that fire, they would've found her body at the house, just like the others.

Unless, of course, her body hadn't been at the house for them to find . . .

CHAPTER 39

Talia stood in Charlie's bathroom, fuming at the way her call with Jeff had gone. Not only had he refused to consider the possibility of another body, he didn't listen to her about the boss—according to Dani, the only one in the business who definitely smoked cigars. The boss must've organized the hit-and-run against her dad. All she needed now was proof, a name. She had to connect him back to the crime scene, back to the house that burned down with the women chained inside.

The missing body might be able to help her do just that.

But she had to find the body first. She needed help from the CPD, and Jeff was the only one she trusted. She had to convince him to listen. And she would. She'd look through her dad's files again and would talk to Dani if needed. She'd find proof that the fourth woman had been at the house, that she died in the fire.

Jeff wouldn't be able to ignore her after that.

Talia left the bathroom and made her way back into the living room.

Dani's position on the couch hadn't changed. She picked another scab on her arm, leaving a smear of blood behind. "What were you doing in there?" she asked.

"Nothing."

Talia went into the kitchen and grabbed her bag. She wouldn't mention that a detective didn't believe her about the body. She and Dani had enough tension between them already. Adding more would only risk Talia's chances of getting information later down the line. "I'm going to the hospital."

"To get my medicine." Dani wasn't asking.

"Yes."

Once Talia's dad was taken out of his induced coma, once he stabilized, Talia would find a way to sneak the medicine out of the hospital. She'd never taken anything from the hospital before, something that could get her fired. But the medicine was there for patients in need. And Dani was in need.

Talia added her cell phone number to Charlie's note.

"Call me if you need anything," she said to Dani.

"Don't hold your breath," Dani scoffed.

"I wouldn't dare."

Talia left and placed the key back under the mat. As she drove to the hospital, all thoughts of Dani were replaced with ones of her dad, with worry over the seemingly endless list of complications that could accompany a head injury—brain damage, speech loss, and seizures to name a few. She didn't know what to expect.

But she'd find out soon enough.

She parked outside of the hospital, grabbed her dad's briefcase, and walked into the building.

The security guard was sitting in the hallway just outside of her dad's door, and the doctor was already waiting by his bed. After reviewing the procedure with Talia, details she'd already heard before, the doctor and a nurse stopped the flow of sedation. They offered Talia a few words of encouragement, and then they left.

Talia sat in the chair next to the hospital bed, willing her dad to open his eyes, to wake up. But that wasn't all. She willed him to forget, too, to forget about the accusation she made at the potluck, about the investigation and the cigar. She wanted him to have a fresh, positive start, to focus on his recovery and nothing else.

She'd worry about the rest.

She opened his briefcase and read the files in the manila folder yet again, finding nothing to suggest a fourth woman's body.

Three dead bodies had been recorded at the scene, and two were identified: Jenny McMahon and Tuco Alvarez.

There was no mention of Abigail, Matilda, or Beth.

She searched for missing persons in Chicago on her phone and selected the Illinois State Police report. There were no Matildas on the list, but a few Abigails and one Beth. If Talia showed Dani the women's pictures, she might be able to confirm whether they'd been in the house.

Her dad coughed, a soft, throaty sound.

She put the files on her lap and reached for his hand, holding on tight. His eyelids twitched back and forth, up and down. She held her breath. His arm jerked.

His left eye opened, then his right.

Talia sat completely still. Part of her wanted to stay in that moment forever, oblivious to what would come next, to knowing the extent of his injuries. The other part of her needed to know just how much of her dad she'd get back.

"Hi, Dad."

He transferred his gaze to her face.

He stared at her, blinking hard. Seconds passed, and then a light turned on in his eyes. His pupils dilated. A tear rolled down his cheek.

"Talia . . ."

"Welcome back." She squeezed his hand while tears blurred her vision. He could speak and he remembered her name. His eyes were functioning just as they should, dilating from the light, scanning the room. He would be okay. He'd survive.

She wiped the tears from her eyes. "You look great, Dad."

He glanced down at his body, at the bandages and his suspended leg.

"You were in a car accident." She filled a paper cup with water from the sink and helped him take a sip—anything to delay his mind from realizing the extent of his injuries, from remembering the hit-and-run. "But everything is going to be just fine."

"An accident." He spoke slowly, as if testing out the words.

"Yes." She set the cup back down and pulled the sheets up to his chest. "Now get some rest, okay? We can talk more when you wake up."

His eyelids started drooping until they fully closed.

She stood, about to grab a nurse.

"Is the other man . . . okay?" her dad mumbled.

She turned back around.

"The other man?" she asked.

He sighed, drifting into sleep. "The man with long hair."

CHAPTER 40

Charlie couldn't bring himself to start his truck, to leave the courthouse knowing Judge Johnson was hiding something about Jenny. But he didn't have a choice. Johnson knew he said too much. He wasn't about to say anything more. Charlie would have to find the information another way. He would have to sneak into Johnson's office and look around. Not today. But he'd be back tomorrow.

In the meantime, he had to check on Dani and make sure she was okay. He wanted to ask her more about the sex ring and also try to persuade her not to go back to the boss. She could have a different life, a better life. She just had to want that for herself.

He grabbed his cell and dialed the work phone he left for her at the apartment.

"Hello?" She answered on the first ring, sounding agitated.

"Dani, it's Charlie."

"I've been waiting to hear from you all morning!" she scolded.

He'd only been gone for an hour. "Did something happen? Are you okay?"

"I'm fine." She inhaled. Her tone softened. "I'm just lonely."

Charlie's cell phone beeped. Another call was coming in, a call from Talia. Finally. "I have to go, Dani. Talia is calling the other line. We'll talk more when I get home."

"Talia is calling you?" Dani asked, suddenly more alert.

"Yes. I have to run."

"What the hell does she want?"

"I don't know. But I need to find out." He hung up on Dani and tried to switch calls, accidently disconnecting Talia's line. "Dammit." He went to call Talia back.

She texted him before he could dial.

He read her message.

She was at the hospital with her dad and planned to grab Dani medicine from there. She wanted to call Charlie later, too, to talk to him about Dani. And that was good. He wanted to hear how Dani was doing from a nurse's perspective. He also wanted to remind Talia about the promise she made the night before to leave the case alone. A promise he had a feeling she'd conveniently forgotten.

But he didn't want to talk to Talia over the phone. He wanted to talk to her in person, to see her in person. The hospital was on his way home. He could stop there before his apartment. He would grab Dani's medicine then, too. Another trip to his apartment was the last thing Talia needed while her dad was still recovering.

He started his truck and drove to the hospital. After dodging traffic for forty minutes, he walked into the lobby and over to the front desk.

"I'm here to visit Mr. Griffin."

"Mr. Griffin." The receptionist typed into her computer. "He's in room 2408."

"Great. Thank you." Charlie started to walk away.

"Hold on a second," she called to his back. "Are you family?"

He stopped and slowly turned around. "No, I'm not." He couldn't pass as family. The only thing he knew about Mr. Griffin was that he worked in real estate.

"Only family members are allowed to visit him."

A doctor approached the front desk from the opposite side of the floor, sounding panicked. "Inna, we have a problem."

The receptionist turned her chair to face him and blocked out Charlie. Their conversation picked up, seeming intense.

Charlie took stock of the lobby. All but empty. He slipped past the front desk and made his way to the second floor, following signs to room 2408.

The door was open and an empty chair stood just outside of the room. He poked his head inside. A man was lying in the hospital bed, fast asleep with his leg suspended in a cast and a bandage wrapped around his head. His face was swollen and bruised. He'd been in one hell of an accident.

Talia was nowhere in sight.

Charlie would wait for her in the hall. He pulled away from the door, but a folder on the chair by the bed caught his eye. Familiar words were written across the front flap: *Galder Fire.*

Jenny died in a fire on Galder.

He couldn't help himself. He went inside and picked up the folder. The first document contained a list of names, first Jenny, then two Jane Does, followed by Tuco Alvarez. Charlie's family was included, too. He flipped past the fingerprint analysis report and details on the fire, details on his dad's pocketknife that Jenny gave the surviving victim—everything.

The folder was a compilation of Jenny's case files.

But how had Talia gotten those?

He reached the end of the folder. Additional notes were written across the back flap, including a list of officers assigned to Jenny's case. Detective Foley's name was marked as lead detective. Charlie moved down the list, but he didn't recognize the others.

He reached the last name.

Support: Detective Keith Griffin

Talia's last name was Griffin.

That had to be a coincidence. She would've told Charlie if a member of her family worked at the CPD, let alone on Jenny's case. And still, that wouldn't explain why the folder was in her dad's hospital room or how Talia had gotten the files.

Unless the files weren't hers.

He grabbed the medical documents clipped to the end of the hospital bed.

Her dad's name was front and center.

Keith Griffin.

"Charlie?"

He spun around.

Talia stood in the doorway, holding a cup of coffee in her hands. Her gaze fell to the folder before jumping back up to Charlie's face. Her eyes grew wide.

"I can explain."

"Your dad doesn't work in real estate?"

"No." She winced. "He's a detective."

"I don't understand. Did you know he was working on Jenny's case?"

"Charlie . . ."

The break in her voice was answer enough. But he had to hear her say the words.

"Did you know?"

Her shoulders dropped. She nodded. "Yes."

CHAPTER 41

Talia had lied to Charlie, but only because she needed more information on the investigation. She hadn't been willing to risk him turning her away, not when her dad had been in danger—was *still* in danger.

"I wanted to tell you he worked on Jenny's case. But I didn't know how you would react."

"Well, now you do." Charlie's tone of confusion was gone. He walked to the room's window and back. "I mean, Jesus, Talia, was all of this just a game to you?"

"A game? Of course not." She took a step toward him, only one, afraid that anything else would send him storming out of the room. "You can't really think that."

"I don't know what to think. You've been lying to me this whole time."

"I was protecting my dad. I did what I had to do."

"I guess so." He stared at her as if seeing her for the first time. "And you'll understand when I do the same." He walked past her and out of the room.

"Where're you going?" She set her coffee down and glanced back at her dad, still asleep and breathing steady. She ran into the hallway just as Charlie stepped onto the elevator and pushed a button.

"Will you just let me explain?" she called after him.

Their eyes locked. He didn't move.

The doors shut.

"Dammit!"

He didn't want to hear what she had to say. She understood that. But she couldn't let him leave without explaining what really happened, that she never meant to hurt him. She had to tell him what she learned from Dani about the boss, too, about Marco, and the fourth woman. The details could help him with Jenny's case.

She ran to the stairwell, down the flight of stairs, and onto the first floor.

Charlie was already in the revolving door, heading outside.

She followed, catching up with him on the sidewalk. "My dad wasn't in an accident, okay?" She hurried her stride to match his. "Marco crashed into him on purpose." At least she'd inferred as much from her dad's question about the man with long hair. If the boss wanted her dad dead, he could've tasked Marco with the hit-and-run. "Marco tried to kill him. And there's more."

Charlie didn't even look at her as he spoke, his eyes trained straight ahead. "Your dad works with Lieutenant Reid. Chances are he's just as corrupt."

"He's not corrupt." She trailed him to his truck. "Will you just give me two minutes? I have details that could help you figure out what happened to Jenny."

"I don't need your help." He climbed into the driver's seat. "Goodbye, Talia."

He shut the door.

Then he backed up.

She watched him drive out of the lot, overcome with a need to go after him. All of this time, she'd pretended she would be able to walk away from him just fine. But now that he was gone, now that he was done, she realized she'd been wrong. She couldn't just let him go. She wasn't ready to say goodbye to him for good.

She cared about him too much.

Pulling out her phone, she went into the neighboring business's empty parking lot, away from the sirens and the noise.

She dialed his number.

The line rang once and connected to voicemail.

She took a deep breath. "Charlie, it's me." She walked toward a line of trees separating the back of the lot from the road. "I'm sorry I lied. But I didn't think you'd tell me anything if you knew he was a detective."

Tires tred on gravel behind her.

She moved away from the sound, stopping when she reached the curb. "I also need to tell you what I learned from Dani."

A car door opened, closed.

She glanced over her shoulder.

A black SUV had pulled up behind her. A man walked toward the front of the car. His hair was in a ponytail—the same man who'd been in the Lonemill house. He had a cut across his forehead, one that could've been from the hit-and-run.

"Marco."

He smirked. "You're hard to find, Talia Griffin."

"Am I?"

She did her best to keep a level voice, to fight the panic rising in her core. Marco would want to know where Dani had been taken. And Talia had a feeling he wouldn't react well when she refused to give him the information.

She stepped away from him, back toward the hospital.

Another man climbed out from the SUV, blocking her path. He was huge, at least three times her size, with muscles bulging through his long-sleeved shirt.

"Going somewhere?" he said.

She backed up. "What do you want?"

"Is that any way to greet someone who just spent hours waiting for you to show up at the hospital?" Marco taunted, ignoring her question.

"Hours," Muscles emphasized, all but bouncing on his toes.

"You must really want to talk to me," she said distractedly, looking everywhere, needing a way out. The hospital was far away, but if she could get there, that was her best bet.

"Unfortunately . . . you'll have to wait a little longer."

She made to bolt for the hospital.

Muscles cut off her path in just one step.

She backed up toward the curb, running out of options.

"Hang up the phone," Marco instructed.

The phone.

She was still on the phone. Charlie might not listen to her message right away, but he was all she had. There was no one else around to help and Muscles was ready to pounce. Her chances of getting past him were slim to none.

Besides, she'd just be leading them closer to her dad.

"Hang up the phone!" Marco looked over his shoulders.

She took another step back. Marco had the upper hand, yes, but she sure as hell wouldn't let him call the shots.

"Charlie, Marco found me. We're in the parking lot next to the hospital. He's driving a black SUV. I need your help, now, please!"

"Get her!" Marco seethed at Muscles.

She turned away from the hospital and the men, and she sprinted toward the trees lining the back of the lot. If she got to the road, she could flag down a car.

"Help!" she screamed. "Help me!"

"Shut up," Muscles panted not too far behind.

She pushed her legs faster, harder. She didn't dare cast a backward glance.

Her foot caught on something.

She tripped and fell to her hands and knees. Branches cut her skin; rocks tore into her shins. She ignored the pain and pushed forward on all fours. Climbing over a root, she forced herself back to her feet, the road just up ahead. She was almost in the clear.

A hand flashed in front of her face, clamping over her mouth.

"No!" she screamed into Muscles's palm as she tried to turn

around and fight. He wrapped his other arm around her torso and squeezed her so tight she could barely breathe.

He lifted her feet from the ground and turned back toward the SUV. She squirmed, desperate to break free of his hold. His hand pushed harder against her mouth and nose.

"I like a woman who screams," he whispered into her ear.

She sobbed. Her stomach churned. She tried to kick, but she felt weaker with each second that passed. She needed a breath of air. She needed to get away.

They reached the clearing. The SUV had moved up to the curb.

Marco stood waiting.

"Nice try, Talia."

She squirmed harder, tried to scream. No one would know she'd been taken or where to find her. She should've listened to her dad, to Jeff, to Charlie.

She should've left the case alone.

But she didn't.

Tears welled along her eyelids. Black spots danced in her vision.

Marco held up a roll of duct tape.

"Let's take a ride."

CHAPTER 42

Charlie sat in his truck outside of his apartment building, phone in his hand. He was tempted to listen to Talia's voicemail, to see what she had to say. But he also knew that her side of the story wouldn't change anything. She lied to him about his sister's case and used him for information. There was no coming back from that, not now, not ever. He cared about her, yes. But she didn't care about him.

The sooner he realized that, the better.

A text message appeared on his screen, one from his work phone, from Dani.

U said u were coming home. Where r u?????

Another text came through.

R u with Talia? U can't talk to her

He sighed and put his phone back into his pocket. He had no idea what was going on between Dani and Talia, but he did know that Dani had survived five years of hell. If constant texts made her feel safe, then he'd try harder to keep her updated.

He got out of his truck and shut the door.

Another car door closed nearby.

He looked around but didn't see anyone as he started walking across the parking lot toward his apartment building.

Footsteps picked up behind him.

He glanced over his shoulder.

A head of black hair ducked behind one of the cars.

"What the hell?" Charlie mumbled under his breath.

He waited and didn't see anything else. No one was there.

I have to get a grip, he told himself before continuing toward his building.

The footsteps returned, exactly in time with his own.

He turned around again.

A man ducked behind a tree before Charlie could get a good look at his face. But half of his body was still visible around the trunk, his jeans and his jacket included.

"You know I can see you, right?" Charlie stood there, waiting.

Seconds passed and nothing happened.

"I can still see you . . ."

The man stepped out from behind the tree.

"Hey, I know you." Charlie recognized his tall, gangly form and his messy black hair. "You're the janitor from the courthouse." The one who was pushing a trash barrel outside of Johnson's office.

"So what? Who're you?"

"Who am I?" Charlie asked. "You're the one trailing me, and doing a pretty shitty job of it, I might add. I think it's only fair I get the first question."

"And I think you should tell me what you know about Jenny."

That caught Charlie off guard. "What did you just say?"

"You heard me."

"How do you know my sister?" He strode toward him.

"Your sister?" The man's face dropped. "Jesus, are you Charlie?"

Charlie stopped. He'd been amused by the man at first, willing to play along. But not anymore.

"Is this some sort of a game? Who the hell are you?"

"I'm Flynn." He closed the distance between them and held out his hand.

"Flynn?" The scrawny man before him couldn't be Flynn. Charlie pictured someone different. Not as wiry, not as lanky.

"Jenny's boyfriend?"

"Of five months. She told you about me?" Hope lit his eyes.

"No." Charlie barely knew anything about Flynn, only that he hadn't been seen since Jenny's murder, at least according to Shevy. And that made Charlie suspicious of him right off the bat. "When was the last time you saw Jenny?"

Flynn dropped his hand back to his side. "On Wednesday. I planned to meet her at the protest, but she backed out. She said she had something else going on."

"Something else?" Shevy told Charlie the same thing.

"That's what she said. But then I happened to see her leave the courthouse. She was sobbing. I tried to catch up to her, but I lost her in the crowd of protesters."

"Did you talk to her after that?"

"No. She didn't return my calls." He stared off into the distance. "I had a feeling something wasn't right. I'd never seen her cry like that before. And then I heard about the fire on the news, that she died." He looked back at Charlie with heavy eyes. "I went straight to the police station and told them about the courthouse. But Lieutenant Reid didn't give me the time of day. He seemed to think I was making everything up, that given my record, I couldn't be trusted."

"What record?"

Shevy mentioned his record, too, but she hadn't known any details.

He lowered his head as if expecting judgment before explaining, "I was caught dealing weed my first year of college . . . I was stupid back then, a real idiot in more ways than one. But I've changed. I'm different now."

Charlie didn't care about the weed. He didn't care about Flynn's past in general. All that mattered was that Flynn's version of events lined up with what Charlie already knew. Still, something wasn't sitting right with him.

"And you just happen to work at the courthouse?"

"Not exactly." Flynn smiled.

"What do you mean?"

"After Jenny died, I couldn't stop thinking about that day, about her crying. The police weren't taking me seriously, so I decided to find out what happened on my own." He shrugged. "I tried getting into the building, but the receptionist wouldn't let me past the front desk. So I had to get a little . . . creative."

"You pretended to be a janitor."

He nodded. "The costume worked like a charm. I got past the front desk on Friday night and I've been snooping around Johnson's office ever since."

That's why no one had seen him since Friday.

"And then this morning," he continued, "I overheard the receptionist tell someone that you asked about a girl named Jenny, that you offered the receptionist a puppy?" He scratched his head. "Anyway, I thought you knew something about Jenny, so I followed you."

"Some advice?" Charlie offered. "Hire someone else next time."

Flynn laughed. "Point taken."

"So you've been looking around Johnson's office," Charlie said. "Did you find anything interesting?"

Flynn lowered his voice. "I sure did. I grabbed a few bank statements before Sara had a chance to take them to the shredder. Let's just say that Judge Johnson deposits a nice chunk of cash into Lieutenant Reid's bank account each month."

"Are you sure?" Charlie asked. "How the hell did you figure that out?"

"I'm an accounting major. I'm good with numbers."

"That bastard."

Johnson was paying the department to keep quiet. No wonder the investigation had been short. But why? What did he have to hide?

"He may have paid others, too. The police could probably dig deeper."

"I don't trust the police." The bank statements were a place to start. But he wanted more before he went back to the CPD. "Did you find anything else?"

"I did, actually." Flynn coughed, avoiding Charlie's eye.

"Well, what was it?"

"Someone else met with Johnson this morning . . ."

Charlie hadn't seen any other names written in the log for that morning. Then again, the receptionist had given him a blank page to sign. "Okay. Who?"

Flynn leveled his gaze with Charlie. "Your dad."

CHAPTER 43

Talia strained against the rope binding her arms and her legs, and the tape covering her mouth. She was blindfolded, and she had no idea where they were going or how long they'd been in the car. If she had to guess, an hour had passed, long enough for Charlie to have listened to her voicemail, to have realized she was in trouble. He was looking for her; he had to be. She refused to believe anything else.

Without him, there was no one else.

Her dad would think she went back to her apartment for the night. Jeff wouldn't expect to hear from her so soon, not after their argument earlier that day. They'd realize she was missing eventually, likely tomorrow. But that could be too late. There was no telling what would happen overnight or where she'd be by morning.

She could be dead.

The car jerked to a stop and she lurched forward, hitting the back of the driver's seat. The front doors opened, then snapped closed.

The back door opened next.

She braced.

"Did you have a nice ride?" Marco mocked.

The blindfold was pulled away from her eyes.

Marco and Muscles stood outside of the car, a rundown ware-house behind them. They were in an alley and dusk was falling. No one else was in sight.

"Get her out," Marco ordered.

Muscles did as he was told and grabbed Talia's arm.

She grunted as he pulled her from the car and threw her over his shoulder.

"Let's go." Marco led the way toward the building.

Talia squirmed and kicked as best as she could. If she went into that warehouse, chances were she'd never come out again. She would never see her dad, Jeff, or her friends again. She'd never see Charlie. She struggled against the rope with everything she had.

"What? You want to get down?" Muscles didn't so much as flinch. His grip around her tightened, painfully so. "Don't worry. I'll have you on your back soon enough."

She kicked harder, grunted louder. It was all that she could do, and it wasn't nearly enough.

Marco unlocked the building's back door. They stepped inside.

The warehouse looked abandoned with its long, dark hallways, closed doors, and sparse lighting. The silence was broken only by the men's footsteps on wet cement, the water dripping from the ceiling, and an occasional scurry from something just beyond the walls—something Talia could picture just fine without seeing. She shivered. The warehouse was as frigid as the October night.

Muscles veered to the right of the hall.

"You're in the way," he barked.

Talia arched her back, straining to see who Muscles had spoken to. They passed a man standing along the wall. Not just any man—the man from the alley, the one who grabbed her bag last night. His purple coat was gone, but she would recognize that beard anywhere. He was there, in the warehouse, and he wasn't swaying from side to side. Compared to last night, he seemed sober.

She widened her eyes at him, desperate for him to do something, to help. And for a moment, she thought he would.

He stepped toward her, but then he stopped. The distance grew between them until he disappeared into the shadows.

Talia was alone, completely alone. All she had was herself.

Marco grabbed another key from his pocket and opened a door.

They stepped into a room. The musty, damp smell made her even more nauseous than she already felt. A single light bulb flickered from the ceiling, but even that was enough to make out the empty syringes and discarded rusty needles scattered along the far wall, the closet in the corner, and the black foam lining the room.

Marco slammed the door shut.

Muscles leaned to the side and slid her off of his shoulder. She landed on the damp cement, hard. The wind knocked out of her lungs and a shooting pain traveled through her ribs. She moaned and pulled her knees up to her chest, curling into a ball as she struggled to breathe through her nose.

"Get the boss," Marco said flatly.

"Can't I have a minute with her first?" Muscles whined.

"You can play with her later."

Play with me? Like hell. Talia tried again to break free from the bindings. The rope dug into her skin. Marco walked to her side and grabbed her by the arm.

He dragged her to the wall and pulled her into a sitting position.

Bending down, he ripped the tape from her mouth.

Her eyes filled with tears as the lower half of her face went numb. "Help me!" she screamed, writhing against the bindings. "Someone help me!"

"Yell as loud as you want. This room has heard worse screams than yours."

She closed her mouth and took in the empty space again, the black foam. The room was soundproof. Dani had mentioned a warehouse that morning, a place the boss used to break women in. This could be it.

Marco was right. No one would hear her screams. She had to think instead and save her energy.

"What do you want from me?"

"Not what. Who. Where's Dani?" Marco asked.

"I don't know." If he thought she'd help him find her, he was wrong.

"You were in the alley last night, watching the house."

"I was," she admitted. There was no use in lying when the man from the alley would've told him that already. But how much more could Marco really know? If she could lead him in the wrong direction, she would. "I took her to my apartment. But she left this morning."

"I don't like liars." He spit on the floor. "And neither does my boss. But you'll learn that for yourself soon enough."

"I can hardly wait." Once the boss showed up, things would only get worse. Talia had to escape before then, make a break for the door, find an exit, a phone.

But first, the ropes had to come off. She couldn't loosen the bindings on her own. She'd already tried. She needed someone's help. And thanks to Dani, she just might be able to trick Marco into being that someone. "I bet the boss really wants to know where Dani was taken, huh?"

"Don't worry. After he's done with you, he'll have all the information he needs."

"Sure." She'd go with that. "But imagine if you were the one to give him the information." She forced her voice to stay steady, to sound conversational, all while praying Dani had been right about Marco's obsession with the boss. She prayed he would take the bait. "He'd be so happy and impressed with you."

Marco's brow furrowed. "He would be . . . yeah."

"You know"—Talia shifted her weight and grimaced for effect—"these ropes are so tight I can barely think. If they were to come off, I'm sure I'd have a better memory."

The door opened.

A man walked into the room. He was big, had dark hair, and wore jeans and a dress shirt. Talia had seen him before, but she couldn't figure out where.

"Boss," Marco said as he strode to the man's side.

So that was him, the man who ran the entire operation, who smoked cigars. The man who Talia was all but positive ordered the hit-and-run against her dad.

He studied her with hungry, beady eyes.

"Hello, Talia."

CHAPTER 44

Charlie couldn't imagine his dad meeting with Judge Johnson, not given his resentment over the *Smith v. Kenton* case. But according to Flynn, he had, five days after Jenny visited the judge on Wednesday. Charlie wanted to know why. He wanted to know the truth. And he wouldn't get that from Johnson.

He had to talk to his dad.

"Dani, I have to run an errand." He grabbed his keys from the kitchen counter.

She stepped out of his bedroom. Her face was even more flushed than before, and her cheeks were splotched with red. "You can't leave now. You just got back."

"I know." But Jenny was his priority. And if talking to his dad could help point him in the right direction, he wouldn't waste another minute. "I won't be gone long."

She crossed her arms over her chest. "You're going to see Talia."

"No, I'm not." And explaining anything else would only take up more time. He grabbed his coat. "Call me if you need anything, okay?" He walked toward the door.

"Talia is a slut," she snapped.

He turned around, taken aback by the venom in her voice. He and Talia weren't on the best of terms, but she certainly didn't deserve Dani's wrath.

"What're you talking about? She's done nothing but help you."

"Oh yeah?" She gestured around the room. "Then where's the medicine she promised?"

Shit, I forgot the medicine.

In the chaos at the hospital, it slipped his mind. But if Talia had proven anything over the past few days, she wasn't one to back down on her word.

"She probably just needs a little more time. I'm sure she'll bring it."

"So you're taking her side?"

"We're both on your side, Dani. Me and Talia." Despite Talia's motives and her lies about her dad, she risked her life going into the Lonemill house and coming back to Charlie's apartment to help Dani. "She's a good person. She cares about you."

"Well, I don't care about her!" Dani yelled, a wild look in her eye. "And I don't want you seeing her anymore." She jabbed a finger in his direction, her hand twitching. "She better stay away from us or else she'll be sorry! Do you hear me?"

"Hey, just take a breath." He walked over to her, having no idea what caused such a strong reaction. Manic, almost. He put a hand on her shoulder. "It's okay. I won't see her anymore." He'd already decided that for himself at the hospital.

Her eyes dropped to his hand on her shoulder and lingered there.

Her breaths started to slow.

He pulled away, unsettled at her mood swing and at what she said, the threat she made. "Maybe you should get some rest."

"Rest . . . right." Her voice had calmed, as if everything were normal and she hadn't just lost her composure only seconds before. She looked up at him, a smile on her lips. "We'll hang out when you're back, then? Just the two of us?"

"Sure." He turned away and couldn't help but feel in over his head, that she might be a little unhinged. Then again, he couldn't judge her too harshly, not after what she'd been through. She could just need more time to adjust. "I'll see you soon."

He left his apartment and drove to his parents' house. No one answered after he rang the doorbell, the same as last time. He opened the door with his keys.

"Hello?" He walked through the kitchen, but no one was there. "Mom? Dad?" He checked the family room next before flipping on the light in his parents' bedroom.

His mom was sleeping in the bed. She didn't stir from the light and he wasn't about to wake her. He was there to talk to his dad, not his mom.

He turned off the light and went to the study. Empty.

He sighed. He'd have to wait for his dad to come back home.

Sitting down in his dad's brown leather chair behind the desk, he turned the seat toward the pictures on the shelves before facing the desk again. A telephone number was written on a sticky note. Maybe his dad had made a note about Johnson, too, something that explained why the two met that morning.

Charlie opened the desk's top drawer, the drawer that used to hold his dad's pocketknife. Now, nothing was there but pens, paperclips, and a notepad with one of his mom's old grocery lists written on the front page.

He opened the second drawer, stuffed with folders, each with a case's name scrawled across the top. *Smith v. Kenton* was front and center. He looked inside of the folder, curious to see what his dad had kept after all of these years.

The folder was full of documents that were highlighted and marked with notes. He shuffled through them. A photograph was caught between two pages.

Three men and two women were in the picture, all of them wearing Loyola University T-shirts. His parents were in the middle of the group, his mom kissing another man's cheek. Charlie read the names printed on the bottom of the picture.

Catherine Lalby, Patrick Kenton, Edward McMahon, Terri James, Isaac Johnson.

He did a double take.

His mom was kissing Johnson.

He examined the picture closer. Sure enough, the man was a younger, thinner version of Johnson. The judge hadn't only known Charlie's dad. He'd known his mom.

Apparently, he'd known her well.

And Johnson's name wasn't the only one that stood out.

Patrick Kenton was in the photograph, too—the defendant in the *Smith v. Kenton* case. He'd been accused of sexual assault and walked away an innocent man. According to the picture, he'd known Charlie's dad and Johnson long before the trial.

Not only that, but Charlie could've sworn that Kenton had been the man with the comb-over that pulled into the Lonemill house before Lieutenant Reid last night. He looked different in the picture, younger. But even back then, his hair was slicked back. If he had been at the house, what exactly did that mean?

He flipped the picture over. A note was scribbled on the back.

I warned you.

None of this made any sense. Not the picture, his mom and Johnson, or the note.

He tried the desk's last drawer, but it was locked. Grabbing a paperclip from the first drawer, he unfolded the wire and slid the end into the keyhole. He jimmied the wire back and forth until it caught, and then he pushed up.

The lock clicked.

He opened the drawer. It was empty aside from a stack of notes. From what he could tell, they were individual pages ripped from some kind of a planner. He grabbed one dated July 3, 1980. His mom's familiar handwriting was on the first line.

Kelly. 1223 S. Harb Ave.

Each page had similar content: a woman's name and an address.

Why had his mom been documenting that, day after day?

And why had his dad locked all of her notes away?

"What the hell are you doing in here?"

Charlie looked up.

His dad stood in the doorway.

CHAPTER 45

Talia forced herself to look the boss straight in the eye. She was afraid of him, of course she was, terrified after what Dani told her that morning. But she couldn't afford to panic. She had to stay strong and think logically. She had to fight for her life. Otherwise, she'd become just another one of his victims.

She'd never make it out of there alive.

"Who are you?" she asked.

"I'll ask the questions." He took his time rolling up one of his shirtsleeves, then the other. "Let's start from the beginning. When did you first meet Dani?"

"When?" She assumed he would want to know where to find Dani, not *when* she and Talia first met. Either way, she wouldn't give him any information, not on Dani, especially not when those details could lead him back to Charlie.

She strained against the rope. "I'm not telling you anything."

"I'll ask you one more time, that's it." His voice was calm, too calm.

She did her best to sound the same. "Don't bother."

He sighed. "We'll do this the hard way, then." He pulled something out of his pocket: a syringe that was the same as the empty ones piled along the wall. Only this one was filled with liquid. "How about a hit of heroin to get you talking?"

Her throat suddenly went dry.

"No?" He tilted his head. "Well then, it's a good thing you don't have a say."

He handed Marco the syringe. Marco smirked as he walked over to the discarded needles and grabbed one that was rusted, used, and exposed. He straightened his form and fit the needle into the syringe.

"Wait." Talia pushed her back against the wall. She needed time to think, to come up with a plan. She'd be defenseless with drugs in her system. "Just hold on a second, okay?"

Marco stepped toward her, still smirking, needle in the air.

"I don't know anything! Really, I promise."

"This will only hurt a little," he taunted, reaching for her arm.

"Okay!" she shouted, her heart pounding. "I'll answer your questions, okay?"

"Good," the boss said as he motioned for Marco to step back. "Let's try this again." He stretched his neck from side to side. "When did you first meet Dani?"

"Last night." She swallowed, trying to calm her racing pulse, to focus.

"At the house on Lonemill?"

"Yes."

He already knew she'd been at the house. She wasn't giving him anything new, but she had to figure out what he was driving at, what he wanted to hear.

"So she wasn't the one who told you about the house?" he asked.

"No."

The boss wouldn't know that Talia's patient had left the note behind. He'd think someone else had given her the house's address, a leak, maybe. And if Talia could convince him of that, he just might forget about Dani. Talia would be able to buy herself some time. "A man told me about the house," she lied.

"A man? How descriptive." Marco snickered.

"Yes, a man." She didn't care what Marco thought. All she needed was for the boss to believe her, or at the very least, to wonder. "A man who works with you."

"A snitch." The boss's left eye twitched. "Who? Give me specifics."

"I don't know his name. He's tall, has light hair." She told him just enough to keep him interested, not enough to expose her lie. "If you untie me, I'll take you to him. I know where he lives." She held her breath. She needed the ropes to come off.

"We're not negotiating. Who is he?" His eyes were pinpricks, dark and cruel.

"I told you. I don't know his name."

"Maybe a few hits will change your answer." He nodded again at Marco.

Marco stepped toward her, syringe at the ready.

"No—don't!" Her muscles tensed. "I'm telling the truth!"

Something buzzed with fast, sharp vibrations.

"What the hell is that?" the boss fumed.

Marco stopped and reached for his back pocket. "Her phone."

Talia's stomach dropped. Her dad would be calling. Or maybe Charlie had listened to her message and was trying to find her. She was desperate for that to be the case. But his name would appear on her caller ID. The boss and Marco would recognize his last name. They'd know he and Jenny were related. They might put two and two together, realize that he and Talia had been working together.

They'd go after Charlie next.

"Wait!"

Marco pulled out her cell and squinted at the screen. "Jeff Foley."

"Jeff?" The boss strode over to Marco. He snatched the phone and looked at the screen. The veins in his neck bulged and he threw the phone onto the ground, shattering the screen on the cement. "Looks like we've found our snitch."

"What? No," Talia said.

But he seems to know Jeff's name, she realized. *Could Jeff be involved with the boss?* Impossible. But if the boss thought Jeff was the snitch, he'd find him. He might even go after Angela and Lucy. Talia couldn't let that happen.

"He's not the snitch."

"First he runs his mouth at the potluck, then he buys airline tickets, now this?"

The boss had been at the potluck. She remembered now. He'd stepped out of the office across the hall from the room her dad and Jeff had been using. He must've overheard her dad mention the missing cigar and suggest they go to Lieutenant Reid. He would've decided to silence him then and there. And now, he was about to do the same to Jeff. "I'm telling you, Jeff has nothing to do with this."

"Stop lying!" the boss yelled. He charged at her, grabbing the front of her shirt as he picked her up from the ground, and pinning her against the wall. "What else did he tell you?" he demanded, his breath warm against her face. "What else?" He shook her.

"He didn't tell me anything!"

"He'll pay." He pressed his forearm against her chest and spoke through clenched teeth. "And this time, he won't end up in the hospital like your dad. He'll be dead."

"Let go of me!"

She struggled against the ropes, against him. She managed to jerk her knee up between his legs. He howled, released her shirt, and fell to his knees.

Marco grabbed her arm, not missing a beat. "You'll pay for that."

"Help me!" She tried to turn toward the door. "Someone, help me!"

"Untie her." The boss's voice silenced the room.

"Untie her? No way! She's lying about Jeff!" Marco looked between the boss and Talia.

The boss put a hand on his knee and pushed himself to his feet. He turned to face Marco.

"What did you just say?" His voice was steel, low and dangerous.

Marco's shoulders dropped. His gaze fell to the floor. "Nothing."

The boss straightened his shirt.

He punched Marco in the face.

Talia cried out at the sound: fist against bone. Marco crumpled to the ground.

He cradled his head, whimpering, and rolled back and forth.

"Get up," the boss demanded.

"I'm sorry," Marco moaned, struggling to his knees and clutching his nose. Blood flowed through his fingers as he stood, swaying. "I'm sorry," he repeated.

"Untie her. Now."

Marco shuffled over to Talia, glaring at her as if she'd been the one to throw the punch, to draw the blood. He removed a pocketknife from his pocket and steadied himself against the wall. Bending over, he grabbed the rope around her legs and yanked her toward him. He cut until the rope dropped to the floor.

Her body shook. She didn't know why the boss wanted her untied. But the ropes would be gone soon. That'd be her chance to run.

Marco cut the ropes around her torso next. He stepped back.

"Now leave," the boss ordered.

Marco's gaze jumped to the boss's face. He opened his mouth, closed it again, and hung his head. He turned away and walked to the door before pausing and glancing back for one last look. And then he left the room.

They were alone.

A shiver traveled down Talia's spine.

"You just couldn't manage to mind your own business, could you?" The boss spoke to her now, only to her. "Snooping around my houses, taking my property." He cracked his knuckles. "You've had your fun. Now it's my turn."

She darted toward the door, taking three steps before a splitting pain tore through her scalp. She screamed as he yanked her back by her hair and threw her onto the floor. Her vision blurred; her head pounded.

"Help me!" she called out.

"Shut up." He climbed on top of her. She writhed under him, trying to push him off, his weight crushing. He grabbed her wrists and used one of his hands to pin them over her head. Reaching under her shirt with his other hand, he squeezed her breast hard and leaned forward, whispering into her ear, "You're mine now."

"Get off of me!" she cried, turning her head to the side.

He moved on to her pants and fumbled with her zipper.

Something fell from his pocket, clattering on the floor.

"Please," she begged. "Stop."

She managed to yank one of her hands free and reached blindly for whatever had fallen. She gripped a set of keys, isolated one of them, and plunged the metal into the fat of his neck. He flinched. She pulled the key out and struck him again.

"You bitch!" He reached for her.

She scratched the right side of his face with the key, pushing the metal as hard as she could into his skin and straight over his eye.

He screamed, covering his eye with his hand, blood on his fingertips. He tried grabbing for her again, but his vision was now impaired. She bit his hand, then punched his throat.

He sucked in air and leaned back.

She pushed her upper body off of the floor, the rusted needles along the wall just within reach. She grabbed a handful and jabbed them into his neck.

He fell over, bellowing profanities, and ripped the needles from his skin.

Standing on shaky legs, she stumbled across the room, opened the door, and ran into the hallway. She pushed herself forward, his keys clutched tightly in her grip.

"Boss?" Marco's voice echoed down the hall.

"Find her so I can kill her!" the boss screamed.

She sprinted as fast as she could. Within seconds, Marco's footsteps followed behind. He was gaining on her. He knew the hallways better than she did.

She rounded a corner. A patch of darkness appeared up ahead: a small alcove. She lunged in that direction and threw her back against the wall.

Marco stopped at the corner.

She held her breath as he decided on a direction.

He started jogging, his footsteps fading into the distance.

She exhaled, pressed a hand over her pounding heart, and tried to catch her breath. Her body was drenched in sweat. Her legs trembled. She wasn't sure she'd be able to keep going, to find an exit. But she had to move. She had to get out of the building.

She stepped away from the wall.

Something shuffled behind her.

She started to spin toward the sound.

A hand covered her mouth, jerking her farther into the darkness.

CHAPTER 46

"Dad." Charlie jumped up from the chair, knocking the picture of his parents, Johnson, and Kenton to the floor. He barely recognized the man before him, his shoulders hunched and wrinkles cut deep into his skin. He looked even thinner than he had yesterday, more vulnerable somehow, more defeated.

"I didn't hear you come in," Charlie said.

"What the hell are you doing here?" his dad asked again, his voice weak. He held a packet of paper in his hands and his gaze fell to the picture on the floor, staying there.

"I came to ask you a few more questions." He came to ask about his dad's meeting with Judge Johnson. But now that he'd seen his mom's notes and the picture with the warning on the back, he wanted more—the full story. He picked up the photograph. "What's this? And what're the notes that were locked in the drawer?"

"They're nothing." His dad's legs started to tremble. He sat down in the chair opposite the desk and set the packet of paper in his lap—a funeral home's letterhead on the front page. "They don't matter, not anymore."

"They do matter, Dad. They matter to me." Charlie had to know what was going on, how Johnson fit into everything. "Please, just explain."

"You wouldn't understand."

"I'm trying to understand."

"Why?"

"Because you're my dad." They'd had their fair share of issues, more than most. But they were family, always would be, and Jenny would've wanted them to get along. This could be their chance to do that, to put their past behind them. "And because I'm the only child you have left."

His dad glanced up at him, not with his usual disappointment, but with a fleeting expression of regret. He looked away, shaking his head.

"I don't know where to start."

"How about here?" Charlie held up the picture. "College."

His dad studied the photo for some time. "You have to understand that your mom didn't have the best childhood. Her parents weren't around much."

Charlie wasn't sure why that was relevant, but he wasn't about to interrupt.

"Speaking of," his dad continued. "As soon as your mom wakes up from her nap, we're done here. She can't find out about this conversation. Understood?"

"She won't find out from me."

His dad leaned back and closed his eyes, pinching the bridge of his nose.

"Your mom had a hard time growing up, in high school, especially. She fell in with the wrong crowd, started skipping school, drinking, and doing drugs." He opened his eyes and dropped his hand. "She barely graduated and almost didn't get into college."

"But she did get into college."

"Yes. That's where she met Johnson. Judge Johnson, now."

"The judge who presided over the *Smith v. Kenton* trial." Charlie wouldn't tell his dad that he met with Johnson that morning, at least not now, a detail that'd only derail the conversation. He set the picture down. "Was Mom dating him?"

His dad nodded. "Johnson noticed her right away, him and every other guy on campus. She was beautiful and confident, but desperate to please at the same time, to be noticed. He liked that.

He saw someone he could mold into whatever he wanted."

"And Mom liked him?" Charlie couldn't imagine why.

"She enjoyed being taken care of, for once. Johnson courted her, in a way. He started paying for her tuition, books, drugs, alcohol, anything she wanted."

"He funded her life."

"For a while, at least. Then he told her she had to start pulling her weight, that he'd love her even more if she contributed to the relationship. He knew exactly how to get into her head. Eventually, he convinced her to help him run his business."

"What kind of business?" Charlie asked.

"A prostitution ring."

"A what?" He couldn't help but raise his voice.

His dad gestured toward the ripped-out page on the desk. "Your mom did the scheduling. She arranged times and places for the women to meet clients."

"How long did she work for him?" Any amount of time was unfathomable.

"A few years. Long enough to realize the girls in the business weren't all that different from herself. They needed money, a way to get through school. Some were just desperate for attention. And that scared her—the similarities. She was sick with guilt. She couldn't sleep, couldn't eat. At some point, she just had enough. She broke up with Johnson and left him and his business behind."

"I can't imagine he reacted well to that."

"No, he didn't. He thought he could win her back with more money, more alcohol and drugs. But she wanted nothing to do with him. She stopped drinking, found another job, and pulled her life together. And that only seemed to enrage him more. His ego couldn't handle the blow. He became obsessed with getting her back. He followed her around campus, threatened her over the phone, and showed up at her work. And Kenton helped him. He was his little sidekick back then."

"When did they stop?"

"When your mom and I started dating. Johnson told us to end things or he'd make us pay. But we weren't afraid of him. And he didn't love your mom, not like I did. So we stayed together. Eventually, he left us alone. We were happy."

"And that was it?" Charlie had never heard his dad so much as utter a nice word about his mom, let alone about being happy. "Johnson just left you both alone?"

His dad picked up the picture. "Until the *Smith v. Kenton* case."

"How did all of you end up on the same trial?"

"I was assigned to represent Caroline Smith even before I realized that Kenton was the same Kenton from school and Johnson the judge." He ran his thumb over the warning on the back of the picture. "Johnson didn't recuse himself from the trial, and Kenton's attorney didn't file a motion, either. So I didn't file one myself. Some twisted part of me wanted to go up against them. And I had enough evidence to win. That's all I cared about."

"But you lost."

"Evidence is useless if the jury doesn't hear it."

Charlie leaned forward. He wasn't following. "What're you saying? You didn't present the evidence?"

Of course he did. That'd been his job—to make a case.

"No, I didn't." He dropped his eyes. "Johnson blackmailed me into losing."

"He blackmailed you? How?" Charlie hadn't expected that.

"Your mom's notes." He waved at the desk. "They showed up everywhere, one by one: in our mailbox, at my work, on my windshield. Johnson said he had more than just the notes, too. He said he had enough to ruin your mom."

"You threw the case on purpose." His dad's descent after the trial hadn't only stemmed from a lost case and a ruined reputation. The guilt of Caroline Smith's suicide after the verdict must've eaten him alive. "Does Mom know about this?"

"She started asking questions once news about the trial and Caroline Smith's death broke. I didn't tell her the truth. I didn't have to. Johnson took care of that on his own." He sighed. "He followed her to the park one day and handed her this picture as she was packing you kids into the car. She started drinking again after that."

"He got his revenge after all."

Charlie's parents blamed themselves for what happened. And yet Johnson carried on with his life as a fraud, a cheat. "Why did he want Kenton to win so badly? He risked his entire career just to keep one friend out of jail?"

"He's not that selfless." His dad shook his head. "He may have moved on from that life, but he still wanted to keep Kenton happy, to eliminate any chance of him ruining the reputation Johnson had built for himself."

"He covered his bases."

If Kenton's visit to the Lonemill house last night was any indication, he hadn't changed much since college. Johnson may have moved on and found a different job, but he was still corrupt. The *Smith v. Kenton* trial was proof enough. And now, he didn't just have Kenton and Charlie's dad to worry about.

He had Charlie, too. "Has Johnson left you alone since then?"

"Yes . . . until last Tuesday night." His dad's shoulders tensed. "He showed up at my North Avenue office, wanting me to get in touch with a prosecuting attorney I used to work with and convince her to back off of his upcoming trial." Anger edged into his voice. "I refused, so he made a show of threatening me and our family and gave me until today to decide."

"And did you?" That would explain his meeting with Johnson that morning.

His dad shrugged. "I told him to go to hell."

"He could come after you again."

"Let him."

"Be careful, Dad. He sounds dangerous." Charlie stood. He now had context for why his dad had met with Johnson.

Still, he had to figure out why Jenny went to see Johnson on Wednesday. "Wait a minute . . ."

His mind caught on something.

"Jenny planned to review her paper with you on Tuesday night, at your office." The same night Johnson threatened their family.

"Yes. I told you already. She lost track of time with Shevy," his dad said.

"Right."

Only, according to Shevy, they hadn't been together. And what if Jenny had been at their dad's office? What if she overheard Johnson's threats? She would've wanted to help their dad. That could be why she met with Johnson.

"What's wrong?"

"I don't know, but something doesn't feel right."

He needed to talk through everything with someone, someone who knew just as much about Jenny's case as he did. He needed Talia. She lied to him, yes. But he still trusted her. He couldn't help himself. Maybe he hadn't cut her enough slack. Maybe he should've heard her out.

He still could.

"I have to go." He walked toward the door.

"Go where?" His dad stood from his chair.

Charlie stopped and faced him, the man he spent the majority of his life resenting, the man he now saw in a more complicated light. "I'll see you soon, Dad."

He left the house and jumped into his truck, taking out his phone to listen to Talia's voicemail. He hit play and heard her apology, then a pause. A long pause.

She came back onto the line. "Charlie, Marco found me. We're in the parking lot next to the hospital. He's driving a black SUV. I need your help, now, please!" Rustling came through the speaker followed by Talia's cries for help. Then nothing.

The message ended.

Charlie pulled the phone away from his ear.

He stared at the screen.

CHAPTER 47

Jeff had planned to look again at the files by now, to explore Talia's claim about the fourth woman, the fifth body. But he hadn't yet had a chance, Lieutenant Reid having monopolized every second of his day. He had to find something on Isaac before he picked up Angela and Lucy. That, or write a confession about their recruiting as kids.

His phone beeped.

He pulled out his cell and saw a text from an unknown number.

My office. Tomorrow. Have your statement ready.

Jeff compared the number to the one Lieutenant Reid called him from the day before. They matched. He stuffed the phone back into his pocket. He'd known Reid would want him to lie about Keith's drinking eventually, to protect Isaac from the hit-and-run by supporting the DUI charge. But still, Jeff thought he'd have more time to beat Reid at his own game.

And now, all he had was tonight.

Tonight would have to be enough. This wasn't just about Isaac. This was about the CPD, too, Lieutenant Reid and Chief Nelson. Jeff had to prove their roles in all of this. He had to prove they were corrupt—them and anyone else involved.

He took the long way back to his office to avoid any chance of running into Reid, and then searched for the Galder case on his computer. The database took longer than usual to load, minutes instead of seconds, an ever-spinning circle.

The spinning stopped.

A message appeared on the screen.

No matches found.

He tried again. Once more, there were no results. *Odd.* The case was still open. The files should've been in the system. Regardless, he had a printed copy he could use. He'd left the folder of files in his desk on Saturday night.

He opened the desk's top drawer.

The folder wasn't there.

He checked the second drawer, the third; he tried the trash, everywhere. The files were gone. They'd been there. He was sure. Someone must've taken the folder from his office. But he didn't have time to speculate on that now, or to keep looking. Detective Strum was managing the documentation and the inventory.

He'd be able to help.

Jeff left his office and found Strum sitting at his desk, his eyes trained on the computer screen. He looked over as Jeff stepped beside him.

"What's up, Foley?"

"I don't see the Galder files in the system. Can you get to them?"

"Sure. I was just organizing them last night." He pulled up the database and clicked around before pausing and scratching his head. "Actually, maybe not."

"Nothing?" He and Strum had been the only ones with full access to the files. If they couldn't get to them, no one could. No one, Jeff was willing to bet, aside from Lieutenant Reid. He'd tampered with the system before by deleting details about the cigar. He could've changed their access now and removed the case. If he was involved, the electronic files were as good as gone. "Have you seen my hard copy?"

"I gave that to Lieutenant Reid."

"You what?" He raised his voice, then checked himself at

Strum's wide-eyed glare. He cleared his throat and tried again. "When did you do that? And why?"

"Yesterday." An edge of defensiveness caught in Strum's tone. "Reid asked me to grab your files. He said he would put them back in your office. Did he not?"

"If he had, I wouldn't be here talking to you." Jeff spoke through clenched teeth. Reid went out of his way to make sure Jeff didn't have access to the case's information. And why do that unless there was something to hide?

Something Jeff must've missed the first time around.

"I can ask if he's done with them . . ."

"Don't." Jeff's interest in the files would only make Reid suspicious. He had to find another way. "Does anyone else have a copy?"

"Just Detective Griffin, as far as I know. I printed one for him myself."

"Great."

Keith's copy would likely be in his briefcase. By now, Talia could have taken that from the hospital. And if Jeff asked her to send him a copy of the files, she'd have a million questions. The folder Lieutenant Reid took could be closer and easier to find. Assuming Reid still had the files, he would've stored them in a secure place, one he could easily access and lock up at the end of the day.

Reid's office was Jeff's best guess. "See you later, Strum."

He walked away and turned down the hall.

Reid's office door was closed, his lights off. Jeff had no idea where he'd gone or when he'd be back. But if the files were there, now was his chance to get them.

He tried the door. Unlocked.

He took a breath and stepped inside. The room was too dark to see much of anything, so he turned on the lights and shut the door. Going straight to Reid's desk, he rummaged through the notebooks, pens, and napkins in his drawers. No folder.

He moved to the file cabinet next and tried each drawer—all locked. He needed a key. Spinning around, he checked under a picture of Reid and his yellow Lab framed on the bookshelf. Nothing was there. The potted plant across the room was his last resort, as good a hiding place as any.

He walked that way and stumbled.

His foot had caught on a slit cut into the carpet, one he never would've noticed had he not tripped. He bent down and lifted the carpet's edge.

A key was there.

He snatched the key and unlocked the cabinet's first drawer, discovering it stuffed with folders. He scanned through the stack and searched for something related to the case. The last folder had his writing across the top.

Galder Investigation.

He removed the folder, shut the drawer, and put the key back under the carpet.

He bolted toward the door.

Someone laughed in the hallway.

He stopped short and heard more voices; there was a group of people just outside of the room, a group that could include Lieutenant Reid. Jeff couldn't walk out of Reid's office with a folder tucked under his arm. But he couldn't just sit there and risk Reid coming back into the room, either. He had to leave. He reached for the door.

A handful of papers fell out of the folder.

"Shit." He bent down and picked them up, stuffing them back into the folder. Something on the fingerprint analysis report caught his eye. He looked closer at Jenny and Tuco's positive IDs, followed by the two Jane Does' inconclusive results.

He scanned the report and stopped cold.

Something was different.

Something wasn't right.

CHAPTER 48

Charlie played Talia's voicemail again. He couldn't believe what he was hearing: Marco's voice in the background and Talia's cries for help. Two hours had passed since she called, two hours since he left her at the hospital. And what had Charlie done since then? He chased his own leads, too stubborn to even listen to her message.

He should've stayed at the hospital and heard what she had to say, just like he should've listened to Jenny outside of the jail. But he wasn't too late to help Talia.

He couldn't be.

The line went straight to voicemail when he called her back. He tried again. Nothing. A third time. No luck.

"Dammit!" He hung up.

He needed help, but not from the CPD; they couldn't be trusted. He needed someone familiar with the business and Marco, someone who'd know where Talia had been taken. And Charlie had just the person in mind.

He started his truck, left his parents' house, and sped back to his apartment. He ran into his kitchen. The lights were off.

"Dani? Are you home?"

His bedroom was dark and the blinds were shut, the only patch of light in the room coming from under the closed bathroom door.

"Dani?" he called again as he crossed the room and knocked on the door. "It's Charlie. Are you in there?"

No response.

He opened the door.

Dani was sitting in the shower with her back against the wall. She was wearing his gray sweats again and her face was pale, streaked with sweat.

She moaned, leaned forward, and dry heaved over the drain. "Shit." He went to her side, crouched down, and placed a hand on her shoulder. Her sweatshirt was damp with sweat and splattered with vomit. She smelled rancid and she was shaking, badly. Her withdrawal symptoms were in full effect. How long those symptoms would last, he had no idea. "Let's get you back into bed."

"Where's Talia?" She pulled away from him, dragging the back of her hand across her mouth. She spit on the floor. "She promised to bring me medicine, that lying whore. She did this on purpose!" she sobbed. "Where the hell is she?"

"She's in trouble." He spoke carefully. He couldn't risk setting Dani off again, not like he had that morning. He needed her to cooperate. He needed information. "Marco found Talia at the hospital. He took her hours ago."

She looked up at him, a shadow of a smile on her face. "She's gone."

"No." He refused to believe that. Talia would survive this. He'd find her, just as soon as he convinced Dani to help. "She's not gone. But we have to get her back."

"She can rot in that warehouse for all I care."

"Warehouse? What warehouse?"

She looked away from him.

"Hey, listen to me." He shifted into her line of vision. "You've been there yourself. You know what she's going through, right? She needs you, Dani."

"What about what I need?" she yelled and grabbed his hand, her grip tight, slick with sweat. "I need you. We're meant to be together. Can't you see that?"

"What the hell are you talking about?" He pulled his hand away and stood. He didn't have time to discuss what Dani needed right now. "Please, just help me."

"I am helping you. I'm doing you a favor," she said, reaching for him.

"You've lost your mind."

He was getting nowhere. She wasn't going to tell him a thing. But she already let the warehouse slip. And that was something. All he needed now was a location, an address. And if pretending he wanted to be with her would give him that, then he'd pretend. He'd do whatever he had to do to get the information.

"Actually, Dani, you're right."

"Of course, I'm right." She pouted.

"We are perfect for each other." He knelt. "And as soon as you get better, we can be together. But you won't get better without Talia's medicine."

"We can get medicine from someone else," she shot back.

"Who?" He raised his shoulders. "We would have to go to the hospital. They'll want to put you in a treatment facility. They'll try to separate us. We need to find Talia so we can be together, you and me. So please, just help me do that. Okay?"

"I can't." She shook her head. "She'll ruin everything!"

"Don't you trust me?" He took her hands, which were shaking, clammy.

"I don't trust her," she seethed.

"She doesn't matter." He inched closer. He would say whatever she needed to hear. "I want to be with you. I'm here now, aren't I? If we find her, you can get better."

"We can be together." She chewed her bottom lip and drew blood. A slow smile stretched across her face. "You and me. Forever."

"Exactly." He let the idea sink in. "So where's the warehouse, Dani?"

She leaned her head back against the wall. "By a McDonald's."

"Okay." That didn't give him much. Every other corner in Chicago had a McDonald's. But she might remember the location in relation to something else. He pulled out his phone and showed her Google Maps as he pointed to 1564 Lonemill Avenue. "Is the warehouse by the house you were in last night? This one here?"

"It's close." Her eyelids closed halfway. She was falling asleep.

He searched the neighborhood for a McDonald's.

The first was located just down the street from the Lonemill house. He zoomed in but saw nothing to suggest a warehouse nearby. The second McDonald's was five miles away from the house. There was a block of space on the corner across the street, West Carline and South Sixtieth Street, a long building, low to the ground.

A warehouse.

He had to get there, now, but he couldn't leave Dani alone at his apartment. She was unpredictable and he didn't trust her. He needed someone else to come by, someone who would help without an explanation.

He called a number he'd been given earlier that day.

The line rang, connected. "Look who's trailing who now."

"Flynn, I need your help."

"What's wrong?"

Charlie glanced down at Dani, now asleep, and stepped out of the bathroom. He made his way into the kitchen.

"It's a long story," he began. "But there's a woman at my apartment. She's sick. I need you to come here and keep an eye on her, make sure she stays put."

"Hold on a minute. Are you trying to hire me as a babysitter?" Flynn laughed. "I'm honored you thought of me, really. But I do have a life, you know."

"This is important, okay? I'll leave my key under the mat, apartment 403. I need someone here I can trust. I can trust you, right?" No response. "Flynn?"

"Does this have anything to do with Jenny?"

Charlie hesitated. After everything Flynn had done for Jenny, he deserved to know the truth. But Charlie couldn't have him getting in the way, wanting to come to the warehouse. Judging by the way he'd trailed Charlie earlier that day, he wouldn't survive one minute with Marco. Charlie needed him at his apartment. And if telling him a portion of the truth got him there, fine.

"It has everything to do with Jenny."

"Consider me hired."

CHAPTER 49

A door shut. Talia couldn't see a thing. The room was dark, the hand still over her mouth. She elbowed the person behind her and heard an intake of breath by her ear, felt the hand slip. She twisted away, broke free, and backpedaled until she reached a wall. Her heart was pounding in her chest and her eyes were wide, desperate for her vision to adjust.

"Who's there?" she called out.

"Don't make a sound," a woman whispered harshly.

"Stay away from me." Talia's voice was pitched, her muscles clenched. A scream lodged in her throat, one she couldn't release, not unless she wanted Marco to come running. But she couldn't just stand there. "Let me out of here or I'll scream."

A light turned on.

Talia blinked, taking in the empty space and the woman holding a flashlight by the door. She had dark, short hair and a bruise under her eye that looked magnified in the shadows from the flashlight's beam.

"Are you trying to get us killed?" she scolded. "Be quiet."

Talia couldn't be quiet. "Who are you?" Her voice shook; her legs buckled.

"Relax, will you?" The woman ignored her question and went to the door. She pressed her ear against the wood. "He's gone," she said, straightening. "But he'll be back soon. We have to go."

She opened the door.

"Go where?" Talia's mind was swimming. One second, she'd

been running for her life. The next, she'd been pulled into a room by a stranger.

The woman peered up and down the hall. "You'll see."

"I don't think so."

The woman seemed to have a plan. But Talia had one of her own: to get the hell out. She had to find an exit and she didn't have time for anything else.

"I'm leaving." She walked toward the door and the woman.

The woman rolled her eyes. "You won't last one minute out there alone."

"I was doing just fine on my own, thanks."

"You were running around like a chicken with your head cut off. Besides, you don't have a choice. Follow me, or I'll turn you in to Marco." The woman gave a terse smile. "Then we'll really see how well you do on your own."

She glanced once more into the hall before leaving the room.

"Hey, come back!" Talia called but stood rooted to the spot.

She wasn't about to follow the woman. She didn't know anything about her, if she could be trusted. Then again, the woman was right. Talia didn't have a choice. She couldn't risk being turned over to Marco and the boss. She'd escaped them once. But that'd been luck. It wouldn't happen again. If she was found, the boss would follow through on his threat. *I'll be dead.*

She cursed and hurried to the door.

The woman was standing across the hall.

"Take your time," she whispered, her sarcasm thick. "We have all night."

She disappeared into another room.

Talia took a deep breath, hoping she wasn't making a mistake. She stepped into the hall and bounded across the floor into the second room.

The woman closed the door and turned on her flashlight.

Three sets of eyes stared back at them—three women, sitting on the ground, propped up against the same wall.

"What the hell?"

Talia stepped back, shocked more than anything. The women just sat there, not saying a thing. Their heads leaned against the wall and their eyes were glazed over. The room's smell was overwhelming: urine, feces, God knew what else.

Talia went to the closest woman. She had dirty-blonde hair, track marks on her arm, and a black eye. Her clothes were filthy and ripped, the same as the others. These must've been the women Dani had mentioned, the ones who acted up. They were drugged. Talia felt the woman's forehead. Her skin was burning up.

"She has a fever."

"They all do."

Talia moved on to the next woman. Her pulse was dangerously low. They needed water, food, and so much more. She looked around the room. Needles and syringes were scattered along the wall. There was nothing she could leverage.

"They need help."

"No shit, Sherlock."

"Oh yeah?" Talia turned around, done with the woman's attitude. "If that's so obvious, then what have you done to help? You look pretty good compared to them." Her jeans were torn and her shirt was stained. But she was conscious, coherent.

The woman put her hands on her hips. "I do what I can. I take care of them when they're sick, grab scraps of food, scraps of anything. It's not much, I know."

"It's nothing. We have to get them out of here."

"I already tried getting them out." She stepped closer. "We were caught. The boss punished them. He had Marco up their dosage so they couldn't even walk."

"Why them and not you?" Talia asked.

The woman's face turned scarlet. "He punished me in other ways."

Talia searched for the right words but found none.

All she knew was that they had to get out of there—all of them, together. "We'll just have to try again."

"He threatened to kill them if I tried again, a threat I'm not willing to test."

"We'll be more careful. He won't catch us," Talia said as she stood. "Besides, the women will die in here if they stay much longer."

"It's too risky, especially with Marco looking for you now."

"Then what exactly do you suggest?" Talia was losing her patience.

The woman held Talia's gaze. "We can't escape. But you can."

"Me? I can't just leave you all here." Not after everything she'd seen. No way.

"We need someone to know that we're here."

The woman was right about that. The boss wouldn't be stopped unless someone reported the warehouse and the women inside. If Talia got away, if she brought back help, the women would have a chance at getting out of there alive.

They'd have a chance at surviving.

"Okay. I'll go," she relented.

"Be quick. They'll move us to a different location once they realize you're gone. That, or they'll burn the place down."

Talia swallowed. "I'll be fast." Anything else and the women would end up like the victims from Friday morning's fire. "How do I get out of here?"

"The exit doors are all locked. We'll have to find a window."

"Maybe not." Talia reached into her pocket and pulled out the boss's set of keys. The metal ring was labeled for the warehouse. "One of these might fit the lock."

"Worth a shot." The woman opened the door. "That's the closest exit." She pointed to a big metal door at the end of the hallway. "Ready?"

"Let's go."

They walked out of the room and tiptoed down the hall. Halfway to the door, the woman grabbed Talia's arm. They stood still, listening. Talia didn't hear a thing.

Then she heard footsteps coming closer, getting louder, faster. Someone was running—running toward them.

"Hurry!" The woman pulled Talia's arm. They ran down the hall until they reached the exit. Talia tried four keys before she found a match and threw open the door.

The woman pushed her outside. "We'll wait for you in the room." She took something out of her pocket and gave it to Talia. "If we don't survive, give this to my brother."

"Your brother? How do I find him?" Talia glanced down at the necklace, a chain with a pendant on the end. She looked closer. The pendant matched Charlie's from the night before. "Who exactly is your brother . . . ?"

"Jenny!" A man called from inside of the building. "Where are you?"

"Coming!" the woman answered. Her eyes locked with Talia's.

"Jenny?" Talia stared. The woman had responded to "Jenny." She had the same necklace as Charlie, the McMahon family crest. Her face transformed before Talia's eyes as Talia began to see resemblance to Charlie in her jaw, her nose.

"Jenny?" Talia repeated. She grabbed the woman's wrist and held on tight. "You're Jenny McMahon?"

"Yes." She tried to pull away. "Now go get us help!"

"But you were at the house. You died in the fire."

Only she hadn't died, because she was standing right there, right in front of Talia. And if she were still alive, then there wasn't really a fifth body. There never had been. Dani thought Jenny was dead.

They all did.

"I was at the house, yes. But the boss needed me here in the middle of the night. He sent someone to pick me up early, before the fire started. I was lucky."

"You have to come with me," Talia pleaded as she tried to pull Jenny outside.

"I can't leave them." Jenny yanked her wrist out of Talia's grip. "Go! Hurry!"

She slammed the door shut.

"Dammit!"

Talia had to tell someone Jenny was still alive. She had to tell Charlie before it was too late. She stuffed the boss's keys and the necklace into her pocket.

Something clicked behind her. She spun around.

Marco aimed a gun at her chest.

He smiled. "Going somewhere?"

CHAPTER 50

Charlie cut his truck's lights and pulled up to the one-story warehouse. Five garages lined the front of the building. There were no other doors, no windows. He parked by the curb and rushed to the first garage. Gripping the bottom of the door, he lifted, but the metal only gave an inch. Locked from the inside.

He tried the next four doors, all secured. "Come on!"

He'd left his Halligan bar at his apartment. He had to find another way inside.

He had to search the warehouse for Talia.

His phone vibrated as he jogged to the side of the building—no points of entry there. He pulled out his cell while moving toward the back of the warehouse.

Dani was calling.

He didn't want to talk to her again, barely thirty minutes having passed since he left the apartment. But she could've remembered something important, something that could help him find Talia. He answered.

"Dani? Is everything okay?"

"I changed my mind!" she cried, speaking in hysterics. "I don't care about Talia's medicine. You need to come back. She deserves to die! Just let that bitch die!"

"We talked about this, Dani. I have to go." He stepped over a pile of bricks.

"And how dare you leave me with Flynn, that skinny-ass loser!" she sobbed. "He's driving me crazy. He talks nonstop. He won't shut the hell up!"

"Dani? What're you doing in there?" Flynn said in the background. "Hey. Give me that." Shuffling sounded. "Charlie?" Flynn came onto the line. "I guess you forgot to mention the woman I'm watching is batshit crazy, huh?"

"You're batshit crazy!" Dani yelled.

"Look who won't shut up now!" Flynn shot back.

Something shattered.

"Jesus! The lamp? Really? What's next? The TV?"

Charlie sighed. "Flynn. The lamp is fine. Just keep her at the apartment, okay? Easy enough." A noise came from the back of the warehouse—a man yelling.

"I have to go," Charlie whispered. "And for God's sake, keep her away from the TV."

He hung up and slid the phone back into his pocket, straining to hear the voice again. The man sounded angry, but he was too far away to make out any words. Charlie moved to the back of the building, crouching low, and poked his head around the corner.

The alley was dark, but he could still make out a man and a woman standing in the distance. Marco and Talia. Charlie stood straight. His heart slammed against his ribcage. Talia was alive. He stepped forward and jerked to a halt.

Marco was holding a gun.

A gun pointed directly at Talia's chest.

Charlie pulled back around the corner. His insides screamed at him to move, to get Talia out of there, but his instinct warned him to wait, to think. He couldn't risk spooking Marco into shooting, not with Talia in his range of fire, not when Charlie had no weapon of his own, no way to protect her.

Marco's back was to him, so Charlie could sneak up on him and use the element of surprise. But still, he'd need something to fight with when he got close.

He went back the way he came and grabbed one of the bricks from the ground, then returned to the warehouse's corner and looked into the alley again. Talia's eyes were wide, glued to the gun. She was scared. Charlie had to get out there, now.

He stepped out from behind the building.

Talia saw him right away and opened her mouth as if about to say something, to warn him. He held a finger to his lips, gesturing for her to keep quiet.

She turned her attention back to Marco. Her shoulders set.

Charlie continued forward, past the row of trash barrels and the fire escape, resisting the urge to bolt ahead. He still had twenty feet to go. If Marco heard him approaching from that far out, he wouldn't stand a chance.

He slowed his step, one at a time.

"You think you're so smart? That you can get away from me?" Marco sneered.

"I'm sorry, okay?" Talia pleaded.

"You're not sorry. But you will be. I promise you that."

A twig snapped under Charlie's foot.

Marco spun around, his gun now pointed at Charlie. He had dried blood on his face, under his nose, and on his shirt. "Who's there?" He squinted. "Don't come any closer!"

Charlie took another step.

"Stop!" Marco grabbed Talia and pulled her toward him. She cried out as he pointed the gun at her head. "Take another step and I'll shoot. I'll do it!"

"I wouldn't shoot if I were you." Charlie's eyes were steady on Talia, on the gun. He held up his hands, brick and all. "Someone will hear the shot and call the police." He took one more step. "Just put the gun down. No one has to get hurt."

"Hey, I know you." Marco frowned. "You were at the house last night." He started backing up, pulling Talia with him. "Get out of here, now!"

"You get out of here!" Talia brought her foot down on Marco's shoe.

"Ouch!" He jerked his foot back.

She pushed off of him and broke away.

Charlie dropped the brick and bolted forward, launching himself at Marco.

They collided and fell to the ground. Charlie grabbed Marco's shirt just as Marco swung at Charlie's head, hitting him above the ear with the butt of his gun. Charlie's grip faltered at the impact, enough for Marco to pull away and get to his feet while Charlie struggled to do the same, his head already throbbing.

Marco started to run.

Talia shoved one of the trash barrels over, into his path.

He tried to jump the barrel, but he tripped and fell.

He got back up, pushing himself forward, but Charlie wasn't far behind. He grabbed the brick and caught up to Marco, tackling him again to the ground. He hit him over the head with the brick, hard enough to knock him out cold.

Marco lay there, unconscious.

Charlie dropped the brick again and took the gun.

He went to Talia and grabbed her shoulders.

"Are you okay?" He looked her up and down and didn't see any blood. "We have to go."

"Wait! I need to tell you something." She grasped his hand.

"There's no time." He started pulling her toward the side of the building.

She planted her feet and yanked her hand away. "She's inside, Charlie." She took a breath, her voice thick with emotion. "Jenny is inside of the warehouse."

He turned back around and stared at her. "Jenny?"

"Yes. She's alive."

"My sister?" He stepped back; he couldn't have heard her correctly. Jenny died. He'd confirmed as much himself. He'd seen her body. "She's dead, Talia."

"She's not. I saw her. She has black hair and gray eyes." She pulled something from her pocket and placed a necklace into his palm. "She asked me to give this to you."

He ran his thumb over the pendant, his family's crest.

He closed his fist and looked up at Talia. "That's impossible."

His sister's body had been at the morgue—what'd been left of her body, at least. Wisps of black hair, one eye melted into the rest of her face, and the other eye closed.

Then again, he'd only seen the body for a few seconds. His vision had been blurred with tears. Jenny's watch had been there. But what if someone planted that on the body after the fire? At this point, Charlie wouldn't put anything past the CPD or Lieutenant Reid. *What if I made a mistake?*

"Jesus Christ."

He crouched over and could barely breathe. He didn't know what to think. If Talia was right, if Jenny was in the warehouse, then he had to get her out, now.

"I'm going inside." He moved toward the door.

Talia grabbed his arm. "You can't just walk in there. They'll be looking for me, and for Marco now, too. They'll find you before you even get to Jenny."

"I have to try." He didn't stop.

She stepped in front of him. "Wait. I have a plan. But you're not going to like it. And it's dangerous."

"Tell me."

"Give me your cell." She held out her hand.

He grabbed his phone. "What're you going to do?"

"I'm going to call Jeff. Detective Foley."

"You're kidding, right?" The detective who wanted to close Jenny's case? "No way." He stepped around Talia and walked toward the door.

She followed. "The boss seemed to know him. He might trust Jeff."

Charlie stopped. "The boss is inside?"

"Yes, and I think Jeff can help us stop him."

"Foley couldn't even manage Jenny's investigation, Talia."

Why she thought he could help now, Charlie didn't understand. "He can't be trusted."

"He can." She took the cell from his hand. "I'll prove it. We'll test him."

CHAPTER 51

Jeff walked into Angela and Lucy's school. The halls were empty, quiet, and dark. The students had already left for the day. He reached Angela's classroom and peered through the open doorway. Her pastel-pink sweater stood out against the black paper bats hanging from the ceiling and the white mummies taped to the walls. She was talking on the phone, her back to Jeff, while Lucy colored on the floor.

He knocked on the doorframe.

Angela glanced over her shoulder and signaled that she'd need another minute.

He shut the door and walked away from the classroom, desperate to get moving, to drop Angela and Lucy off at the Thompsons' guesthouse. Considering what he found in the fingerprint analysis report that Lieutenant Reid had hidden, Jeff's night was only just beginning.

He had more digging to do.

His cell phone rang and he rushed to answer the call. "Jeff Foley."

"Jeff. It's Noel."

"Thanks for calling me back." He'd worked with Noel on plenty of cases before and trusted her more than anyone else at the lab. He walked farther down the hall. "I wanted to ask you about the Galder fingerprint analysis report."

"Sure. I helped with that one. Go ahead."

"A sentence on the analysis is typed in a different font than the rest of the template. Have you ever seen that before?" The fonts were similar enough that Jeff hadn't noticed the difference the first few times around. But tonight, he had.

"A different font?" she asked. "No, but I can guarantee you that the report's integrity is still there. Tuco Alvarez's prints did match the body."

Jeff closed his eyes. "What about Jenny McMahon?"

"The two female bodies at the scene were too burned to pull any prints. We didn't get a comparison." She paused. "Surely, Lieutenant Reid told you that?"

Jeff's grip on the phone tightened. According to the sentence typed in a different font on the CPD's version of the report, not only had the lab compared the prints, but Jenny McMahon's had matched. "He must've forgotten. When did you talk to him?"

"He called me Friday morning and asked me to send him the report before anyone else. After that, he had some pretty detailed questions about the results."

Jeff hung up without another word.

He stuffed his phone back into his pocket. At some point after leaving the lab, the report had been altered, made to look as if Jenny's prints did match one of the bodies. Isaac must've had Reid make the change. That would explain why Reid asked for the results before anyone else. But why had they wanted the report altered at all?

Why Jenny McMahon?

He didn't know. But despite the fact that the McMahons were planning a funeral for the wrong body, there was a silver lining to all of this. He now had something he could use against Isaac and Reid. The altered fingerprint report combined with the missing cigar had to be enough to start an internal investigation.

Now, he just had to talk to someone at the CPD.

He couldn't go to Chief Nelson. According to Reid, Nelson was a player in the sex ring. But he could try Nelson's boss, Superintendent Lee. And in the off chance that Lee was also corrupt, Jeff would be sure to let slip that the media had already caught wind of a botched investigation and were sniffing around for leads. He'd remind Lee that they would love nothing more than to break a story of police corruption and incompetence. The media didn't actually know about the case, not yet.

But they would.

Jeff would deliver the content to the reporters himself. He'd built enough contacts over the years to know who had the most credibility, the widest audience.

With the added visibility, Superintendent Lee would have no choice but to save face and follow protocol. He'd have to set up an internal investigation, one that would start with Reid and inevitably lead to Isaac. Reid's and Isaac's crimes were connected, everything from the sex ring, to the falsified documents, to the hit-and-run.

The investigation would ruin them.

Jeff was playing with fire. Once Isaac learned what he'd done, he would react. He'd come after Jeff and his family. But Angela and Lucy would be at the guesthouse by then, and Jeff would be careful himself. He'd stay at work late. He wouldn't go home until Isaac was arrested. And after that, his brother would be done.

His business would be over, the investigation sure to uncover others involved in the sex ring, too. A new team would be assigned to the Galder case, and they would start fresh with the information. The McMahons would finally get answers.

Jeff's family would finally be safe.

The classroom door opened.

Angela stepped into the hall and walked toward him, lines of worry on her face becoming more visible as she approached. She looked around before she spoke.

"Did you take care of everything?"

"Yes." He wanted to give her the details then and there. But he'd wait until they reached the guesthouse, until she and Lucy were out of harm's way. "I found something on Isaac and Lieutenant Reid. Isaac will be behind bars soon enough."

"How soon?" she asked.

Once he turned in the report and told Superintendent Lee everything he knew about Isaac and Reid, arrests could be made within hours, a few days at most.

"Maybe tonight. Maybe tomorrow. I don't know for sure."

"You had until tonight, Jeff."

"I know."

His phone rang again.

He tensed, but he didn't move. The last time he took a call in the middle of their conversation, Angela walked away. He wasn't about to risk that now. He had to convince her to give him just a little more time, that everything was under control.

"I'm close, Angela. I promise. I just need you to hang in there for one more day, okay? One more day and all of this will be over."

Another buzz.

He winced.

She sighed. "Just answer it."

"Are you sure?" He pulled out his cell and checked the screen. He didn't recognize the number. "I'll be quick, one second." He accepted the call.

"Hello?"

"Jeff, it's me."

"Talia?"

"I need your help," she whispered over static. "The boss found me at the hospital. He kidnapped me. He's holding me hostage. Other women are here, too."

"Slow down. The boss? Other women?"

She had to be talking about Isaac. He hadn't been happy with her snooping. He would've taken matters into his own hands, just like he had with Keith.

"Where are you, Talia?"

"I'm at a warehouse on West Carline and South Sixtieth Street." She inhaled sharply before speaking faster, in a panic. "The boss is coming back. Please, Jeff, help me."

The line cut.

"Talia? Are you still there?" He pulled the phone away from his ear. The screen was black. She was gone, just like that.

"Go."

He looked up. "What?"

"You have to help her," Angela urged.

"I will. But not until I drop off you and Lucy at the guest-house."

They were his priority. He had to drive them first.

"Talia may not have that time."

"Yes, she will." He wasn't sure who he was trying to convince, Angela or himself. "I can't leave you and Lucy until I know you're both safe."

"I'll drive Lucy to the guesthouse myself. I know the way there." She placed her hand on his arm and squeezed. "Just go, Jeff. Hurry. Finish this, tonight."

He didn't move, terrified to leave them. But Angela was right. Talia was in trouble. There was no telling what Isaac would do to her in a warehouse. Besides, if Isaac was focused on Talia, then Angela and Lucy wouldn't be on his radar.

They'd be safe.

Jeff would finish Isaac, tonight.

"You'll call me once you're there?" he asked.

"Yes." She hesitated, then took his hand. "Be careful, Jeff."

He kissed her cheek. "I'll see you tonight," he said as he pulled back and started walking away. After a few steps, he stopped and turned around.

"I love you, Angela."

She didn't reply. But he could see it in her eyes.

She still loved him, too.

CHAPTER 52

Charlie followed Talia to the front of the warehouse. He wanted to go inside, to find Jenny. But Talia was right. He had to think logically, and he couldn't just run into the building only to be caught. He needed her help. But she'd barely said a word since calling Detective Foley, since they tied an unconscious Marco to the fire escape using cables from Charlie's truck.

"Tell me the plan, Talia."

"I will." She reached the front corner of the warehouse and glanced up and down the road. Not a single car in sight. "Just as soon as Jeff gets here."

"I'm not waiting for him. We're wasting time."

She seemed to think Foley would solve all of their problems. She trusted him. And Charlie knew better than that.

"Just give him one more minute," she said.

"That's too long. We don't even know if he's coming." Charlie had lost Jenny once. He wasn't about to lose her again. Not to mention, the boss would send someone outside to find Marco soon enough. And when he did, when Marco woke up, Charlie didn't want to think about what would happen next.

"Forget the plan." He turned around. "I'm going inside."

He stepped toward the back alley.

"Wait." Talia grabbed his arm and pointed at a car driving down the road. "That's him." She looked at Charlie. "See? He came. You can trust him. At least trust me."

She walked out to meet Foley.

Charlie stayed put, still tempted to try to find his own way inside. But he did trust Talia. And with Foley here now, she'd tell him her plan and what to expect.

She'd tell him where to find Jenny.

Foley parked and stepped out of his car. He strode toward the warehouse, toward Talia. "Thank God," he said as he pulled her into a quick embrace. "Are you okay?" he asked.

"I'm fine."

"No thanks to you." Charlie joined them.

"Charlie?" Foley did a double take. "What're you doing here?"

"I'm doing what you should've done from the beginning." Charlie turned to Talia. He didn't plan on engaging Foley any further. "He's here. Now what's the plan?"

Foley looked between them. "The plan? The plan for what?"

"For getting my sister out of the warehouse alive."

"Jenny?" Foley raised his eyebrows.

"Yes." Charlie faced him and squared his shoulders. "She's still alive. That seems like something the case's lead detective should've known, don't you think?"

"That's impossible." Foley paused. His face lost some color. "Or not . . ." He started pacing. "That bastard! He wanted us to think Jenny was dead."

"Who did?" Charlie asked.

"Lieutenant Reid." Foley looked at Charlie. "I think he changed the fingerprint report to make the results look like Jenny's prints matched another body."

"And how long have you been sitting on that information?"

"I only noticed the change an hour ago. And still, I assumed she was one of the Jane Does. I never thought she was still alive. I was planning to turn Reid in tonight."

"Bullshit."

Talia jumped in. "Reid isn't the only one we need arrested. Jeff, listen, when I was in the warehouse, the sex ring's boss seemed to know you somehow."

"Yeah, well . . ." Foley looked away, then back at Talia. "He does know me." He ran a hand over the lower half of his face, red stubble having grown over the past few days. "Unfortunately, he happens to be my brother."

Talia and Charlie stared at him.

"You don't have a brother." Talia spoke first.

"I do. A half-brother. Same mom, different dad."

Charlie could barely process the information. "Let me get this straight . . . You knew this whole time that your brother was involved? That he was running the goddamn sex ring?" He was yelling now. "That explains the shit investigation. You were protecting him!"

"It's not what you think."

"It's exactly what I think!"

"It's perfect," Talia added. "If he's your brother, then he might talk to you. You could help us bring him and his business down, help us stop him from hurting anyone else."

"Help us? You think Foley will side with us over his own brother?"

She can't possibly believe that, Charlie assured himself. "We can't trust him, Talia. He's lying. He's setting us up. Can't you see that?"

"I'm not setting you up." Foley held his ground. "My brother threatened my wife and daughter. I need this to end just as much as you do. I'll do whatever it takes."

"It's a little late for that," Charlie shot back.

"It's not." Talia pulled a set of keys from her pocket. She held them out for Charlie to see. "These will get us into the warehouse. I'll show you where to find Jenny. Then Jeff and I will distract the boss while you and Jenny get the women out."

Charlie took the keys. "You're not going back in there." Not with Foley, on top of that. "You've already been in enough danger for one night."

She ignored him and said to Foley, "Your brother will want

to know why you're here. You can tell him that I called you, maybe buy us time by acting conflicted about what to do, whether to arrest him or not. We'll get him to talk and incriminate himself. My phone is gone, but we can record the conversation on your cell."

"You're staying outside, Talia," Foley said, echoing Charlie.

"If I'm not in there, he'll think I'm still on the loose. And then what?" she argued. "Do you really think he'll sit around and talk to you? No. He'll be too worried about covering his tracks and getting rid of the women."

"He'll make a run for it," Foley agreed.

"Exactly. We can't let him get away. He'll hurt more people."

As much as Charlie hated to admit it, Talia had a point. They needed the boss to feel confident, like he had the upper hand. If he felt threatened, rescuing Jenny and the other women would become that much harder. But still, Talia wasn't thinking through the risks. "How will you get out of there? He won't just let you go."

"We'll make a deal with him," she said with a shrug. "If he lets us go and leaves our families alone, we'll stay quiet about his business. We'll do whatever he wants."

"That's it?" Her safety hinged on the boss accepting a deal? There was only one problem. He didn't sound like the compromising type. "And if that doesn't work?"

"We can use Jeff's gun."

"No." That left too much up to chance, way too much. "We need something else."

"If you have a better plan, now would be the time to share."

He didn't have a better plan. He didn't have another plan at all. But still, he wouldn't sit by while Talia put herself in harm's way.

"I'll think of something," he said.

"We're wasting time, you said so yourself." She turned to Foley. "You'll protect me, right? You'll shoot if you have to shoot?"

He didn't hesitate. "Of course."

"Great. Decision made."

Only the decision hadn't been made.

Charlie put his hands on her shoulders. "I can't lose you."

"You won't." She took his hands in hers. "This isn't just about you, Charlie. If we don't finish the boss tonight, he'll hurt my dad. He'll hurt Jeff's family."

"He'll hurt you if you go back in there."

"I'll be fine." She let go of his hands and stepped back. "I've made up my mind."

"I guess you have."

She was going into the warehouse whether Charlie wanted her to or not. He didn't trust Foley and he never would. And yet he had to. Talia's life would be in his hands. All the more reason to plan for backup.

"I need a second." He stepped away, pulled out his phone, and dialed.

Flynn answered the call. "Please tell me you're on your way home."

"Is that Charlie?" Dani yelled in the background.

"No! It's my mom!" Flynn shouted, then lowered his voice. "I can't take this much longer, man. She's delusional. She said you're dating! That can't be true, can it? I know I just met you, but still, I pictured you with someone a little more . . . chill."

"Flynn, I need your help."

"No offense, but after the past hour, I'm not too keen on helping you again."

"Listen, if you don't hear from me in thirty minutes, call the police and the Humboldt Park Fire Department."

He wasn't sure who from the CPD would show, but he trusted the fire department, Chief Freeman, and his squad. Worse come to worst, they'd find Talia, Jenny, and the women. They'd get them out.

"Tell them I went into a warehouse on West Carline and South Sixtieth Street with Talia Griffin and Detective Foley."

"The police and the fire department? What the hell is going on?"

"Just make sure they know that women are inside, okay? That Talia is, too."

Charlie looked over his shoulder. Talia and Foley were talking. She glanced Charlie's way and their eyes locked. "I need to know you're on this, Flynn. You're possibly the only one protecting someone I care about."

"Someone you care about?" Flynn asked.

"Yes." Charlie turned away from Talia. "Will you remember everything?"

"West Carline and South Sixtieth Street, women inside, Talia Griffin," Flynn recited.

"Talia Griffin?" Dani's voice came over the line again, sounding closer than before. "That's not your mom, you lying piece of shit! Give me the phone!"

"Get off of me, crazy lady!" Flynn yelled.

"Thirty minutes, Flynn," Charlie spoke over the noise and ended the call.

He turned to Talia and Foley.

"Let's go."

CHAPTER 53

Jeff walked to the warehouse's back door. His shirt was damp with sweat, his shoulders tense. Everything he stood to lose was riding on this rescue. One mistake and Isaac could walk away. But Jeff wouldn't let that happen. He couldn't afford any mistakes. Their plan would work. Isaac would be behind bars later that night.

His games would finally be over.

"Let me see those keys." He took the set from Charlie. After finding the key that fit, he turned the lock until a click echoed into the night. Then he opened the door. The inside of the warehouse was dark with long, empty hallways and closed doors, no one else in sight.

But that didn't mean Isaac wasn't close.

"Stay here," Jeff said, stepping into the building first. He leaned his back against the wall by the door and stood still, waiting for his vision to adjust. Water dripped from the ceiling. He didn't hear anything else and didn't see anything, either.

"It's all clear."

Charlie walked in next, then Talia. Charlie was holding a gun of his own.

Jeff stepped away from the wall. "Where did you get that?"

"While you were sitting on your ass, trying to close a case that never even started, we were busy here."

Charlie didn't offer anything else. And that was fine.

"Which way?" Jeff asked Talia.

"Jenny was down this hall."

Jeff led the way, his gun at the ready. Talia followed behind him and Charlie took up the rear. They stayed along the wall, stepping light and walking slow.

"Stop." She paused where one hallway met another and pointed straight ahead. "Jenny and the others are in the last door on the right." She took the keys from Jeff and handed them to Charlie. "You'll need these to get the women outside."

Charlie closed his fist around the keys. "Right."

He and Talia stared at each other, long enough that Jeff felt like he was intruding on a private conversation.

Talia pushed her shoulders back. "Be careful, Charlie, please."

Charlie pulled her into an embrace. "We'll meet by the trash barrels in the back alley." He stepped away and glanced at Jeff. "You'll keep her safe."

"Yes."

Talia was family. Jeff would protect her with everything he had.

Charlie looked once more at Talia. "Okay, then . . . I'll see you soon."

He walked toward the room.

Jeff and Talia went down the other hall, Jeff's pulse increasing with every step he took. This was his one shot to put his brother away. Isaac would try to get into his head, to use Angela and Lucy to control him. But Jeff couldn't fall for that, not tonight. No matter what threats Isaac made, he had to remember that Angela and Lucy were safe.

Talia slowed. "This is the room."

"Let's hope he's still here." Jeff took out his phone and started to record. He tucked the phone into his back pocket. "Stay close to me in there."

Once they opened that door, there'd be no turning back. Jeff was ready.

With his gun pointed at the ground, he reached for the knob and opened the door.

He stepped inside. "Isaac?"

Talia followed.

Isaac stood in the middle of the room, his phone to his ear. He had dried blood on his face, his neck, and the collar of his shirt. His right eye was cut and swollen shut.

He glanced at Jeff and ended the call. "You're right on time."

"Right on time for what?"

Something didn't feel right. Isaac should've been more surprised to see them. He should've been asking questions, demanding answers, not acting like he'd been expecting them. Jeff took in the closet in the corner, the syringes and needles on the floor.

"Do you remember Ruby, Jeff?" Isaac tilted his head.

Jeff balled his fists. "You have some nerve saying her name."

"That's when I first realized that you were weak: the day she was taken." He started walking around the room, moving at a leisurely gait. "Still, I never knew that you were a complete idiot, too. Not until you decided to try and fool me tonight."

Jeff felt Talia stiffen beside him.

Isaac was speaking as if he knew about their plan. But that was impossible; it couldn't be the case. "I don't know what you're talking about."

Isaac stopped walking and looked at Jeff. "I think you do."

Jeff forced himself to breathe, to stay calm, in control. Isaac was playing games, again. But whether or not he'd been expecting them didn't matter. As long as he didn't know about the phone recording and Charlie, they were fine. As long as he talked, they could still buy time.

"You kidnapped Talia. I could arrest you for that," Jeff said, playing his part.

"You won't arrest me."

"What makes you so sure?"

"You'll be dead." Isaac smirked. "Both of you."

"What? You're going to kill us?" Jeff stepped in front of Talia and raised his voice for the recording, his gun still at the ready. "People will notice that we're missing, Isaac. They'll look for us. They'll find us here. And then what?"

"You were in the wrong place at the wrong time."

"That's the best you can come up with?"

"I could spin a double suicide, if you prefer that." He scratched his chin in mock thought. "Come to think of it, that will work nicely. An officer who let the job get to his head, a woman so in love with him that she couldn't live without him."

"You've lost your mind. No one will believe you."

"The evidence will speak for itself. Lieutenant Reid will help with that." Isaac spoke calmly, as if he'd had this conversation a hundred times before.

"You won't get away with this." A tremor broke in Talia's voice.

"Oh, I think I will." His beady eyes settled on Jeff. "Chief Nelson will be surprised to hear you've been distracted at work lately, a little depressed, too." He shook his head. "It's a shame. From what I heard, you were one of his favorites."

"You son of a bitch."

According to Lieutenant Reid, Chief Nelson was also corrupt. But the fact that they would have to convince Nelson of Jeff's staged suicide had to mean he wasn't really involved in the sex ring. Jeff could've gone to him for help. Had he realized that sooner, he could've avoided this whole situation.

Talia and Charlie wouldn't have had to get involved.

A thud came from the closet.

Jeff swung his gun that way. "What was that?"

"I'm glad you asked."

Isaac sauntered over to the closet and opened the door. Four women were crammed inside. They didn't move. They seemed drugged.

Talia gasped.

Jeff saw red. "Let them out."

"If you say so." Isaac grabbed a handful of black hair.

He dragged a woman out of the closet and into the room. She shrieked as he threw her onto the floor.

Jeff went to the woman. He knelt on the ground, reaching for her arm.

She looked at him.

He froze. She had a gash on her forehead and seemed dazed. But that wasn't all. He recognized her from the investigation's pictures. "Jenny McMahon."

He glanced back at Talia, her face white. The women were here, with them.

Where had Talia sent Charlie?

"Let's get this over with," Isaac droned.

He whistled and the door opened. Two men stood in the doorway, one muscular and one small, both with guns.

"What the hell is this?" Jeff said as he helped Jenny stand. Talia joined them and wrapped an arm around Jenny's torso. They backed up to the wall as the men filed into the room.

"What, this?" Isaac gestured to the men. "Let's call it a welcome party."

"Don't do this, Isaac." Jeff stepped in front of Talia and Jenny. He trained his gun on the men, on Isaac. "This is between me and you. Just let the women go."

"Always the hero." Isaac sighed. "Superman, right?"

"Let the women go," Jeff repeated, barely able to hear his own voice over the blood pounding in his ears. "Now."

"I can't do that."

The men aimed their guns at Jeff.

Isaac's eyes turned cold. "There won't be any heroes tonight."

CHAPTER 54

Jenny and the women weren't there. Charlie shut the door, took out his cell, and turned on his flashlight. Aside from syringes and needles discarded on the floor, the space was empty, but it reeked of sweat and urine. He was in the right room. He had to be. Talia had told him where to go. She said Jenny and the women would be here.

But they were gone.

They couldn't have left the warehouse, he told himself. Talia and Charlie had been outside. They would've heard them leave and they hadn't heard a thing. And if the women hadn't left, then they were still in the building. They were close. He refused to believe anything else.

He had to find them.

He left the room and moved up and down the hallway, opening each door he came across and finding nothing, no one.

A man's voice echoed up ahead.

Charlie darted into one of the rooms. He slid behind the door and pulled the knob toward him, peering into the hall through the sliver of space between door and frame.

The footsteps came closer.

"I trapped her in the alley," Marco bragged.

"Shit," Charlie cursed under his breath. Marco was supposed to be outside, tied to the fire escape. He must've broken free from the cables. Charlie should've hit him harder. At the very least, he should've tied him tighter.

He didn't hear a second voice, but there was a second set of footsteps.

"You should've seen the look on her face." Considering the circumstances, that Marco had been tied to a fire escape moments before, he sounded a little too smug. His steps grew louder. His shadow appeared first, then his body.

He was walking with a man—the man from the alley, Gus.

"She was terrified," Marco added.

Gus rolled his eyes while scratching his beard. He didn't seem to be enjoying the conversation.

Marco didn't seem to notice. "Had her boyfriend not showed up, I would've made her pay for hurting the boss." He took on a more solemn tone. "I'll get her back eventually, that bitch. Then the boss will see how loyal I am, that I can be trusted."

They passed the room.

Charlie moved to the wall on the other side of the doorframe and watched them from behind as they continued down the hall. He had Marco's gun. He could catch up to them and force them to tell him where to find Jenny and the women. But if one of them yelled or managed to get away, his chance at staying undetected would be over.

Gus cut toward an adjacent hallway up ahead.

Marco stopped. "Where are you going?"

"Anywhere but here."

"But I'm not done with my story," Marco huffed with his hands on his hips.

"You suck at telling stories." Gus didn't offer so much as a backward glance.

"Oh yeah?" Marco called after him, fuming. "Well . . . at least I don't think I'm a stupid captain!"

"What was that?" Gus turned around and strode toward Marco with a raised fist.

Marco shrieked and jumped back. "Don't touch me!"

Gus stopped just inches away from him.

He leaned forward. "Boo."

Marco flinched.

Gus laughed and lowered his fist. "I don't *think* I'm a captain, you dumbass, I *am* one. My shrimp boat fell on hard times and I ended up in Chicago. But I'll get back on a boat some day, once I get my shit together. Just you wait and see. "

He turned away from Marco and made for the other hallway.

"By the way," he called over his shoulder, "you shriek like a little girl."

"Yeah . . . well . . . I hate shrimp!" Marco stumbled over his words as he clenched his fists. "I'm in charge of you, you know. I can make your life a living hell!"

"You already do." He flipped Marco off and disappeared down the other hall.

Marco gasped. "You'll regret that!" He took two steps in Gus's direction, but didn't go any farther. He stood there a few seconds more, then huffed again.

He walked three doors down and let himself into a room.

Charlie stepped into the hallway.

He could follow Marco into the room and hope he led Charlie to Jenny and the women. But Charlie had no way of knowing what was behind that door. He couldn't risk running into the boss or someone else and blowing their entire cover.

Besides, Marco wasn't the only one with information.

Gus was involved in the business, too. He had to know about Jenny and the women. With a little convincing, he just might point Charlie in the right direction.

Charlie trailed Gus down the hallway. He couldn't tell if he had any weapons, not from behind, so he picked up his pace; he had to catch him by surprise.

"Stupid piece of shit," Gus muttered. "In charge of me, my ass."

Charlie stepped up right behind him. "You sure told him."

"Christ!" Gus jumped and spun around.

Charlie put the gun to his temple and grabbed his shirt. He shoved him against the wall. "Make any noise and I'll put a bullet in your head."

"Who the hell are you?" He threw his hands into the air.

"You must not have heard me." Charlie jabbed the gun into his forehead. "I'll ask the questions. You'll tell me what I want to know. Got it?"

"Screw you!" Gus stood up taller and glared at Charlie, straight in the eye. "I'm so sick of you people thinking you own me. You want to shoot me? Fine!"

"You sure?" Charlie cocked his gun.

"Do it! At least then I'll be done with this shithole. I can't live like this anymore."

"What? You want out of this life? You want to get back on a boat and work an actual, honest job?"

"Maybe I do."

"Good." Charlie dropped the gun to his side. "Then you'll tell me exactly where I can find Jenny McMahon and the other women being held hostage here."

"Who did you say you were . . . ?"

"I didn't." Charlie checked over his shoulder. The coast was clear. But that didn't mean they had all night. "Listen, you want a better life, right? You want a chance to redeem yourself for all of the bad, messed-up shit you've done?"

Gus shrugged. "So what?"

"So this is your chance." He let go of Gus's shirt. "I'm helping the women escape tonight. But I need to find them first. Help me do that."

"They'll kill me if they find out I talked to you."

"Then don't let them find out."

A door slammed in the distance.

Charlie had to go. "What'll it be? A new life or the same old shit?"

Gus studied Charlie. He sighed. "Oh, what the hell?"

He pointed the way they came, saying, "There's a room in the hallway back there."

"The room Marco just went into?"

"Yeah," he confirmed. "All of the women are in there."

Charlie bolted in that direction, slowing to glance over his shoulder halfway down the hall. Gus was still there. "Are you going to stand there all night?" Charlie asked. "Get the hell out of here while you still can."

Gus started moving.

"And don't even think about telling anyone I'm here," Charlie added. "Or trust me, you'll wish I shot you in the head." He left Gus at that and jogged back into the other hall.

Something darted in front of him—someone.

They collided. A woman cried out and fell to the ground.

"Are you okay?" Charlie helped her stand, then stepped back. "Dani?"

"Charlie!" She stumbled, seeming disoriented, and yet somehow better off than she'd been at his apartment. "There you are!"

"What the hell are you doing here? You're supposed to be with Flynn."

"He wouldn't leave me alone! I couldn't take another second of his hovering." Her hair was matted with sweat, and she'd changed back into her tank top and mini jean-skirt. "I convinced him to come here after you called."

"Flynn is here, too? In the warehouse?" He couldn't be.

She shrugged. "He didn't want to wait in the car."

"Dammit, Dani! You shouldn't have come at all."

"I was worried about you!" She grabbed his arm, reaching for his shoulder.

He pulled away. "Find Flynn. Go back to the apartment. Do you hear me?"

Her eyes narrowed into slits.

He didn't care. He turned around and continued toward the room.

A beat passed.

"You're going the wrong way."

He faced her again. "What're you talking about?"

"Talia is outside," she spoke in an eerily calm voice, holding his gaze. "I just saw her and the other women leave the building."

"Outside?"

Gus had said the women were still in the room. And Charlie had believed him, easily—maybe too easily. Gus could've been lying. He could've told Charlie what he wanted to hear, just enough to get away.

Charlie stepped toward Dani. "Was Jenny with Talia, too?"

"Jenny?" Dani hesitated. "Yes."

He glanced back at the room; he could always double check.

"In fact," Dani added, "Jenny didn't look so good."

"What do you mean?"

She shook her head. "There was just so much blood . . ."

Charlie didn't wait to hear another word.

He took off running for the exit.

CHAPTER 55

Talia's plan had backfired. Isaac wasn't about to make a deal with them and let them go. And Jeff couldn't shoot Isaac, either. They wouldn't stand a chance, not with two guns against one, and Marco in the room now, too. If they wanted to get out of there alive, they had to change the dynamic and take back control. The recording could help; it could give them leverage. But Isaac had to say more for that to be a sure threat. He had to talk about the sex ring.

So Talia would get him to talk. "Why're you doing this?"

"Because I can."

Isaac had a glint in his eye. He was enjoying himself, the moment, the power. And that was good. With any luck, he was in a bragging mood.

"You're hurting innocent people." She spoke loudly as she inched closer to Jeff and his phone. "These women did nothing to you. Why kidnap them and hold them here?"

"They're weak . . . just like you."

She bit the inside of her cheek, a reminder to stay in check. She wasn't there to argue. She was there to trick Isaac into incriminating himself. And for that to happen, she needed him to give more than just a few vague answers. She needed him to fill in the gaps. "So you bring them here and what, drug them? Rape them?"

"Among other things."

That might be enough for an arrest. But she wasn't about to leave anything to chance. "Is that why you started the sex ring?"

The glint in his eye disappeared. "I started the sex ring to remind women of their place in this world . . . I'll remind you of that, too, soon enough."

"You won't touch her." Jeff steadied his gun on Isaac.

"And you're going to stop me?" Isaac chuckled. "What exactly is your plan, Jeff? Shoot me and go back to a family that doesn't even want you?"

Jeff's arm dropped, only an inch, but it dropped all the same.

Talia put a hand on his shoulder. "Don't listen to him."

"Am I wrong?" Isaac looked around the room, palms up, putting on a show.

Marco snickered. Muscles and the shorter man did, too, their guns still at the ready.

"How could they love him?" Isaac continued. "He can't even protect them. What kind of a man is that?"

"Shut up, Isaac." Jeff's muscles tensed under Talia's hand, the air growing more charged by the second. One of them would snap, soon. And Talia didn't want to find out who that would be, who would fire the first shot. If the recording was going to get them out of there alive, now was the time to use it.

"You're a failure. A fraud," Isaac taunted.

"You're the fraud, Isaac," Talia said as she pulled Jeff's cell phone out of his pocket and found her dad in his contacts. "And once this gets out, everyone will know who you really are."

Isaac glared at the phone. "What the hell is that?"

"A recording." She texted the recording to her dad, then smiled at Isaac. "Sent. Now you have to let us go. Unless you want to be tried for the sex ring and murder?"

"You stupid bitch." Isaac lunged forward.

Jeff blocked his path.

They came head to head, the barrel of Jeff's gun now inches away from Isaac's chest. "Shoot me," Isaac dared through clenched teeth. "You don't have the guts."

"You sure about that?" Jeff challenged.

One of the women in the closet moaned.

Isaac's eyes stayed on Jeff. "I'm positive."

"Hey. What the heck is that?" Marco pointed at the ceiling, at a line of smoke snaking into the room. He opened the door and peered into the hallway.

"There's a fire!" he yelled.

"A fire?" Jenny looked at Talia.

"Just down the hall," Marco said, his voice growing shrill. "We have to leave. Now!"

Muscles and the shorter man inched closer to Marco and the door. The smaller one stuck his head into the hall. "I'm out of here." He bolted from the room.

"We're not done yet!" Isaac yelled.

"Just let us go, Isaac," Jeff demanded. "It's over. Can't you see that?"

"You're right." Isaac walked to the door and snatched the gun out of Muscles's hands. He faced them, aiming the barrel at each of them in turn. "It is over."

"You can't shoot us." Talia's heart was pounding. Smoke was coming into the room. They had to leave. "I sent the recording. You'll be charged for murder."

"Maybe." Isaac's eyes were black, deadly. "But at least I'll be alive. And that's more than I can say for the three of you." He stepped closer to the door and paused. "Oh. And Jeff, don't worry. I'll take good care of Angela and Lucy once you're gone."

A gunshot exploded.

Talia dropped to the ground, pulling Jenny down, too. Her ears rang. Jeff was still standing, but Isaac had fallen to his knees. Blood was spreading on his shoulder.

He smiled at Jeff. "You shouldn't have done that."

Raising his gun with his uninjured arm, he aimed at Talia and Jenny.

"Get down!" Jeff shouted as he stepped in front of them and shot at Isaac again.

Talia screamed and ducked her head, pulling Jenny close.

Three gunshots followed, then nothing.

A click interrupted the silence, another. "Useless piece of shit!"

Talia peered around Jeff's legs as Isaac threw his gun to the side. Marco and Muscles helped him stand. Then they left the room, slamming the door behind them.

"He's gone." Talia stood. Jenny didn't. Blood pooled around her leg. Talia knelt back down and put a hand on her shoulder, looking closer. "Jeff, she needs help."

Jeff didn't respond. He stood there with his back to them, his gun at his side.

He collapsed.

"Jeff!" Talia reached for him and turned him onto his back as fast as she could. "No. No, no, no."

Blood was blooming over the left side of his shirt, his chest. Another wound was on his opposite arm. His eyes were open, darting from left to right.

"Hang on, Jeff. I'm here. I'm right here." She placed a hand over his chest wound and applied pressure.

Jenny's gaze settled on Jeff, on the blood. "Oh my god."

"It's okay. We'll be okay." Talia didn't know that. If Jenny got help soon, yes, she'd be fine. But Jeff was a different story. They had to stop the bleeding, but they couldn't stay in the room much longer. The smoke was rushing in now, stinging her eyes, her lungs. "We need to call for help." She grabbed Jeff's phone from the ground.

The text to her dad was still on the screen, the recording undelivered. "No service." That was impossible. She tried to call 911. Nothing happened. "Come on!"

"What do we do?" Jenny's voice shook.

"We move." Talia stuffed the phone into her pocket. She'd have to drag Jeff outside and come back for the other women. Jenny would have to walk. Talia grabbed Jeff's arms, raised them over his head, and tried to pull him across the floor.

He was too heavy, and he barely moved an inch.

He moaned. His eyes rolled back into his head. "Stop," he mumbled.

She dropped his hands and fell to her knees, watching helplessly as more blood pooled on his chest, too much. Even if she were able to pull him, he'd die before they reached an exit.

The building's fire alarm blared.

She exhaled and reapplied pressure to his wound. Help would be on the way. But someone would have to tell the firefighters that they were inside.

"Can you stand?" she asked Jenny.

"I think so."

Just then the room's door flew open. A man stepped inside. He pushed his black hair away from his forehead and coughed into his arm. "Is everyone okay?" he asked. "I heard gunshots." He took in Talia and Jeff, then Jenny.

His mouth fell open. His face turned white.

He reached for the wall and steadied himself.

"Flynn!" Jenny cried, her eyes filling with tears.

He ran across the room and dropped to the floor by her side, wrapping her in an embrace and rocking her back and forth. "Jenny. Oh my god."

"You found me." They sobbed into each other's arms.

"Hey." Talia tried to get their attention but received no response. "Hey!"

They turned her way.

"We don't exactly have time for a reunion." She glanced at Flynn. She didn't know him, but she planned to use him. "Can you carry Jenny? And one of the other women?"

He followed her gaze to the closet and blanched. "What the hell?"

"You'll have to move fast."

"Are they dead?" His eyes grew wide. He ran a hand through his hair. "Jesus Christ. They look dead. How did this happen?

We need help. They need help!"

"Flynn!" Talia snapped. "Either grab one of them or get the hell out."

"Right." He shook his head and took in a ragged breath. After pulling one of the women out of the closet and lifting her into his arms, he helped Jenny onto his back. He looked at Talia.

"Let's go," he said.

"You two go ahead. I'll catch up."

"Are you crazy?" Jenny asked. "You can't stay here."

"I'm not leaving him behind."

Jeff was like family. He'd been there for Talia and her dad through the worst. He risked his life for her and Jenny just now. He stepped in front of Isaac's gun to protect them. She'd wait with him until help came.

"The fire is spreading pretty fast," Flynn warned.

Jeff grabbed Talia's hand, his grip weak. "Go," he whispered.

Talia ignored him. She locked eyes with Jenny. "It's your turn to bring back help, okay? We need someone to know that we're here."

Jenny didn't say a thing.

"Tell the firefighters where to find us. And look for Charlie outside. If he's not by the trash barrels in the back alley, then he's still in the building. They'll have to find him, too." The thought of him still in the warehouse was too much to bear.

He was safe. She had to believe that.

"Charlie?" Jenny's eyebrows furrowed.

"I'll come back for you," Flynn offered.

Talia allowed herself that bit of hope. "Great."

"Okay." Flynn nodded. "I'll see you soon, then."

He left the room.

And just like that, they were gone.

A sob escaped Talia's mouth. Forcing her lips shut, she closed her eyes, and failed to steady her shaking limbs. She had to hold herself together.

She had to be strong.

She opened her eyes and coughed from the spreading smoke.

Jeff tried to say something, but he made no sound.

And she didn't need to hear him.

She could read his lips just fine.

Leave.

She pressed harder against his chest.

CHAPTER 56

Charlie circled the building a second time, stopping in front of the trash barrels in the back alley. Talia, Jenny, and the other women were nowhere in sight. They could've left and gone for help. But until he knew that for sure, until he confirmed with his own eyes that they were safe, he couldn't make any assumptions.

He ran over to Dani.

She was standing by the fire escape, staring at the building with a soft smile on her lips—singing under her breath. "Ashes . . . ashes . . . they all burn down."

"Dani," he said as he put his hands on his knees, struggling to catch his breath, "they're not here. We have to find them." Based on the gunshots he heard a minute before, and the fire alarm blaring, the sooner they found them, the better. "Let's split up."

"I already know where they are.'"

"I'll check the side streets. You stay here in case they come back." He started walking away, but stopped short. He turned around and faced her again. "What did you just say?"

"I know where they are." She scratched at the back of her hand, at a newly enflamed track mark on her vein. Her eyes were bloodshot.

And that could only mean one thing. "You took a hit."

"I did." She shrugged and dropped her hands to her side. "And that's exactly how I know that they're still in the building."

"Still in the building? No." They left. Dani was on drugs, confused. But again, she seemed more coherent now than she had the last time he saw her, dry heaving over his shower drain. "You said you saw them leave. Remember?"

"I said that, yes." She nodded. Her smile disappeared. "And you said that we would be together forever, that Talia meant nothing to you."

"What does that have to do with anything?"

"I guess we all say things we don't really mean."

"I don't understand." He stepped toward her, his frustration mounting. "Are you saying you didn't really see them leave the warehouse?"

"That's exactly what I'm saying."

"You lied?"

Of course she lied. She despised Talia. She wanted Charlie all to herself. He knew that. And yet, he'd been stupid enough to believe her, to follow her outside. He left Talia and Jenny in the warehouse while he ran around the building, wasting valuable time. "What've you done?"

"Please." She rolled her eyes. "The lie was nothing compared to the rest."

He clenched his fists. "The rest?"

"When Flynn told me that you, Talia, and the cop were going back into the warehouse, that you might actually have feelings for Talia, I knew I had to do something." Her voice had a bite, an edge. "So I took matters into my own hands."

"What did you do, Dani?" he asked through gritted teeth.

"I called the boss." Her words were starting to slur. "He was angry with me for running away. But once he heard what I had to say, he came around."

"And what exactly did you have to say?"

"Nothing about you."

"You told him about the others?" That explained why Jenny and the women hadn't been in the room. The boss would've moved them when he heard about the rescue. He would've been waiting for Talia and Foley, just like Dani had wanted.

They would've walked right into his trap.

Charlie bolted toward the door.

"Wait!" Dani followed, but tripped over her feet.

She tumbled to the ground.

A red box of matches fell out of her pocket.

He stopped and picked up the box. "What's this?"

"Nothing." She stood and snatched it from his hand.

"Did you take that from my apartment?" The box matched the one he had on his fireplace mantel. Why would she have bothered to bring the matches here?

They stared at each other—fire alarm blaring in the background.

He looked at Dani, at the box of matches, at the building.

"You started the fire."

Her soft smile returned.

"Ashes, ashes . . ." He repeated her words from before.

Her smile stretched. "They all burn down."

"You did this . . ."

She set the building on fire, knowing people were still inside. Hell, that's why she set the fire, *because* people were inside, because Talia was inside.

"Jesus Christ, Dani, how could you do that?" He raised his voice, shouting, "You already told the boss about Talia. What, you didn't trust him to finish the job? You wanted one last guarantee that she wouldn't walk out of there alive?"

"No one will walk out of there alive, not this time."

"This time?"

She was speaking as if she'd done this before. And maybe she had. Her jealousy wasn't new. It was a pattern. *First Jenny, then Talia,* he reminded himself.

"Wait a minute." He stepped back. "Did you start Friday morning's fire, too?"

She jutted her chin into the air. "Jenny was trying to take my spot."

"So, what, you tried to kill her?" he yelled.

"Until tonight, I thought I had."

"You framed Tuco with the note. You murdered three people, Dani!"

And now, after tonight, there could be more.

But Charlie wouldn't let that happen. He'd get them out.

He turned to the door and touched the back of his hand against the knob: warm, but not hot. The fire had yet to reach the back of the building. He opened the door with the boss's key and stepped aside as a burst of smoke rushed out of the building. He coughed, waited for the smoke to clear, and went back to the door.

"You're making a mistake," she warned.

"No. I'm fixing yours."

"After everything I did for us, you're still choosing her?"

"There's no us, Dani. And it's always been her."

He stepped inside.

The smoke was thick, dark gray and expanding by the second, just as deadly as the flames. Crouching down low, he took off his sweatshirt and held the fabric over his mouth. He started moving forward, the temperature hotter with each step.

"Jenny? Talia?" He shouted as loud as he could, but his voice was muffled. He couldn't see anything past a few feet in front of him, nothing but the fire's glow in the distance. "Jenny! Talia!"

Then he heard a cough. One single heavy cough.

He pushed forward as a faint outline of a body appeared up ahead, growing clearer until Flynn's gangly form broke through the smoke. He was holding a woman in his arms and another on his back—a woman with black hair and a pale face.

"Jenny!"

Charlie ran to them and placed a hand on Jenny's shoulder. She didn't stir and her eyes were closed. He felt her neck for a pulse, relieved that she had one. Throwing his sweatshirt over her head, he glanced at the other woman in Flynn's arms.

He pulled back; he didn't recognize her.

"Where's Talia?" he yelled. She should've been with them. What if she hadn't been able to keep up? What if she'd been injured, shot?

"She's back there." Flynn jerked his head over his shoulder. "She's waiting in a room with the others for help to come." A coughing fit racked his body.

Charlie steadied him. "Get Jenny outside. Stay with her there."

"Got it." Flynn moved toward the exit. Charlie watched them go.

Jenny would be okay once she got some fresh air.

He turned back toward the fire.

Talia would, too.

CHAPTER 57

Talia and Jeff couldn't stay in the room much longer. The smoke grew thicker by the second and the room was hot, the heat heavy. Her arms ached from applying pressure to Jeff's wound, pressure that wasn't working. His face was gray and slick with sweat. His breaths came in long, drawn-out wheezes and he'd lost too much blood.

"Stay with me," she croaked, not knowing if he could hear her.

She talked in case he could. "Please, Jeff, stay with me."

Something crashed.

She leaned forward and threw her arms around him, covering his chest. A larger crash followed, a rumble that built in her ears and blocked out all other sounds. And then there was nothing, nothing but the quiet roar of flames coming closer.

She sat up to find the left side of the doorframe gone, the door lying on the ground, and debris piled high in the hallway. Something snapped, and the ceiling just outside of the room crumbled to the floor. The building was falling apart.

They had to move.

Jeff was weak. He might not survive the strain. She already knew that. But he'd die if they stayed in that room and waited for help any longer, help that might never come. The room's ceiling could cave in next. And that would be the end, assuming the smoke or the flames hadn't killed them first. Jeff would never see Angela and Lucy again. Talia would never see her dad, her friends. Charlie.

She couldn't let that happen.

She stood. "I'm going to move you, Jeff." She grabbed his arms and pulled. He felt heavier than he had before, and he didn't budge. "Come on!" She tried again, pulling with everything she had, everything she could muster. Nothing happened.

"Dammit!"

"Talia . . ." Jeff managed.

"It's okay!" she sobbed. She had to try harder. "I can do this!"

"Stop . . ."

She dropped to her knees. His face was cold to the touch and his pulse dangerously low—bad, but she'd seen worse. She'd seen patients on their deathbeds pull through. And Jeff wasn't there yet. He couldn't be there yet. She just had to remind him to fight. "I'm going to try again, Jeff. I need you to hang in there, okay? Angela and Lucy need you to hang in there. They'll be waiting for you to come home tonight."

A smile tugged at his lips. He opened his eyes, only a sliver, and he tried to speak. She leaned in closer, but couldn't make out what he was saying.

"It's okay. I'm here. I'm right here. I'm going to get you outside."

"Tell Angela and Lucy . . ." he managed to whisper, "I love them."

"No." She shook her head as tears rushed to her eyes. He wasn't fighting; he was giving up. "Don't do this." He still had time. He had to believe that.

"Tell them . . . I love them." He winced after each word. Taking a deep breath, he held the air in his lungs, then exhaled. "So much." A single tear rolled out of his eye.

"You'll be able to tell them that yourself." She hugged him and held him tight. "Your family needs you. Do you hear me? I need you." She felt him struggle to take in air, his heartbeat slow. He was drifting away, the man with a wife and daughter who loved him, the man who'd become family to Talia and her dad over the years.

"I'm sorry," he whispered.

"Don't you dare start that." Her tears mixed with the blood soaked into his shirt. She'd been the one to call him tonight, to ask for his help. She suggested the plan—the plan that failed. This was her fault. She sat up and grabbed his hand. "You saved our lives, Jeff. Now I'm going to save yours. So just stay with me."

He coughed twice, soft coughs, almost peaceful. He grimaced, only for a second. And then the pain was gone. His face relaxed. His chest stopped moving.

"No." She moaned and wrapped her arms around him again. She didn't let go.

"Come back," she begged, even though she knew he wouldn't open his eyes again. He wouldn't say anything else. He'd been with her a second before.

And now he was gone.

"Talia?"

He was gone forever.

"Talia!" A hand grabbed her shoulder and pulled her back. Charlie was there.

He felt Jeff's pulse and shook his head.

"He's dead," she whispered, more to herself than Charlie.

"Let's go." Charlie grabbed her hand and helped her stand. He led her toward the door but she turned around. Jeff's body was surrounded by blood. She felt numb. She couldn't stop the tears. He was gone, no longer in pain.

Charlie pulled her hand. "We have to move, Talia, now."

"Wait." She broke away and went to the closet. Two women were inside, their eyes still glazed over. They weren't fully there, not with the drugs in their system. And the smoke would only be making things worse. Charlie joined Talia and grabbed the closest woman's arm. But then he hesitated and felt her pulse.

He glanced back at Talia. "She's gone."

"Gone?"

He grabbed the other woman, threw her over his shoulder, and took Talia's hand. He led her toward the door.

She tried to stop. "We can't just leave them here."

They both looked back at Jeff.

Charlie repositioned the woman on his shoulder. "We'll come back for him, for them, okay?" He didn't wait for a response and guided her to the door. "Step where I step." He led her through the collapsed frame, over the rubble, and into the hallway.

They turned toward the exit.

Angry flames licked the walls and the ceiling, engulfing the space.

They wouldn't make it through; they had to find a different way out. Talia didn't know of another exit. She looked at Charlie in a panic. She couldn't think. "Now what?"

"Stay low!" he yelled as he took them in the opposite direction. His head jerked left and right as they moved. Talia became more disoriented with each fumbling step.

The hallway emptied into a long room with five garage doors spanning the far wall. Low ceilings and built-up heat made the space unbearably hot.

Fire was spreading on the opposite side of the room. It was only a matter of time before the flames came their way, before the fire consumed everything in its path.

Everyone.

Charlie rushed to the first garage door, letting go of Talia's hand and placing the woman on the floor. He knelt and grabbed the metal lock securing the door to the cement. He yanked the lock a few times, but he didn't break the hold.

He looked around.

Talia pulled the gun out of his back pocket. "Use this."

"That'll work." He took the gun and turned to the door.

An arm wrapped around Talia's chest and yanked her back. She tried to scream, to push away, but no sound came out of her mouth. Her muscles refused to work. She felt a sharp point press against her neck.

"Charlie!" she managed to screech.

Charlie glanced over his shoulder. Confusion flashed across his face.

He stood, yelling, "What the hell are you doing here?"

"Good to see you again, Charlie," the boss said with a raspy voice.

CHAPTER 58

Charlie couldn't believe his eyes, couldn't believe who was standing right in front of him. Judge Johnson was there, the man who blackmailed Charlie's dad into losing the *Smith v. Kenton* case, the man Jenny met with two days before she disappeared. He looked different now than he had in his office that morning. His eye was cut and swollen, and he had blood on his arm. He was holding a syringe full of liquid.

He was holding a needle to Talia's neck.

Charlie raised his gun. "Let her go."

"Drop your gun." Johnson jerked Talia back.

Charlie mirrored their step. The flames were spreading fast and the smoke was growing thicker, darker. If they didn't get out of there soon, they'd die, all of them, Johnson included. Surely, he understood that.

"Are you trying to get all of us killed?" Charlie asked.

"Not all of us." Sweat dripped down his face. "And if your gun isn't on the floor in one second, I guarantee you, I won't be trying anything. Your girlfriend will be dead." He ran the needle's shaft down her neck. "Heroin overdoses are quick, so I hear."

Talia stiffened.

"Put the needle down." Charlie spoke through clenched teeth. His finger hovered over the trigger. He wanted to shoot. But he didn't have a shot, not with Talia between them. "I'm warning you."

"And I warned you . . ." Johnson pressed the needle's point to her neck.

"Okay!" Charlie held up his hands. "You win. I'll drop the gun. See?" He bent his knees and set the gun on the ground. He tried to catch Talia's eye, to assure her that everything would be okay, but her eyelids were drooping and her shoulders slouched. She needed air, soon.

He stood, empty-handed. "There. Now let her go."

"Slide me the gun."

Charlie didn't move. He wasn't about to give Johnson something he could use to kill them on the spot. But he had to do something. Their time was running out. He could barely think. The heat was too heavy, the fumes getting to his head. He had to get Talia outside. He had to get her away from Johnson so he could shoot.

"Let her walk over here first. Then I'll slide you the gun."

"How stupid do you think I am?"

"Boss!" Marco ran into the room. "I found another way out!" He stopped and looked at Talia, at Charlie, at the gun. "Oh, shit."

"You're the boss?"

Charlie knew Johnson was hiding something, that he was a liar. But how the hell could a judge be running a sex ring undetected? Then again, that would explain Johnson's payments to Lieutenant Reid each month, incentive for Reid to turn a blind eye to his business.

"You're Foley's brother?" he asked next.

"The one and only."

"I should've known you were behind this."

Johnson ran a prostitution ring in college, a ring that had apparently only grown over time. According to Charlie's dad, Johnson had moved on from that life. But he hadn't moved on; he was still living it. Hell, Kenton was probably one of his clients. "You've had Jenny this whole time."

"I wanted her all to myself." He smirked. "The next best thing to your mom."

"You sick, lying bastard." Charlie stepped toward him.

A piece of plaster fell from the ceiling and hit the ground with a thud.

Johnson flinched. "Enough! Give me the gun or Talia dies!"

Talia would die if Charlie gave Johnson the gun. He needed a distraction, fast. His eyes settled on Marco, his best bet. "Hey, Marco, you're on fire!"

"Oh my god!" Marco looked behind him, hopping up and down. "Where is it?" He ran at the boss, fanning at his behind, at a flame that wasn't there. "Put it out!"

"Get away from me, you idiot!" Johnson swung Talia in front of Marco.

And that was all the distraction Charlie needed.

He launched himself forward and knocked Johnson and Talia over. Jumping to his feet, he stomped on Johnson's hand, on the syringe in his grip.

Johnson screamed. He dropped the syringe and pulled his hand away.

Charlie brought his foot down on the syringe again. The plastic cracked.

"I'm on fire! Someone help me!" Marco rolled around on the floor while Talia pushed herself into a seated position. Charlie had to get the gun.

He turned.

Johnson slammed the piece of plaster into Charlie's face.

His head snapped to the right. Blood exploded in his mouth. He fell to his knees and Johnson kicked him in the ribs. He hunched over, pain tearing through his side, but he forced himself to stand.

Johnson made to dart back toward the gun.

Talia reached for his ankle and grabbed on, almost tripping him. "Get off of me, you slut." He kicked Talia in the head. She moaned and let go of his ankle.

Johnson rushed for the gun. Charlie did, too. They dove at the same time. Charlie grabbed the gun but felt Johnson grip the other end. They wrestled back and forth. Charlie rolled onto his side, kicked Johnson in the gut, and yanked the gun away.

He stood, took aim. "It's over."

Johnson held up his hands and rose to his feet. "We can work this out."

"How stupid do you think I am?"

Charlie pulled the trigger and fired a shot.

Johnson screamed. He clutched his knee and dropped to the floor.

Charlie stumbled to the garage door, steadying himself against the metal.

He aimed the gun at the lock.

Sirens sliced through the night, help just on the other side of the door.

Charlie blinked and fired.

The bullet broke the lock in half.

He gripped the bottom of the door and lifted.

Fresh air hit him in the face. The night was black—red, yellow, blue. Fire trucks, police cars, and ambulances sped down the street and parked. Charlie went back for Talia and grabbed her under the arms. He pulled her out of the garage and to the road.

A medic met him there and swept her away.

"Charlie?" a familiar voice called. Reggie Howell came into view. He put a hand on Charlie's shoulder. "Shit. We need another medic over here!"

Charlie shrugged out of his grip. "There's a room down the hall with a collapsed door. Two bodies are inside: Detective Foley and a woman in the closet."

"That son of a bitch shot me!" Johnson pointed at Charlie as he was carried past on a stretcher. "Do you idiots have any idea who I am? Call my lawyers! Now!"

"Someone call his lawyers, now!" Marco trailed a few steps behind, patting at the back of his pants. He hurried to keep up. "I'm right here, boss, if you need me."

Howell raised an eyebrow at Charlie.

"Just don't let them out of your sight." Charlie left Howell and went to Talia.

She'd been loaded onto a gurney and had an oxygen mask over her mouth. She was covered in Foley's blood.

He grabbed her hand. "You're going to be okay, Talia."

"Jeff saved us," she whispered.

Us.

Charlie spun around. The street was crowded, chaotic. Jenny was nowhere in sight. Neither was Flynn. They'd be behind the warehouse. They had to be.

"I'll be right back." He stepped away from Talia and stumbled around the side of the building. The alley was empty.

"Jenny?" he called, his pulse picking up. The warehouse was fully in flames. If they hadn't reached the exit by now, they'd be dead.

"Jenny!" he yelled again. "Flynn!"

"Charlie?"

He turned toward Flynn's voice and ran that way, rounding the trash barrels.

The woman Flynn had carried in his arms while Jenny had been on his back was lying on the ground. Her eyes were closed and her chest moving. Flynn and Jenny sat next to her, clutching each other's hands. Jenny stared up at Charlie. She had a gash on her forehead.

Her eyes brimmed with tears. "Charlie."

"Jenny." He dropped to his knees and pulled her into his arms. He held her tighter than he ever had before. "I thought you were gone." He choked on his words.

"I'm sorry," she cried. "I heard Johnson threaten Dad. He promised to leave our family alone if I worked for him.

He said he'd kill you, Mom, and Dad if I told anyone, so I tried to leave clues behind. I thought Dad would notice his missing knife . . ."

"You did good, Jenny."

"I was stupid," she sobbed. "So many people are hurt because of me."

"Hey, you were not stupid." He pulled back but held on to her arms, waiting for her eyes to meet his. "Because of you, Johnson will never hurt anyone else again."

She sniffed and wiped her eyes.

She didn't look like herself. A hollowed-out version, maybe, with gray eyes that lacked their usual light. After what she'd been through, he wasn't sure he'd ever see that light again, the same with her smile, and her laugh. But she was safe.

And for now, that was enough.

He placed a hand on Flynn's shoulder. "Thank you, for everything." He'd underestimated Flynn from the start. He'd been wrong. "You saved her life tonight."

Flynn puffed with pride. "My pleasure."

Charlie stood and reached out to Jenny. "What do you say we get you home?"

"She needs a doctor, first." Flynn pointed at her leg. Charlie's sweatshirt was tied around her calf, covered in blood. "She was shot."

"I'll get help." Charlie stepped away from them.

"It sounds nice." Jenny's voice stopped him.

He turned back around. "What does?"

She looked at him with a fresh set of tears in her eyes. "Home."

He smiled. "Welcome home, Jenny." She was right; it did sound nice.

She smiled back at him.

And she laughed.

CHAPTER 59

Five days had passed since the warehouse fire, five days filled with ups and downs, anger and tears, laughter and relief that Jenny was still alive. And now, Friday morning had come too soon, a morning of loss, and of pain, a celebration of life.

Charlie held the door open for Jenny and Flynn.

They stepped into the church and sat down in the last pew.

The space was small and packed with family and friends, with CPD officers clad in uniform—the same uniform Detective Foley wore in his photograph on the altar. His face was serious in the picture, his mouth a straight line. A child's drawing was taped to the bottom of the frame, a drawing of Superman flying through the sky.

The music started, slow and soft.

A hush fell over the crowd.

They stood and turned to the back of the church.

Angela and Lucy held hands as they led the rest of their family down the aisle. Angela looked better than she had when they saw her last, when she asked Charlie and Jenny to come over and tell her everything. Her face was still swollen and her eyes were puffy. But she had a strength in her step. She held her head high.

Lucy stared at the people staring back, her eyes curious, wide.

Per Angela's wishes, Talia and Mr. Griffin followed behind.

Talia pushed her dad in a wheelchair, his leg still in a cast and his head bandaged. From what Charlie had heard, recovery would take some time. But Mr. Griffin was getting stronger every day, especially with Talia by his side. And that morning, she was just as beautiful as always, wearing her brown hair pulled back and a black, long-sleeved dress.

They reached the front of the church.

Angela, Lucy, and their family sat in the first pew, Talia in the second with her dad next to her in the aisle. The priest gestured for everyone to sit. He started talking about loss and grief. He assured them that Jeff would never be forgotten, that he'd live on in their hearts as they moved forward with their lives—one step at a time. Then he spoke of gratitude, of finding things to be thankful for in this crazy world.

Charlie had an endless list.

He had his sister back. She wasn't the same girl she'd been. How could she be? But she started taking classes again and her leg would be better in a few weeks' time, would heal just fine. Flynn had been there every step of the way.

Jenny's return had also given their parents a second wind, a renewed energy. They wanted to rebuild their relationship with Charlie and Jenny. And they were slowly and surely taking steps to do just that. Their mom was in rehab and their dad finally reported what happened in the *Smith v. Kenton* case. He'd be disbarred. But that was okay with him. He was ready for something new.

He was ready to be someone new.

Charlie had Talia. They were taking things slow, as slow as they could in a relationship that'd seen so much already. She worked only night shifts now, spending the days with her dad. And Charlie's shifts at the firehouse would start again on Monday, his medical suspension cleared as of that morning. The doctor advised him to take the weekend and relax. This time around, Charlie thought he just might listen.

He had closure. Chief Nelson took up the investigation. Johnson, Marco, and Lieutenant Reid were behind bars. And they weren't alone. Dani showed up at Charlie's apartment the night before. She was in hysterics, begging him to take her back, reminding him that they were meant to be together, forever.

He invited her inside.

He called Chief Nelson's direct line.

Nelson tracked down Johnson's other thugs, too, everyone but Gus. And Charlie was okay with that. He liked to think that Gus had found his way back into the captain's seat, that he was creating a better life out on the water.

The priest stopped talking.

Talia stood. She made her way to the podium, holding a white piece of paper in her hands. She adjusted the microphone and looked up. Her eyes found Charlie in the back.

His chest swelled with pride.

She scanned the crowd, her cheeks flushed. "Jeff Foley was many things," she said, her voice echoing against the walls and the ceiling. She glanced at Angela and Lucy. "He was a devoted father and a loving husband." She smiled at them. Her gaze shifted to her dad and the CPD. "He was a fierce friend, a fighter for justice."

She paused, looked at the back row, at Charlie, Jenny, and Flynn in turn.

"He was a hero."

The rest of the funeral passed by in a blur. Charlie, Jenny, and Flynn joined the procession to the cemetery. Once the burial was over, Jenny and Flynn walked back toward the car, arms linked. Charlie waited on the outskirts of the lot.

Talia saw him and walked over.

He pulled her into his arms. "Are you okay?"

"I will be." She stepped back and held his gaze. "I just wish he were here."

"He is here, Talia. He always will be."

She nodded and looked off into the distance.

She took his hand. "Let's go."

They walked back into the crowd, together—one step at a time.

ACKNOWLEDGMENTS

Thank you to the incredible team at Hadleigh House Publishing. Anna, Allison, and Alisha, your guidance and support were everything throughout this process. From writing, to editing, to marketing my work, you were there every step of the way. Thank you for taking a chance on me, and believing in *Ashes Ashes*. Erin and Brenna, your critical eyes and honest feedback helped me shape my story into what it is today. Thank you for your encouragement as I polished my work.

Thank you to Mary Carter and the Chicago Writers' Loft for teaching me how to transform my writing into a story. Mary, your class was a turning point for me, and Wednesday nights quickly became the highlight of my week. I used to rush home after class and transfer my notes into a second notebook, just in case I ever lost one of the versions. I'm beyond grateful for your guidance over the years, both in and out of the classroom. Thank you for being an amazing mentor, and for never hesitating to offer me help or your opinion.

I'm blessed with family and friends who supported me since day one. For those who sent messages, checked in on my writing, and went out of your way to make connections for me, thank you. To everyone in the Culligan, Morrison, LeFevour, and Butler family, your words of encouragement did not go unnoticed. Sue and Andy, thank you for your constant support. Mary Clare, thank you for answering random questions about nurses and hospitals at all hours of the day.

Connor, Morgan, Tate, and Josey, how did I end up with such loving, supportive, and talented siblings? Thank you for volunteering to be early readers of my work. You all inspire me every day. Morgan and Tate, thank you for reading my drafts, providing honest feedback on all things writing, and responding to my panicked text messages during the editing process.

Dad, thank you for introducing me to crime fiction, and for reading every manuscript I ever wrote. Your constant excitement and support throughout the writing process motivated me to keep going. Years ago, you told me that my writing wasn't just a hobby. That validation meant more to me than you will ever know.

Mom, I don't know where to start. You believed in me from the beginning and made my goal your mission. When I was stuck on this storyline, you sent me feedback on every chapter, every sentence, and every word multiple times over—morning, day and night. You became my editor, therapist, and cheerleader, all in one, and I'll never forget the time you set aside to help me with my dream. Thank you for making the writing process less lonely and more fun. Thank you for being the first person to talk about my characters as if they were real people. Thank you for the time and love you put into these chapters, and for pushing me to never quit, to ask for what I want, and to believe in myself, always.

Last, but certainly not least, this book would not exist without my husband, Andrew. Thank you for never questioning the time I put into this story, even when it seemed like these pages would stay as a Word document on my computer. You didn't so much as bat an eye at the early alarm clocks, the nights you watched TV on mute while I wrote at the kitchen table, and so, so much more. Thank you for being there for me (and Birdie!), and for always knowing what I need—whether that be a sounding board, a reminder to take a break, or a hug and a nudge to keep going. The hard work and dedication you put into everything you do will never cease to inspire me. I love you, and I can't wait to continue chasing our dreams together.

Murphy Morrison is a crime-fiction author who grew up in the Twin Cities. When not writing, she can be found spending time with family and friends, reading, or plotting ways that her characters can get away with murder. She currently lives in Chicago with her husband and French bulldog.

Visit her at MurphyMorrison.com or follow her on Instagram at @MurphyMorrisonAuthor and Twitter at @MMorrisonAuthor

Made in the USA
Monee, IL
11 November 2020